S
Volume Two

M.M. Kin

1

Seeds Volume 2 Copyright © 2013, 2019 by M.M. Kin

Books by M.M. Kin

Seeds
Volume One
Volume Two
Volume Three

Interludes in Myth
Worthy of Love
Khthonios
Tapestry

Moonshadows

This has been a long journey, but well worth it. My heart goes out to Madame Thome, Elke, and Marit, who have been a cherished source of encouragement and inspiration. I would also like to thank everyone else who has given me encouragement or feedback when this book was still in progress. I could not have done it without your help and feedback, you have my undying gratitude.

I would also like to thank Lani Rush, Sophia Luo (Sorelliena), Teresa Dec and Zele Jones for their feedback and editing help, and Moranyelie Osorio Morales for the incredible cover she designed for this book.

I would like to thank everyone for reading and enjoying the first book. I could not have done this without the support of my readers. Without further ado, the next installment of Seeds.

FLOWER

HUNGER

Chapter XX

oOo

Persephone's heart fluttered in anticipation as she stared at her reflection in the mirror. She had never been to a banquet, at least like this. Yes, there were the festivals that the mortals had held when her father was still alive, but there had been nothing formal about them. Games had been played and jokes told, and songs were sung as the men had races and the girls danced. She touched the collar she wore, feeling the myriad diamonds under her fingertips. Despite her relative youth, there was no denying the effect the jewels and fine material had on her appearance.

She certainly didn't want all these ancient and dark deities to think she was a child, which she was, in comparison to these august entities. It was odd how she wanted to escape the Underworld, yet she cared about the impression she made on its residents.

I am doing this for myself, she rationalized. If she could make a good impression on them, one of them might be inclined to offer her assistance...

When she emerged from her chamber, she was pleased to see delight and approval in his eyes.

"Nobody could ever question that you are Queen of a mighty realm, my darling. You look *splendid.*"

"Thank you, my lord." She took his proffered arm, hooking hers through it and resting her diamond-ringed hand on his forearm.

The grand dining room opened onto a garden that had a large pond in it. There were a rich variety of flowers, many of them looking like the ones above, but all were flush with deep and ethereally vibrant colors. Daffodils, lilies, marigolds, crocuses, irises, and other flowers she had plucked many times from the earth to make a crown or bouquet had their colors magnified in a brilliant palette. The gray light from outside poured in evenly to fill out the shadows cast by the impressive chandelier above.

Its lights were made of diamond and hung in seven tiers that seemed were crafted from the same sort of branches as the ebony trees outside, sending brilliant prisms of light against the wall and illuminating the table and its appetizing contents. The long table lay parallel to the garden, with half a dozen comfortable divans along the sides, and another at either end. All of the divans were crafted to look alike, with black cushioning, but the one at the end of the table had the three heads of Kerberos wrought into both of its arms, marking it as Hades's own.

"You will sit with me," Hades instructed. Persephone found herself seated on that very divan, the Lord of the Dead settling down at the other side. The space was comfortable with ample room for two, and she leaned back against the arm, ignoring the wrought-iron snarling dog-heads.

Persephone wondered why the introductions weren't more formal, as she was certain they would have been on Olympus. She had imagined Hades and herself in the throne room, receiving their guests and Hades making his introductions, as she imagined Zeus doing with Hera at his side. As she settled herself, she let her attention move around the room.

The walls were adorned with ornate tapestries, deep and rich swirls of color that didn't exist on the surface world, like the flowers in the garden. Standing out amidst the dark marble it hung in front of. The scent of the food overwhelmed her senses. The cushions she sat on and her own clothing was softer than anything she had ever felt. It almost felt as if this world were... hyper-real, at times. The world of Dis was just as real as the one above, according to Hades. It certainly felt so, much as she tried to tell herself otherwise.

The doorway to the dining room was wide and arched, so it was easy for her to see who was coming through the portal before introductions were made. The first guest was a tall and elegant-looking woman with skin darker than anyone that Persephone had ever seen. Her long, straight black hair flowed down her shoulders, barely distinguishable against the gauzy ebony layers of her veil and clothing. She had a long, oval face with a straight and graceful nose and sensuously full lips. Her eyes were nearly half-lidded, fringed by long and thick lashes.

Hades rose from his seat, motioning for her to do the same. Obediently Persephone stood, staying at Hades's side as he approached this mysterious and elegant goddess. She was the first of the ancient *Protogenoi* that Persephone would become acquainted with.

"Lady Nyx, it is always a pleasure to have you here." Hades's tone was warm and welcoming, "I would like to introduce to you my queen, Persephone."

"Greetings to you as well, Lord Aidoneus," Nyx replied in a smooth, almost purring tone. Her eyes were black surrounded by clear almost-blue white, giving her an open, penetrating gaze whenever she opened her eyes wide. She extended her hands, fingers long and the white of the nails almost blue in stark contrast with her deeply-tanned skin.

Persephone lifted her own almost without thinking, touching Nyx's fingers. Before she could pull back, dark fingers wrapped around her own.

"I have known that this day was coming for a long time. Yet it almost feels strange that that time is already here. Time does fly when you give it no notice, does it not?" Nyx's gaze moved from her to Hades, and he slowly nodded. The older goddess returned her attention to the Queen of the Dead.

"Welcome to Khthonios, Persephone. I look forward to seeing what you think of this kingdom." A faint smile appeared on Nyx's face as if she were speaking of a secret.

"...It is nice to meet you too," Persephone replied, bowing her head. Only then did the ebony-haired goddess release her hands, and she slid over – indeed, to Persephone it didn't look as if she *walked* – to the other end of the table, though she made no move to touch the food yet. A shade – there were several of them hovering about – poured her a glass of wine, which she sipped.

Another guest arrived almost as soon as Nyx made herself comfortable. Persephone recognized him as Aeacus. More greetings, a deep bow from him, a lighter one from her, and he was seated. His robes were somber, but they were edged with red along with a bit of gold. And then Minos, garbed in black with no colors, having only a gold belt as ornamentation. She knew they weren't full-blooded gods, but Hades seemed to regard them as so.

The next man had shoulder-length blond hair, so pale it was almost silvery. He smiled at her, his face looking youthful yet somehow ancient at the same time. His skin was as pale as Nyx's was dark, but he was a strikingly handsome man, garbed in black and various shades of pale blue. Despite their physical differences, Persephone had the feeling that there was a resemblance between Nyx and Hypnos. Perhaps it was the long face, or the full lips, or that almost sleepy expression.

"Hypnos, God of Sleep," Hades whispered before the newcomer approached them.

"My lady Persephone." Hypnos fell into a graceful and sweeping bow, almost as if he were trying to charm her. She had to fight back a small smile, thinking about how easily the nymphs she had known might be captivated by this suave display.

"Thank you for coming, Hypnos. I hope you enjoy yourself," Persephone replied neutrally, shielding herself against his charm by playing the role of hostess. He righted himself and as he strode past her, she could almost swear that he winked at her. Unlike Nyx, his eyes were pale blue, the blue so light it was almost invisible against the white, leaving his pupils floating in a great pale expanse. This might have made for an unnerving effect, but somehow, it suited Hypnos.

Rhadamanthus was the next person to arrive. Knowing her true paternity, it felt a bit odd to know that the Judges of the Dead were her half-brothers. Being the daughter of Thermasia – the name Demeter used in her mortal guise in Enna – and Iasion, she was an only child. But as the daughter of two of the mightiest gods of Olympus, she had how many siblings? Perhaps Zeus himself didn't even know just how many children he had, if all the tales about him were any indication.

She was still getting used to the fact that she was a goddess. A real, actual Goddess, rather than merely a demigoddess, a divine offspring still destined for mortality. Yet without means to use her Gift, she might as well be mortal down here in the Land of the Dead.

Hades's voice cut into her thoughts as he drew her attention to their newest guest. This woman had light tan skin like many Hellenic women, and her locks were dark and wavy, another relatively common occurrence in this part of the world. However, her eyes were a curious balance between purple and gray.

"Hekate, welcome. My dear, this is Hekate, the Goddess of the Crossroads," Hades whispered as he gestured towards the other woman, who was clad in indigo and muted violet, with silver threads woven into the hems. Her hair flowed loosely down her shoulders and back, held in check only by the sash that ran around her head in a thick headband. The older goddess smiled at her, revealing a set of dimples.

Mortals often spoke of Hekate as a mysterious,

hooded or dog-faced character, clad in shadows. Demeter didn't have much to say about her, either. But this woman looked open and friendly, and Persephone found herself smiling back."

"Welcome to our home, Hekate. Allow me to introduce to you my queen, Persephone."

"Pleasure to meet you, my lady. I trust Lord Hades has been a good host to you." Her eyes twinkled, and Persephone heard Hades snort.

"The wonders of this kingdom are many," Persephone said after a moment's hesitation. As she did, she took the opportunity to scrutinize the other woman. Hekate's physical appearance gave her the appearance of being in her late twenties or early thirties, beauty in full bloom but tempered with almost imperceptible signs of wisdom and age.

"I am not what you expected," the older goddess replied in a friendly tone, and Persephone blinked as she registered this rapid shift in subject.

"No. Not at all. Not that I object, of course," Persephone admitted. Hekate shot her a brilliant grin and winked at her.

After Hekate's arrival, Persephone was ushered back to the divan she shared with Hades. There were other gods, and Hades assured her that she would eventually come to know them. There was no need for her to meet everybody at once, he had said. She appreciated his concern but also felt annoyed because these deities had already been told that she was queen, that she was now the bride of Hades. What would they think of her if she told them she was a captive?

Could she appeal to Nyx, who was smiling at her in a mysterious but kind way? Or Hekate, who seemed to truly want to be her friend? The Judges, would they rule that her kidnapping wasn't fair? Hypnos looked as if he might consider it, but it was hard to read that half-lidded, distant expression of his. And they had all known Hades longer than she.

Music played, and lovely women danced around them, trailing sashes that seemed as diaphanous as wisps of smoke.

"Musicians and dancers from Elysium," Hades whispered.

"And cooks," Persephone added, glancing towards the food. He shrugged and smiled.

"I have access to the finest workers in Elysium, and they are happy to please their lord."

She smirked faintly as one of the women twirled around the divan where they sat, slender chains with silver discs wrapped around her waist, making a light, chiming tinkle as she wiggled her hips. However, the dancer made no apparent overture towards the Lord of the Dead and moved towards Hypnos instead.

"That man has a way with women, as I am sure you will see. Although he seems to prefer to use his charms on the women in Dis."

Persephone wasn't the center of attention, but she didn't feel excluded. Hades slid a goblet of wine in her hand, and she held onto it for appearance's sake. She did not sip the wine and shook her head when Hades offered her a savory-looking morsel off his plate, and he wisely made no further attempt to induce her to eat. She was grateful whenever someone asked her a question because these provided her with momentary distractions from the empty feeling of her stomach.

She was mentally debating which one of these deities might be willing to help her when she felt a hand lightly touch her arm. She turned from Hades to face Hekate.

"I am full, and not in the mood to watch these sirens dance around and sing. Let the boys have their fun, I was hoping we could take a walk out in the garden?"

"That sounds lovely."

Hades glanced curiously at them but shrugged as Hekate led Persephone down the steps and into the garden, which spread out into what looked like a moor, bathed in the light of the Underworld's perpetual twilight. There were several streams running near the edges of this one, making for a charming landscape.

"I knew you were coming. I have known for a long time. Before you came, our circle of Khthonios was incomplete. The visions kept telling me that there was one more. I am glad you are here. I was hoping for another goddess, to balance out the gods we already have." She grinned. Persephone was happy that she was at least welcome here, but she had to let this goddess know the truth.

"I... I did not come here on my own. Hades kidnapped me," she replied in a quiet but clear tone, staring off at the weeping willow trees that marked the edge of the garden. The leaves were rich and dark-green, and made for a lovely screen for anyone who sought its shade and privacy.

"Really? My visions never said anything about that." Hekate was now glancing at her with open curiosity. Persephone shrugged.

"Could you help me escape the Underworld? Mother is doubtless worried about me, and I do not belong here."

"But Hades... he clearly cares for you. I have never known him to be interested in any women before. And I have known him for a long time."

"Oh, Hades *is* very kind. I... do not hate him or wish him ill. But I cannot stay here. Please help me. Surely you must know a way out of here. You are able to travel to the surface, are you not?"

o0o

Hekate held back a frown and kept her face as calm as she could. On one hand, if Persephone had been kidnapped, a wrong had been committed. But Hades was an honorable man, and this captive bride admitted to the Lord of the Dead's kindness.

She had known Hades for many centuries, and not once had he expressed any need for a bride or even a lover. Yet this daughter of Demeter had caught the Lord of the Dead's attention – not for a simple tryst but to stay at his side as Queen. Hades was serious about this union, that much was plain. And she could not go against her longtime friend, not if Persephone wasn't harmed in the very least. There was more to this situation than met the eye.

15

"I belong down here. I cannot go to the surface as often as I would like," Hekate replied. It wasn't quite the truth, but close enough.

"But when you can, could you...?"

"But you said that Hades was kind. Is it so terrible being with him?" Hekate asked, evading the question with increasing discomfort. Hades was Lord of this realm, and she could not meddle in his affairs.

"No, it is not. But..."

"He has not forced himself upon you, has he?"

"... No. No. He promised that he would never force himself upon me. He has been..." She glanced at a point beyond Hekate's shoulder as she carefully considered her choice of words, "very respectful."

Hekate nodded in relief and approval.

"I did not believe he was capable of such a thing, but I must be certain." She swallowed. "Your husband is a powerful man, and lord of a mighty realm. It is not my place to interfere with his affairs."

Persephone cast her gaze to the ground.

"I am not unmindful of your plight. But sometimes solutions to a problem are not always as apparent as they seem, and may lead to consequences," Hekate explained. The younger goddess looked back at her.

"Count me as a friend, Persephone. I have my own affairs, and need not tell Hades everything."

"You will answer my questions?" Persephone asked. Hekate nodded.

"Please tell me about the circle of Khthonios deities?"

"After expecting a question related to escaping

16

the Underworld, the older goddess was happy to answer this one.

"Unlike the world above, there is no one high king. Each of us has our own realm, and when in other realms, we respect the lords or ladies of these places. Hades is the king of the Underworld. Hypnos's realm is sleep, and Morpheus, that of the Dreaming. The dead and sleeping of the Hellenes come to them. Of course, we can not forget Erebus and Nyx, the first of us, of the darkness and the night. Hypnos is their son, as well as Kharon, guardian of the border between the dead and the living."

Persephone's brow creased in thought as she took in what was said, stroking her chin.

"And there's the Styx, who is Oblivion. And then there is you, of course. Would you care to guess who else makes up the circle?"

"Hmm." Persephone pursed her lip for several moments. "The Fates?"

Hekate shook her head. "The Fates are not of this world or the other, but it is an intelligent guess. There are three, though..."

"The Judges?"

"Justice is a necessary part of Dis, and the Judges, however many Hades might have, are a part of that circle, serving a vital part in Khthonios. As do the Furies, which are their own three-in-one. And Kampe, guardian of Tartarus. There are many parts of Khthonios, and Hades can not oversee them all on his own, mighty as he might be."

"Are there many other gods besides you? Like there is on Olympus?"

Hekate shook her head in the negative. "And thank Gaea for that. It's much quieter down here."

Their stroll led them under the wide canopy made by the weeping willow. Several fireflies buzzed around lazily, glowing in the semidarkness, and Persephone smiled faintly. Their light was more white-blue than the yellow she had seen in the world above, and also brighter, seeming more like hovering lamps than insects. Their buzz was also smoother and more sibilant than their earthly counterparts.

"The gardens down here are beautiful," Persephone whispered as she lifted one hand, palm upraised. One of the fireflies drifted over, landing on the preferred palm. "It is a lot like the surface world, but when you look closer...."

"That is what I like about this place. Places like this are familiar, but... different. The food, the material, the plants, and animals..."

"Do you ever miss the surface world?"

"No. I was born and raised up there like you, but I had the constant feeling that I did not fit in. I did not hesitate to eat the food of the Underworld. I have never regretted my decision."

o0o

"Why does the food bind you here?" Persephone asked. What was its unique property?

"It is not so much the food itself as... the commitment you make when you eat it. Hades' kingdom is not an ordinary home. He is host, and to accept his food is to make a sacred agreement."

"Xenia," Persephone whispered. The other goddess nodded. It was a sacred covenant between host and guest, that one would not harm the other, that the guest would follow the rules of the house, and the host would not take advantage of his guest. Naturally, down here, the rules would take on a new dimension.

"Your vision said that there was one more person left to complete the circle. But it did not say who, am I correct?" she asked. Hekate nodded.

"Then it could be *anybody*."

"Yes, it could have been anybody, but that time is past. It is you."

"Just because Hades brought me down here..."

"Visions are fulfilled in a variety of ways. Things happen. If Hades did indeed make the wrong choice, it will be apparent soon enough." She paused. "Why would Hades resort to kidnapping you? Had he made no attempt to court you?"

Persephone remembered her dream. "Mother. She was very... protective, and refused to allow any man near me."

"Any man?"

"*Any* man. God or mortal. I was surrounded by nymphs or under Mother's watch."

"And you *want* to go back to the surface?"

"I... yes. It is not because the Underworld is a terrible place. It is just... down here, there is no warmth, no life. However comfortable Hades keeps me, there is a certain... coldness to this place. Up there is the sunshine and the earth. I have the same Gift as my mother, and I cannot use it down here."

19

"Mmm. Now I understand your problem a little better. Demeter's Gift is part of the life-energy up there. You are right, there is none down here." Hekate seemed genuinely concerned. "Have you talked to Hades about it? He loves you. He *should* make accommodation for that, as a reasonable lord and a loving husband."

Yes! Thank you! Persephone almost cried out. Before either goddess could speak further, she heard Hades call out their names. Persephone frowned. It was almost as if Hades had known what they were talking about and had decided to stop the conversation from going further. Mind-reading wasn't part of Hades's Gift, was it?

Hekate lifted her arm, making an opening in the screen created by the drooping branches to see Hades standing near the steps, his eyes moving along the garden.

"I suppose the other guests bored you," Hades said to Hekate. The goddess in question just grinned and shrugged as she and Persephone walked down the small path.

"It is not often we get a new god down here. Much less often that you choose a bride."

"True enough. I trust the two of you had a pleasant time together." Hades commented. Persephone slowly nodded.

"Doubtless you have been working on corrupting her," Hades added as he glanced at his longtime friend.

"Maybe." Hekate smiled at Persephone before she looked back at Hades.

Persephone spent a bit more time with the other gods, familiarizing herself with them. The Judges were relaxed in this setting, and she suspected that they welcomed a reprieve from the judging of souls. After so many years, it must get boring, but when she asked them if they enjoyed their work, Minos nodded.

"It is necessary, my lady. But that does not mean we do not take satisfaction in our jobs."

"You could come and watch, if that would please you, Dark Queen," Aeacus offered.

"I would enjoy that very much, thank you," Persephone replied. There were still plenty of things to see and learn about the Underworld, and it emboldened her that despite her youth, she was being treated with respect by the elders of this shadowed realm.

o0o

Persephone stifled a yawn and felt a hand on her shoulder.

"If it pleases you, you should go on and take a bath. I will be there to join you shortly," Hades whispered. Not surprisingly, the thought of a bath with Hades sent small frissons of warmth and delight rippling through her body. She held back a low moan as she felt fingers slide up her hand and wrist, and looked down to see a shadowy hand stroking her. To be sure, Hades had a unique and exciting Gift. The last guest had just left, the performers were returned to Elysium, and she was eager to simply turn in for the night. It had been a long day, and she looked forward to the welcoming embrace of the soothing hot bath.

Before she left from the room, she glanced over her shoulder at him. He licked his lips in blatant lasciviousness, and she smirked before she disappeared from sight.

oOo

Hades's eyes followed her as she left the large chamber before he turned around, seeing Hekate standing next to a pillar. A thoughtful frown settled across his features.

"What is it, Hekate?" he asked, not wasting any time. The Goddess of the Crossroads lifted her chin and slid away from the pillar, approaching the Lord of the Dead.

"You announced that you had a bride, but you never mentioned the fact that you had to kidnap her."

"Oh, did I forget to mention that?" Hades asked dryly.

"What of her mother? Do you think that this will go unnoticed?"

"Demeter will have to accept it. Her father gave his blessing," A weak excuse, he knew. But he just had to say it. Daughters were given up all the time in marriage in Hellas. What of it? Yet this rationalization rung bitter in the back of his head, leaving a lingering taste of cold metal at the bottom of his mouth. He could not allow Hekate to see this, and schooled his face into the austere calm he was known for.

"Is that all you have to say?" Hekate asked incredulously, placing her hands on her hips.

"Yes," Hades replied shortly. He had no desire to try to defend his actions, especially with his old friend, nor did he want to waste the time when Persephone was waiting for him.

"Demeter will not rest until she has her child back."

"Persephone is not a child."

"You know very well what I mean!"

"I do, and I have no desire to discuss this matter."

"You stole a girl from her mother."

"So."

"You have no concern for Demeter's feelings?" Hekate pressed.

Hades kept his expression inscrutable as he looked at her. Yes, he cared for his sister. If Demeter hadn't been so hardheaded in protecting her daughter, the Lord of the Dead would have been glad to approach her for permission to court her daughter and give her whatever honors she might demand. He honestly had wanted to do the right thing, and if Ares hadn't pulled off that shitty stunt of his, then Demeter might have been more willing to consider a suitor for her precious child. After Persephone had been nearly raped, one couldn't blame the Harvest Goddess for her protective measures. But enough was enough.

"I will *not* discuss this matter further. And you will not try to intervene or get anyone else to. Understand? Persephone is *mine*," Hades growled. The temperature in the chamber suddenly dropped, and the shadows in the corners and around Hades's body were now pulsating and writhing. The Dark God's eyes were dark, so dark as to be fathomless black instead of their usual dark blue. His jaw was set in a tight line as he glared at Hekate.

oOo

Hekate had seen many things and was a powerful deity in her own right, but she was taken aback by the anger and fierceness she saw in his eyes. Hades was never a god to be trifled with.

She hadn't thought he would respond so angrily. Heaven forbid that anybody ever try to come between Hades and his bride.

"Yes, my lord." Hekate lowered her head in a respectful bow before retreating, her heart pounding.

oOo

Hades exhaled, the shadows stilling and the coldness fading away, shaking his head slowly as he made his way to his apartments, seeing the door to the bath chamber slightly ajar, admitting faint wisps of steam into the main room.

He closed the door behind him and stalked across the room. As he opened the smaller door all the way, he did it quietly so Persephone wouldn't hear him. She looked up anyway, already submerged in the water up to her shoulders, her hair pinned up loosely. Her eyes remained on him as he approached the edge of the gemstone-lined pool. She was sitting at the far

24

side, her head leaned against the edge as she relaxed. The rippling and bubbling of the water distorted the rest of her body, leaving no clear detail of her form to study from this vantage.

The Lord of the Dead wondered if he should say anything at all about the matter that Hekate had just broached. Persephone continued staring at him, her expression relaxed and pleasant. She then lifted a hand out of the water, curling a finger in a clear invitation. If she looked so at ease, why dredge up the subject that was the biggest point of conflict between them?

"Come on in, or are you just going to stand there looking all somber? You wanted a bath, have you changed your mind?" she asked.

"Oh no, not at all." He smiled at her.

Chapter XXI

oOo

Several days had passed since the banquet, and Persephone had not broached the subject of leaving the Underworld. Rather, she focused on spending time in the library and learning as much as she could, or asking him questions about this or that, particularly the Olympians. She wanted to know what to expect when she finally met her family, which was something that she determined would happen, one way or another.

It was when he was her tutor that he was at his most avuncular demeanor, and sometimes it felt a bit odd to know that he *was* her uncle. Despite knowing how closely tied their family was and how natural this was within Gaea's brood, she could not help but remember the mortal notions Iasion and his family had raised her with.

With many of the things she was learning, her perspective inevitably changed.

oOo

When Persephone woke up, Hades was already out of bed and sitting in front of the fire, deep in thought with his chin propped up on his hand. He leaned back against the divan, clad in a deep blue robe that was tied loosely, revealing his chest.

"It feels strange waking up alone. Already I have grown used to waking up beside you," Persephone admitted as she glanced at him. He looked up at her with a small smile before he rose from his seat, stalked over to the bed with several long, smooth strides, and blanketed himself over her form. His long hair framed his face and fell on her bare shoulders in silky black rivulets.

"It comforts me that you want my presence upon waking," he said as he looked down at her. She smiled faintly before he leaned his head down to kiss her cheek. She let out a quiet coo of delight as he nuzzled her, burying his face against the side of her head and her rumpled locks. She arched against him, feeling the hard and warm planes of his body through the thick blanket. He groaned softly and pressed back, his need making itself known. She delighted in being able to arouse him so easily.

She alone had this power over this sexy, handsome, powerful death-god. Death itself was mysterious, faceless. It decided when a soul would be cut off from his or her living flesh. The Greeks had a word for it, *thanatos*. Assigning it a name gave them a concrete concept to talk about, to identify. Hades was inevitably linked with this *thanatos* even though he actually had no part in people dying, making him an especially fearsome God.

Yet all she felt was comfort and security in his arms. She let him hug her tightly, one of his hands trailing along her face.

"Aidoneus..." she sighed as his thumb trailed along her lips.

"Yes." Hades sealed her lips with a kiss.

"There is something I would like to do today."

"You have but to name it."

"I want to see Tartarus."

Hades stared at her for several moments. Persephone gazed back at him calmly. After her encounter with the Fates and with Hekate, she decided to be more serious about her explorations of the Underworld. She had kept herself to the safety of the library and gardens after what had happened to her in the Styx. There had been plenty of things to do – she was never bored – but she knew she couldn't just stay in Hades's Palace forever.

"You... are certain that is what you want?" he asked. There was concern in his tone, but he wasn't at all patronizing or condescending as many others would have been.

"I am mindful of your warning. That is why I asked you to take me." She could have gone by herself while Hades was off performing his godly duties, but after her encounter with Styx, she was more cautious. She didn't want to be overwhelmed and unable to respond to her surroundings, and she knew that the tortured screams she heard the other day were but a glimpse into the hell of Tartarus. She trusted Hades to keep her safe, and to also be honest with her.

"Very well then. After breakfast, we will go."

Persephone sighed softly, not wishing to sit through another tantalizing meal, but Hades gazed down at her steadily.

"I will permit you to remain in your room and amuse yourself while I eat," Hades said in a surprise concession. She maintained a placid expression to hold back the quick grin that nearly flashed across her face, not wanting to make her relief too obvious.

"Thank you."

He nodded.

oOo

After Persephone had chosen an outfit, she examined some of her treasures until Cloe nudged her, signaling that Hades was done with his meal and it was time to leave.

With her destination in mind, Persephone chose a black chiton over a deep red silk tunic. The rich variety of garments gave Persephone plenty of room to experiment, and she found pleasure in mixing colors sometimes. The deep red of the tunic peeked out from her chiton, which was held up by gold pins and cinched by a matching plain golden girdle. The black garment ended at her elbows, tastefully displaying her lower arms, which were free of adornment. Her hair was pinned up in a bun, swept up off her neck gracefully in a coil held by black ribbons.

"Is Tartarus hot? Or do I need a cloak?" Persephone asked. Cloe was unable to make words, but the servant understood her commands and found ways to answer her requests. The wispy head shook 'no', and she briefly nodded.

As if he had read her mind, Hades was also clad in black and deep red. He was dressed regally, with a golden crown atop his dark hair, and his clothing was trimmed with gold.

She showed no apprehension when the Lord of the Dead led her to the chariot and climbed into it before he could offer her his hand. She held the chariot railing with calm confidence, her head lolling back against his chest in a relaxed and trusting manner. He lowered his head to nuzzle the top of her own, and felt one of her hands leave the railing to lie atop the hand that was resting over her stomach.

The gray sky turned crimson as the chariot sped along the road. The trees reached out with clawed branches, seeming almost alive. They passed souls being led by shades, most of them struggling against the faceless specters of Dis. Persephone noted to herself that she had yet to see a judging. She could only imagine how it must be for the mighty Judges to condemn someone to an eternity of suffering.

They crossed the bridge, heat radiating from the river to envelop them and bringing a flush to their cheeks. The thick brass doors rose before them like a monolith, its burnished face hard and cold. The design of the doors was deceptively simple, with no indication as to what horrors waited within, but a sudden, terrified wail from beyond the walls caused her to shudder. *Do I really want to see what's in there?* With firm resolve, she stared ahead, raising her chin.

The chariot stopped, but Hades made no move to get out. The condemned souls they had passed now approached the bridge, dragged along by the silent and efficient shades. A few were silent, resigned to their fates as they were led along, but that was not the case for the majority of souls here. They screamed and pleaded with Hades, giving him all sorts of praises and lavish titles, bemoaning the injustice of their sentences, and swearing up and down on all sorts of gods that they were innocent. Even without solid flesh, she saw the fear and desperation in their eyes. She felt Hades's hand on her arm before she felt his warm breath at her ear.

"Do not be swayed by their pleas. Their crimes in life were heinous, and the justice they escaped in their lives awaits them here. Even now they do not wish to admit their guilt."

She silently nodded, watching as the heavy gates opened. There had been several blackbirds perched atop the gate, their eyes glowing balefully as the souls approached. When the gates started to open, they flew off their perch and dove at the souls, undeterred by their terrified shrieks. The screaming of the birds melded with the cries to create a harrowing symphony that caused her to shudder. As the souls were admitted, Hades flicked his reins, and the horses pulled them into Tartarus. Even as he did so, more souls were dragged down the road behind them to swell the ever-increasing numbers in this cursed region.

Persephone let her eyes move around, seeing pits of flame here and there, and more gateways leading in different directions, lacking doors. She didn't see anyone being tortured in this open space, and the souls that had just been admitted were flung into a firepit. She wondered what the purpose was, but was quickly answered when solid forms climbed out of the flames, making various sounds of terror and pain

31

as they sought to escape the heat.

"These firepits create fleshy shells for the condemned souls so that their punishment can be administered in a more... effective manner."

"I see." Shades were at hand to collect the newly 'born' prisoners, and she noticed that the shades assigned to Tartarus had a reddish tint to their wispy forms, and some of them even looked solid, with well-defined boundaries to their bodies. In a few moments, she realized why.

The more solid of Khthonios's servants had various features that were menacing, like clawed hands, barbed tails, or jagged maws lined with sharp and ragged teeth. Some of them even bore objects such as pitchforks, spears, whips, or other instruments of pain. The newly fleshed souls were poked and prodded by these, and ushered off through different gates.

"What do the different gates lead to?" Persephone asked.

"It depends on their sin. Some have let greed or sloth take over their lives. Others betrayed their family and friends. Some were so consumed with vainglory that they did evil deeds, thinking they could escape justice. All punishments are determined by the nature of the sin. Though the Judges decide which of the three realms of the dead a soul goes to, Kampe and the Furies determine these particular punishments and the shades of Tartarus mete them out as ordered."

"I am positive that if mortals could actually see Tartarus, it would be a good deterrent to evil behavior," Persephone commented, already impressed, even though she knew that she had barely begun to see Hell.

"Some of them would continue their wicked ways nonetheless. There are always those who think they can escape the consequences, however great the risk," Hades shrugged as he stepped down from the chariot. A couple of shades came forward to attend to the horses as Persephone let Hades help her out. She was perfectly capable of doing it herself, but she had to admit, she enjoyed his chivalry.

Suddenly, she heard a slithering sound and turned her head. Through one of the gates, she saw a large and serpentine form emerge, its scales reflecting the flickering light from the firepits. The creature was massive, standing at nearly twice Hades's height, and that didn't include the length of tail winding along the stone floor. As she got a better view of this creature, she realized that it was actually a she. Though the female traits weren't very obvious, Persephone noted the difference between chest and waist, one she had only ever seen on women. The chest was covered in what appeared to be a brass breastplate, and armbands adorned the she-creature's arms, which were just as flexible as her tail and ended in clawed hands.

The face was lacking in delicate feminine features, but there was still something about the set of lips and the shape of the face that marked this creature as a woman. Her hair was made up of a writhing mass of scaled coils, much like a Gorgon, though these coils did not terminate in snake-heads.

Nevertheless, they coiled and whipped around as if with a mind of their own, and Persephone felt a shiver pass through her body as this creature cast her slitted amber eyes at her.

"Welcome, Lord Aidoneus," she said in a voice that was an odd mixture between a rumble and a hiss, giving her words a sibilance that Persephone had never heard before.

"Greetings, Kampe," Hades said as he looked up at the impressive demoness. Persephone did not miss the mutual respect that the two underworld deities held for one another, their gazes relaxed and polite as they regarded one another, no differently than any other Underworld deity might interact with Hades.

"This must be our new queen," Kampe stated, her gaze moving to Hades's companion.

"Indeed. This is Persephone. Persephone, this is Kampe, keeper of the keys to Tartarus and warden to all of our condemned souls."

Kampe's gaze was penetrating, and the young goddess lifted her chin, gazing back, trying to not make it too obvious that she was studying the serpentine deity, having never seen such a creature like this. She had imagined Kampe to have human form like all the other chthonic deities she had met thus far. Hekate had never said anything about this! The two held one another in silent regard as Hades smiled faintly with amusement. Finally, the serpentine goddess gave out a grunt before she nodded.

"One who can look upon me without flinching is worthy."

"I am not a condemned soul. I should not be afraid of you, correct?" she asked. She saw the barest of smiles tug at the demoness' lips.

"A fine bride you have chosen," Kampe hissed to Hades. He smiled, pleased with her approval. As the demoness turned away to lead them deeper into Tartarus, Persephone felt him squeeze her hand.

"Kampe does not take to many people," Hades whispered. She smiled.

"I suppose spending all day around screaming and tortured souls does that."

Hades chuckled softly and shook his head.

"Where are we going?" she asked.

"Tartarus is a big place. It would be impossible to see all of it within a day. But we could show you a few things, and Kampe can answer your questions."

The gates leading off the firepit area looked the same, and Kampe chose the center one to lead them through. Persephone let her eyes wander along Kampe's tail as it slithered along the ground. Even with the redness of the sky and the light from fires, Persephone could tell that Kampe's scales were of varying shades of copper, which reflected the fires of Hell beautifully and adding to her appearance. She could easily imagine the impression that the guardian of Tartarus made on her prisoners.

o0o

Because of the sights in Tartarus, Hades had been reluctant to take her here, but she seemed so calm as she asked Kampe questions or was shown several condemned souls being subjected to various punishments. Her eyes might widen, and she would wrinkle her nose a bit at the gore of several displays, but she did not flinch or turn away.

Tartarus was divided into various regions, each of them suited for the punishment of a certain sin. Kampe referred to them as 'levels' and 'circles'. She listened attentively as the Warden explained what they had done in their mortal lives, and why they were punished that way. Persephone didn't seem at all put off by Kampe's brusque manner of speaking.

"So far I have seen mortals being punished for their wicked deeds. But..." She frowned thoughtfully, "I thought that the Titans who went against Zeus were also held here."

"Indeed," Kampe replied, "But for practical reasons, they are kept apart from mortal souls in a level all their own."

"What about Prometheus?" the younger goddess asked. "I heard that he was punished for bringing fire to humans."

"That is another example of where the myth differs from fact," Hades explained, "It was not Zeus who punished him. This was the time of the Titanomachy. They were not like the Olympians, as you well know. Kronos and his allies were tyrants who enjoyed exercising their power over the mortals, simply because they could. Back then, the Titans guarded the secret of fire. If the mortals wanted fire, they had to petition Kronos and his brethren and give them many offerings."

"...and Prometheus showed the mortals how to

make fire on their own?" Persephone deduced. Fire was precious. It was difficult to start, but with enough efforts and the right ingredients, just about anybody could spark a fire, especially if they had a good flint. The general practice in Enna at nights was to bank the fire to ensure that there would be embers in the morning to refresh the fire or create new ones. Nonetheless, Iasion had taught her how to spark a fire on her own with not just a flint, but also with the older and more time-consuming process of rubbing wood, saying that such knowledge was valuable.

"Indeed. They chained him to an open spot on Olympus so that the eagles could feed on him day after day. Since he was a Titan, he could not die, and so his flesh regenerated every night."

Persephone swallowed thickly as she imagined herself in that position. That poor man!

"He is not among those down here," Kampe hissed with what appeared to be a small smile on her reptilian face.

"I would hope not." Persephone quipped.

"Zeus broke his chains and freed him. However, he is not one of those who wish to be recognized. He lives somewhere among the mortals and has been lost to us for many years. But his legacy remains, though the tales that the mortals tell of him are now mangled." Hades shook his head.

Persephone nodded in rapt interest, absorbing everything that Hades or Kampe told her.

"If some of these tales are wrong, then why not set them right? Why not tell the mortals what really happened to Prometheus? The mortals think he is still being punished for teaching them the secret of fire." If Mother knew the truth of these tales, why didn't she share them with her daughter?

"It is the nature of humans to embellish the myths to make them more interesting. Just you wait," Kampe said, wagging her finger in the manner that a stern grandmother might, "In a thousand years, the tales you know today, and the tales that will be created will change again. Humans have the tendency to change history to suit their own purposes."

"That seems rather... deceitful."

"Sometimes, yes. There are those who deliberately change the stories, especially to benefit themselves. But at other times, such as with old stories, they change in subtle ways, without any deliberate twisting around."

Persephone nodded before glancing at Hades. "Thank goodness for your library, then!"

"Indeed."

"Who is that?" Persephone asked as she pointed just past Kampe's arm, seeing a steep and jagged hill in the distance surrounded by a moat of fire-water. The silhouette of a man was illuminated against the vermilion-hued sky, and she could make out his struggle against a large boulder that was nearly at the top of the hill.

"That is Sisyphus, now a prisoner of his own avarice and prideful cleverness," Kampe replied.

"Will you tell me about him?"

"Certainly. In life, he was a proud king who founded the city that mortals now known as Corinth. He was the son of a king of Thessaly but was so prideful that he wanted a kingdom of his own. He was a clever man and managed to accomplish it, but he was so arrogant as to consider himself above the law of mortals. The fool did not bother to consider that even he was subject to the laws of Death." Her hiss was one of clear disdain. "He lured travelers and visitors deep within his Palace and killed them."

Persephone gasped softly. "Why?"

"Pride. He thought himself above the laws of hospitality. He cleverly hid the bodies and even fed their meat to his guests, saving his own animals for himself. He wove a web of lies and tried to deceive even the gods themselves. But his ego was his undoing. And even in death, he refused to face the truth."

"And the punishment?"

"He accomplished much in life. Despite his faults, he *was* an intelligent man." Kampe's lips twisted into a fanged smile, "Down here, his skilled mind serves no purpose. See the boulder? His task is to push the boulder up the hill. If he stops, the shades are there to poke and whip him along. And when it nears the top of the hill, it rolls down. And he must start all over, for eternity."

Persephone smirked. She could easily imagine how menial and mind-numbing such a task was, especially to an intelligent person. To have to repeat it over and over and *over*, with no results or success...

"Did you think of that punishment?" Persephone asked. Kampe nodded.

"How fitting that Sisyphus had his punishment decided by someone more clever than he." She wasn't trying to flatter Kampe – it was clear that the guardian of Tartarus cared little for honeyed words – but she could see that her comment pleased the serpentine deity immensely.

"Are there any other prisoners you would like to show me?" Persephone asked, making it clear that she trusted Kampe's decision.

"Yes. Follow me." As she slithered off, Persephone caught Hades staring at her with a small smile. She smiled back and took his proffered hand.

"You look like you are enjoying yourself," he whispered.

"Yes. Immensely so."

"Tartarus is not a place for enjoyment," he shot back lightly.

"I do not enjoy this in the same way that... I enjoy the gardens or other such things. It is just... I find this place-" She waved her hand, looking for the correct word. "Enlightening."

"I was afraid that this place would be too frightening for you," he admitted.

"I appreciate you being honest with me and not hiding anything from me."

They came to a pond, its waters dark and clear. At the edge stood a large tree bearing several varieties of fruit, most of its branches hanging over the pond. Several shades hovered around the edge of the pond, and it became apparent why. There was a naked man in the water, the pond level with his waist. Near the pond, the air felt rather hot and oppressive, even worse than the hottest summer day on the surface world.

"This man was once a great king. Zeus sometimes invites kings to Olympus to share his Council with them, to impress them and learn from them." Kampe said, gesturing towards the man.

"He must have angered Zeus..."

"The fact that he had been invited to Olympus filled him with arrogance. He stole ambrosia, using it to extend his own lifespan. That in itself might have been forgiven in due time. But when Zeus invited him back, he had already become so arrogant, falling to the same faults as Sisyphus. He murdered his own little son and brought the meat to the table of the gods, disguising it as animal meat, having his cooks prepare it with spices. He presented the remains of his son to Zeus. The meat was cleverly prepared, but Zeus still saw it for what it was. He was so disgusted and outraged that he threw a thunderbolt at Tantalus and killed him on the spot."

"And what is this punishment?"

"He was a king who enjoyed the finest things in life and demanded every comfort, however trivial, at the cost of others. Here the air is always searing and the water icy, and he longs for the most basic comforts. He is always hot, hungry, thirsty, cold, bored, and lonely. He cannot leave the pond, but he may lie down in the shallows. But the rocks are hard and sharp, so whether standing, sitting, or lying down, he is ever uncomfortable."

As Kampe spoke, Persephone saw Tantalus reach for the fruit above him, jumping out of the water to do so. But the branches lifted the tantalizing food out of his reach. The sand surrounding the pond was soft and fine, which would be welcome to sleep on even if one hadn't been spending centuries on sharp rocks. The dark-haired man lowered himself in the water until it ended at his underarms. However, when he tried to lower his arms – whether to cup his hands or simply splash the water – the level receded, staying out of reach of his hands. He could not splash his face, much less try to drink from the water! The shades were there to make sure he did not leave the pond, and since they did not speak, Tantalus had nobody to talk to, but she was certain he screamed and pleaded with them. How ingenious.

At one side of the pond was a thick forest of black trees, and at the other side of the forest was a large stone tub with a decently sized pile of brass urns near it. However, there was nobody in sight, and Persephone tilted her head, stopping. She wanted to know about this before she went on. At the other side of the clearing was a river. Its size alerted her to the fact that this might be one of the important rivers of the Underworld. Thus far she had only seen two, the Styx and Phlegethon. She knew there was still the Lethe, Acheron, and Cocytus rivers to see.

"Wait, Kampe. I would like you to tell me about this." She waved her hand at the tub and pile of urns.

"The prisoners here are one of few who ever leave Tartarus," Kampe replied as she turned around.

"Excuse me, but I thought that Tartarus is... permanent."

"Most of the time, it is. But not every crime is committed with malice in the heart. The ones here committed their crime out of fear and obedience, and they were further provoked by the ones they had been told to murder. The crime was grave indeed, so punishment was necessary, but not an eternal one."

"I want to hear the story," she replied firmly. Kampe nodded.

"There was a king named Danaus. He had many daughters by a nymph, and they were all of great beauty, and renown through the land. Their father guarded their virginity closely, for he had ambitions to take his twin brother's kingdom for his own. This brother, Aegyptus, had sons of his own. So Danaus offered him his plethora of daughters as brides for the princes. But before they were sent to their grooms, he gave them each a dagger and told them to kill the princes. That way, Aegyptus would have no heirs, and Danaus intended to murder him right after the wedding banquet. Thus, both kingdoms would become his."

Mother had never discussed such stories with her, Persephone mused.

"All but of the girls killed their grooms as their father had ordered, for he was a powerful and despotic king who did not hesitate to punish or execute his subjects whenever he saw fit. The lone innocent maiden spared her husband because he had honored her wish to not give up her virginity to a man she did not know, and thus their wedding night was peaceful. Because murder is a severe crime, the others had to come here to Tartarus. However, they had no malice in their hearts and were fearful of their father not without reason, and being forced into their wedding beds by their grooms only exacerbated their terror. Though these men were murdered, they had their own crime, that of forcing themselves upon innocent maidens and planning to take Danaus's kingdom for their own. Had they not, they might have been spared just as their brother was spared by Hypermenstra. So her sisters' punishment was to draw water from the Cocytus and fill up the tub so they could bathe in it and wash away their sins."

Doesn't sound too bad, Persephone thought to herself. The river looked placid, and she didn't see any instruments of torture. She knew better than to voice that assumption.

"There is more to it, is there not?" Persephone asked as her eyes moved to the pile of urns, noticing tiny perforations around their rounded shapes.

"By the time they got to the tub, most of the water had leaked out. It took them many years to complete the task. They could complete this task on their own time since there were no shades to push them along. Every time they stepped into the Cocytus, they were overcome with incredible sadness and lamentation. Some of them lamented more than others, but as you can see, all finished the task in due time."

"Does this river run through other parts of Tartarus?"

"Indeed. Through Tartarus, the Cocytus cuts a winding path, as does the Acheron and the Phlegethon, flowing where they are needed."

It was a unique punishment indeed, but she could see Kampe's wisdom. Persephone could understand how having a cruel father who threatened your life, and a groom you had never met before taking you by force, could reduce a woman to such measures. Had she had a sword or dagger when Ares tried to force himself on her, Persephone wouldn't have hesitated to stab or castrate him.

She felt appreciation to Hades for honoring her wishes, and as if he was aware of her feelings, she felt him squeeze her shoulder as the trio continued down the path.

oOo

Persephone's stomach had been bothering her for most of the day. It was something other than hunger pains, and it had been located below her stomach. Having a scrumptious-looking feast in front of her as Hades had his supper only increased her discomfort. She curled up on the divan, her back to the table as she tried to ignore the tantalizing scent of the dishes. She heard him coax her to come and eat, but she covered her ears with her hands. Damn Hades!

Finally, the door to her room swung open. She retreated into it without so much a glance over her shoulder, closing the door behind herself. How dare Hades try to coax and tempt her with the food when he saw her discomfort! In her anger, she slipped off her sandals and flung them against the wall. Cloe appeared in a moment to pick up the shoes and put them away, which only vexed her all the more.

Tartarus had been a wonderful distraction, but she had also felt moody this morning, wishing to see something darker than the library or one of the gardens. She couldn't explain why she had felt so impatient and frustrated even when Hades hadn't forced her to sit with him for the morning meal.

With an angry mutter, she pulled the pins out of her chiton, letting the soft black material fall to the floor before pulling her tunic over her head, becoming aware of a hot slickness on her thighs as the cool air caused goosebumps to rise along her naked flesh. With a thoughtful frown, she reached down.

Her fingers came away wet, and Persephone stared down at the crimson slickness on her fingertips.

Chapter XXII

oOo

Persephone stared at the bloodstains on her trembling fingers, her heart beating rapidly as she tried to process what had just happened to her. Why was she bleeding? She wasn't bleeding from... *there*, was she? Hesitantly, she turned toward the mirror and approached it, barely conscious of her shallow breathing.

With her other hand, she reached down, careful to not touch anything until she reached her most private part. Tentatively, she slipped her finger between the soft folds of flesh down there, discovering slickness that didn't come from arousal.

No no no. She felt as if she might faint. Why was this happening to her? Had her body somehow responded to the horrors of Tartarus?

Those who enjoyed inflicting pain upon others in life were rewarded with torture for eternity. Some were chained while various abuses were inflicted upon them – whippings, stabbings, needles, fires, hot oil – while others were allowed to run around in a confined space, but this provided no reprieve because there was always a shade to punish them, driving them on with nail-studded whips. The flesh would tear and fall apart. The souls were tossed into the firepits to regenerate their flesh, and the pain would be inflicted anew. A few of the inmates of Tartarus even had their bodies removed, leaving them nothing more than heads stuck on poles, screaming and wailing, denied their bodies until the shades decided to toss them back in the firepits, which might be the next day or several centuries hence.

Her first thought was to panic and go to Hades for help. A brush on her arm caused her to gasp and shudder, and she looked over her shoulder, seeing Cloe. She blushed even though she knew that her servant was merely a shade, with no mind or personality of its own.

The shade floated there, waiting for a command. Apparently, it had sensed her distress, but this was a situation it had never encountered, and it was waiting for her directive. That gave Persephone something to focus on, and she took a deep breath, focusing on practical matters, grateful for the shade's silent efficiency as it fetched her what she'd asked for.

Once the immediate crisis had been addressed, she sat down in front of her mirror, clad in a chiton and robe of dark indigo and violet, recalling memories from her childhood in Enna. That part of her life seemed almost like a dream sometimes.

It had been over a decade since her father died and she had been taken away from her family. It didn't matter if Zeus was her sire, she would always consider the people she left behind as her family. She had been treated with love and warmth by everyone. She missed them and often reminisced about them even though Mother said that that part of her life was past.

One day, she and Alestis had gone to one of the ponds near the farm with Ptheia to collect berries. Her aunt had taken a basket of laundry with her and while the girls romped and collected blueberries as well as herbs, Ptheia washed clothes, beating them against a rock and hanging them up on the branches of a tree.

By chance, Persephone – Kora back then – noticed that her aunt had a rag at the bottom of the basket that was dark with blood. She wondered if Ptheia had hurt herself, and watched silently as her aunt scooped up some water into a clay bowl and washed the rag in it before wringing it out on the grass, so as to not dirty the pond. She repeated this process a few times, refilling the bowl and dumping its contents on the grass.

"Did you hurt yourself?" Kora asked, breaking the silence. The older woman looked up, startled.

"Are you well?" the girl asked, concern evident in her tone.

"No, But thank you for being so concerned. You can go collect some more blueberries."

"What happened, then? Did someone else hurt themselves?" Kora could not help but ask.

"No," Ptheia sighed quietly, shaking her head. "It... comes with being a woman. You and Alestis will learn about it soon enough."

"Why would a woman bleed? Does it hurt? Where do you bleed from?"

"So many questions, Kora. Your husband will have to be a very smart and patient man," Ptheia replied. Now, as Persephone thought about it, her aunt's statement had been uncannily prophetic.

"Do men bleed?" Kora could not help but ask.

"It would be nice if they did," her aunt replied

ruefully as she wrung out the rag one more time before hanging it up to dry.

"Why?"

"It would make them more humble, for one thing. But no, it is a woman's burden. You will learn about it in a few years and your mother or I can explain it. For now, just enjoy your girlhood. It is short enough as it is, so do not dwell upon such matters." There was a tone of finality to her voice which made it clear that she would not answer any more questions about the subject, at least not until the right time came.

When she had asked Mother about why a woman bled, Demeter had become tight-lipped, refusing to speak of the matter at all.

Persephone stared at her reflection in the mirror, admiring the swell of her breasts under her tunic, and the graceful curves that were replacing her almost boyish angles. Oh yes, she was finally taking on a woman's form. She wished that Ptheia had been willing to discuss the subject further. How often did this happen? How long? Did Ptheia experience the same pain she felt in her lower abdomen? Did all women feel vaguely cranky or irritable when they bled? She tapped her chin, pondering the fact that her breasts had felt slightly tender the last couple of days, especially her nipples. Was that from her the effects the Underworld, had on her, or did it have something to do with this bleeding?

The underlying irritability she felt fed her resentment towards Mother. If Mother had been honest with her, then she would know exactly what to do and what to expect.

It was something all women went through. Ptheia took care of her husband and children like any other woman did. Evidently, this bleeding wasn't dangerous or harmful, though she still needed to know why and how. Who would answer her questions? She would simply figure that one out on her own if she had to, and rose to her feet, feeling more confident.

At least, until she thought about leaving her room. She would have to face Hades. How long could she hide this from him? How did women deal with this around males, anyway? How much did men know or understand of this? Oh dear, there were more questions than she had originally thought...

Staring ahead, she picked up her brush and ran it through her hair in slow, idle strokes. Normally she would have Cloe do her hair, but she was looking for an excuse, any excuse, to delay facing Hades, since she was still angry with him about supper, and her overall grouchiness certainly wasn't doing any favors for the Dark God.

She tugged her brush through several tangled locks and felt the wispy, ethereal fingers of her attendant brush against her hand.

"No!" she growled. Obediently, Cloe drew back.

oOo

Hades had already changed into a comfortable robe, ready to relax for the night with his bride. At least, he hoped she would want to relax with him. They'd had a pleasant time today in Tartarus, but her

51

attitude towards him had deteriorated at supper. He had heard the rumble of her stomach, why did she have to be so damn stubborn? What was she afraid of? She seemed to enjoy everything she was shown, including Tartarus.

She had even shown disappointment in the fact that the Furies had not been in Tartarus at that time – they sometimes went to the surface to torment mortals and drive them mad – and had seemed eager to come back to Tartarus at a later date so she could meet them. Her interest was genuine – she wanted to know things and her questions were interesting, rather than seeking knowledge merely for the sake of escaping the Underworld. How could he convince her to take a bite of the otherworldly food?

He waited for a while before he rose from his bed and approached the door to her room. He wouldn't let her sulk. He hated seeing her angry or perturbed, and he paused before her door. Never in his entire existence had the feelings of somebody else affected him in such a way. He was generally cold and aloof, yes, but he was also fair, and deep down inside, compassionate. But he had never been moved as he was now, and it was a feeling he was far from used to. He was upset with himself for upsetting her, angry that she continued to be defiant, and baffled at her refusal to eat his food.

"Persephone," Hades said loudly before giving the door a couple of sharp raps. No response came from within, so he opened the door without hesitation. She sat on a stool in front of the mirror, staring ahead blankly as she brushed her hair. He stared for several moments as the brush went down her hair slowly, tugging at the thick waves. She did not acknowledge him.

Like the shadows that he controlled, the Lord of the Dead moved across the floor smoothly, dark and regal as he approached her from behind, his pale face standing out amidst the muted light of the chamber. Persephone's eyes flickered as she noticed his reflection in the mirror before looking down.

"I do not like to see you unhappy," He placed his hands on her shoulders. She continued to brush her hair, and he grabbed her wrist, holding it in a firm but gentle grip.

"I do not want to see you go hungry. I am sorry you are upset, but I cannot sit by and watch you starve yourself."

"If you would bring food from the surface world, you would not have to watch me starve. Then you would not have to be so concerned," Persephone replied primly, trying to tug her wrist from his grip, but he did not budge. Being the daughter of the Goddess of Bounty, it was a certainty that she had never before known hunger, so her resolve was as impressive as it was vexing.

Already her self-denial was not without consequences. Free of her mother's magic, her body was molding itself to what it should be, but not without signs of her deprivation. There was a slight hollowness in her cheeks and shoulders, and she was becoming paler.

"I have told you before that I will not be doing that. The only way to sate your hunger is to eat what I offer you," he replied calmly and resolutely.

Persephone sighed, shaking her head in irritation.

"We had such a lovely day today. Please do not sulk."

"Then kindly refrain from setting all that food before me!" she replied petulantly.

"I cannot let you starve yourself. Must I tie you up and force you to eat or stand by and watch you waste away? I do not relish the thought of either," Hades scolded.

"I have no desire to talk about it," Her eyes were downcast

"... Very well." He slowly let go of her wrist to stroke her hair. "Come to bed, then, and sleep." All he wanted was a night of peace.

"Do not tell me what to do."

Hades raised an eyebrow. Was she *looking* for a fight? Hmm. He smirked wryly. Normally, he did not respond to deliberate provocation, but this might be what was needed.

"I am your husband and master," he stated imperiously, biting back a smile as he saw her cheeks flush in indignation.

"You are not! We are not even married!"

"Oh, is it a ceremony you want?" Hades did want one, but he hadn't wanted to force her into one, so the subject had not been approached. He would prefer her to eat the food of the dead first and accept her place here so she would be a happy bride for the wedding. "I will be all too happy to oblige. The tailors will make a glorious wedding dress for you. What color would you prefer? Oh, this is so exciting.

This will be the first wedding we have ever had in Khthonios." In a rare moment of playfulness, he clapped his hands together like an excited child.

"Hmph! I think not. Go away," she pouted.

"Such behavior is not fitting of the Queen of the Dead," the Lord of the Dead retorted, dropping his hands.

Persephone whipped around to glare up at him. "You sound like Mother. 'Such behavior is not fitting for the daughter of a goddess', she would say when I did not want to listen to her orders."

"Yet you refuse to eat my food so you can go back to the surface, and you know what your mother is likely to do."

"I want to see the world."

"Accept what I offer you, and you *will* have the world."

"I am not in the mood for riddles."

"Then what are you in the mood for?"

"I don't know." Persephone huffed softly, setting down her brush. It was clear she was frustrated about something, and that she didn't know how to – or didn't want to – voice it.

"How about a bath? I will massage your back," Hades offered. Perhaps being in the hot water would ease the perturbed and unhappy glint he saw in her eyes.

"No." She looked away, as if afraid by the thought of a bath.

"Perhaps I could... *soothe* away your frustrations..." His voice dropped lower, taking on a velvety tone.

"*No!*" This idea seemed to bother her even more than a bath with him.

"Why are you so upset?"

"Hmph."

"Come now, love. Talk to me."

"No."

Hades let out a quiet huff. Women could be so... baffling sometimes. Rather than seek further engagement, he decided a graceful surrender would keep them both in better spirits.

"I hope that you know you can talk to me," he finally said after several moments of terse, awkward silence. She nodded briefly.

"Leave me alone," Persephone stated after several more moments of silence. "Please," she quickly added.

o0o

In the mirror's reflection, she saw a flash of hurt in his eyes, but she regarded his pain with frosty silence. He looked down at her, his gaze lingering on her face before he retreated from the room.

Chapter XXIII

oOo

On Olympus, nobody knew of Kora's disappearance but Zeus himself. Once in a while, he would send one of his eagles to check on Demeter, and they always returned with the news that she was still looking for her child, which suited him since there was no other living soul that was capable of telling Demeter where the girl was.

Let Demeter keep looking, as long as she didn't cause trouble. Hopefully, after a while, she would be more receptive to the news that her daughter was now the companion of Hades once she was assured of her safety. After all, the Dread Lord really wasn't a bad man. Kora would be treated well. Things would be fine, at least eventually. It was not even a moon after Kora's disappearance, and what were a few weeks to the gods, who had existed for many centuries?

Zeus was relieved that she hadn't gone to the Olympians for help. He expected her to, after a while, but was glad for her to wait as long as possible. If the young gods of Olympus knew Kora was missing, he did not doubt there would be a mad scramble for what they would view as a prize.

Not that Hades would permit it, of course. But he had no doubt that his elder brother could handle things well. Hadn't he always?

oOo

Demeter was a powerful Earth-goddess, much like Gaea herself. She could find secrets deep within the earth – like she had discovered Ouranos – but the location of her daughter eluded her. Nymphs continued to report back to her with empty hands. Even the reclusive nymphs who lived in the most remote mountain ranges and underground springs or rivers yet unexplored by man had no news to offer.

Demeter hoped that she would not have to go to Olympus, but the earth offered her no clues to Kora's whereabouts, and Cyane would not appear out of her pond. She had been hoping that she could find her daughter on her own, but that prospect was fading every day. If Kora wasn't being held prisoner on or within the earth, she dreaded to think who might be involved.

It was something she never wanted to contemplate. She had pushed the knowledge of Kora's paternity into the deepest recesses of her mind, content with the illusion that her daughter was the child of the man she loved, not the god who had tricked her.

If Kora could not be found in the earth, did that mean she was on Olympus? Surely Zeus wouldn't... She felt her jaw tighten as she processed the implications of this deed and what it meant.

o0o

Iasion moved away from the shore, strolling along the white sand as the azure-green waters of the Sea of

Eternity sparkled under a nonexistent sun. He'd been dead for over ten years, and while Elysium was a pleasant place to live in, he still felt at times that this place was lacking despite its pleasures. Any newly dead mortal was comforted in the fact that they would eventually be reunited with their loved ones. Mother had led a good life and Father was here, waiting to welcome her when her time came. His brothers would come here too, he was sure of it. His nephews and niece...

His thoughts went to his wife and daughter as it often did. One day, he might see Kora. She would be twenty-five years old now. Was she already married? She had been a beautiful little girl, and he had no doubts that she would have blossomed into a lovely maiden. He spent a lot of time thinking about her. Never in his mortal life would he have dreamed that he would have a child with a goddess. Demeter had lifted the curse from his life and loved him, and he had worshiped her freely.

Demeter would be gone for days at a time, performing her duties as the Goddess of the Harvest. Her absences made him appreciate her all the more, and he always welcomed her back with ardor. Sadly, he knew that he could never be with her here in Elysium. This was one of the consequences of loving an immortal being.

The man stared out at the Sea of Eternity, contemplating what had come to be since he had settled for a nap under the olive tree at the edge of his farm, intending to rest after feeling some tightness in his chest.

Anytime a person felt that Elysium was not the right place for them, they could petition to go to the Lethe Court, where they could drink of the waters of oblivion and be reborn in the mortal world.

This place was nice, but it wasn't one that he wanted to stay in forever. He had met new people here and made friends, but he still missed his goddess. He could not forget her as long as he remained here. This would mean meeting the Judges again, or possibly Hades himself face-to-face as he made his case. He could only be honest and wondered what Hades might say to know of his relationship to Demeter. But he had heard that the Lord of the Dead was a stern but fair ruler.

This was something he had considered for a few years. He saw lovers being reunited with one another, joy filling their eyes as they saw cherished ones, rushing forward and kissing and hugging often. Every time he saw such a thing, he felt wistful.

What's the point of living in Paradise if I do not have somebody to share it with? His mind was made up. He would go to one of the shades who kept an eye on this blissful haven and wait to be summoned before the Judges or even Hades himself. He already knew what he was going to say.

oOo

The sun was setting, and the view from Olympus – no matter what side one was looking from – was spectacular. Zeus's residence took advantage of the light and air, being a stately structure of white stone and marble, along with tiles of light blue and gold amongst other cheery colors. When his children had been growing up, the halls and courtyard were filled with the sound of little feet. Zeus had not heard that sound for a long time.

A set of footsteps almost as light as a child's met his ears as he sat on the roof, gazing across the parapet, where one had a full three hundred-and-sixty angle view of Olympus and Hellas. This was one of his favorite places to be, where he truly felt as if he was on the very top of the world. He was currently reclined on a divan, being fed grapes by his newest lover, a dryad. Just as he was about to close his mouth on the grape that dangled from her fingers, another nymph emerged from the staircase.

"My lord, I hate to interrupt. Lady Demeter is here, and she will not be denied."

The nymph yelped softly when Demeter herself emerged, wrapped in a somber brown cloak, the hood pulled from her head. Her tresses were braided around her scalp in a severely tight coronet that added austerity to her demeanor. With his hand, Zeus waved the nymphs away, and they scuttled down the stairs.

"Whatever it is, it must be very important to you to interrupt my quiet evening at home, or wait for my assent," Zeus said in an impatient tone, masking his nervousness. Demeter frowned at him, but the King of the Gods maintained his facade, knowing he would have to pull off a convincing performance so she wouldn't suspect that he might know where Kora was.

"It is of dire importance, indeed. Do not take that tone with me," Demeter stated reproachfully, "Kora is missing! She is to be found nowhere on the earth."

"She is missing! My goodness, for how long?" he asked, immediately shifting to the role of a concerned relative.

"Twenty days. I have searched far and wide and enlisted the help of all the spirits of Nature, but nobody knows where she is. I have used all the magic at my command, to no avail. If she is not on earth, she must be here!" She approached Zeus, towering over him, her hand shooting out to prevent him from rising off his seat.

"If she is, I have heard nothing of it!" Technically, that was the truth. After all, part of charm was choosing a genuine fact and working around it when flattery was not called for.

"Truly?"

"Truly, I swear by the Styx. I know nothing of our daughter being here on Olympus. I have left you and Kora in peace as you have asked."

"Yet there is now no trace of her."

"I can have other gods look for her."

"I do not want to spread this all around Olympus! I don't want her harmed..."

I don't either, Zeus thought, a plan forming in his head.

"Hermes is the one who found Kora and revealed her existence to the other gods. Why not use him to look for her? After all, he is the speediest of the gods, and good at discovering secrets. I know you are still angry with him, why not let him serve penance to you?" the King of the Gods offered astutely. As much as Hermes might search, he wouldn't look in the Underworld. He was as much wary of that place as any other god was. Additionally, this task would keep him occupied for a good while.

Demeter nodded slowly, finding that agreement suitable, and Zeus relaxed.

"I will send Hermes to you the very next time I see him. I expect to see him this very evening. Does that suit you, sister?" he asked, turning his palms upwards in a gesture of agreeability.

"It does, indeed," the Harvest Goddess replied.

"Very good. I do wonder where she could be, though. But if anyone can locate her, it can be none other than Hermes!" Zeus replied brightly.

oOo

The weak, pained cries of the child rang through the room and its mother leaned over her, making soft hushing sounds as she stroked the soft, downy hair of his scalp. Despite his clean diapers, warm blankets, and the loving attention of his mother, he still cried. He appeared to be in constant pain, often crying fitfully for no apparent reason however he was held, rocked, fed, or simply left alone in a soft nest of blankets. Sometimes he would exhaust himself from crying and would just whimper, flailing his small arms in frustration. The best physicians could not diagnose his malady, and all kinds of remedies had been tried, to no avail. It was doubtful the child would even make it to his first birthday.

Her child's pain baffled Metaniera. She and her husband already had five children, a son and four daughters. All of them had been healthy and were growing up to be a fine prince and princesses. Triptolemus, the older son and oldest child, was just past twenty and was a handsome and ruddy-faced youth. Her daughters, in various states of maidenhood, were all of pleasant if not beautiful appearances, with agreeable personalities and each with a talent of her own.

Instead of having a wet-nurse as queens usually did, Metaniera had breastfed each and every one of her children. After all, what better nourishment was there for a child than its own mother's milk? But Demophon drank fretfully, sometimes spitting up his milk when a fit of pain seized him.

Metaniera felt frustrated even though she knew that this wasn't Demophon's fault. Perhaps the gods had cursed him, and the rest of the family. Eleusis's harvest was not looking good this year, for a drought had bitten into the crops, and the dry summer heat was stunting the growth of the harvest that was to feed the city-state. Even though her older son wouldn't admit it, she sensed that Triptolemus was unhappy. A plague had gone through the city last year, and even though this year had been thankfully free of disease, their army was still depleted, with minimal manpower for the city's defenses. A warlord was threatening them, and would only consider backing off if the four Eleusinian princesses were given to said warlord as brides. No decision had been made, but the toll of stress was visible in the lines of her husband's face.

Celeus loved his family and city and had no desire to hand over any of his children. Yet he had the welfare of his city to consider. He was not really in a position to fight, but giving the girls over might cause the warlord to make more demands, perhaps even for the crown itself. To make matters worse, his own little son was dying.

They had prayed at the temple and made sacrifices to various gods, only to receive nothing for their efforts. Metaniera shook her head sadly as she looked down at her son, wishing she could alleviate his pain. His cries turned to whimpers as she stroked him, humming a soft song. It was only within the refuge of sleep that any of them could escape their problems.

o0o

Thalassa was the eldest daughter of Celeus and Metaniera and was well aware of the warlord's threat against her parents. She had no desire to marry him and knew that her parents didn't want to force her into marriage, either. But with the welfare of the city at stake, Thalassa was afraid that she might have to steel herself and agree to be the wife to a man who would in all likelihood mistreat her and betray her father. All of them had prayed to the gods, but to no avail.

The princess knew she should not be out here at night, but her bedroom felt confining, and she liked having fresh air and walking while she thought. She knew better than to roam the city after dark, especially without a guard, but the walled courtyard of the small Eleusinian Palace afforded safety and privacy. Despite the lackluster results of Abas's work – a gardener could no more control the weather than a King – the garden was still an enjoyable place. She had grown up here in the palace and dreaded the thought of leaving it.

As she sat down on a bench, she saw a figure move furtively through the shadows. After a moment, she recognized the lanky and small figure of the gardener. Ever since she had first set eyes upon Abas, she had fostered an intense dislike of the squirrelly-looking boy and preferred to avoid his company, all the more when he became a man. Whenever she wanted to take a walk in the garden, she would look around to see if he was working, for he had a way of looking at her that made her feel dirty inside. Aethra, her younger sister, reported the same thing, calling his eyes 'beady'. It was an apt description, and she wondered what he had to do at night. He disappeared around a corner, apparently unaware of her presence, and Thalassa frowned to herself.

oOo

The River Styx churned on as it had for all time, standing as the border between the realm of the living and the dead. Unlike the tales told above, coinage was not required to cross the Styx, but the deities of the Underworld did nothing to dispel that rumor. Wealthy and poor souls alike were admitted onto the ferry, for in death everyone was the same. The coins that Kharon received were whisked out of sight, disappearing under the cloak of his robe, presumably never to be seen again.

Kharon slid out invisibly from his cloak, leaving his doppelganger to operate by itself, shadowy hands gripping the oar. One of the nice things about being such a powerful deity was that he did not have to be on his boat for all Eternity. That would be a boring prospect, indeed. The doppelganger was an effective simulacrum of himself and an extension of his will, performing his duty without his physical presence. The passengers were never the wiser.

He followed the course of the Styx, disappearing into its blackness. A body wrapped around him, arms and legs hooking around his limbs, softness pressing against his chest. Styx's flesh was cold, but then, Kharon had never liked the heat. Her lips were like ice, but he became impassioned, feeling her hands roam along his body, fingers scraping along like icicles as she welcomed him into the abyss.

o0o

Hades stared out one of the windows of his bedchamber, peeking through the heavy curtains as Persephone made her way out from the main room, her feet gliding along the dark marble as she came to the railing. Her pale skin stood out amidst her dark clothing and the shadows that surrounded her, making her seem like a ghost, her skin glowing almost ethereally due to the loss of her light tan. The sky above, dark to represent night as it was on the surface world, glittered with the diamonds Hades had cast up there for his bride-to-be to enjoy. She looked despondent, her gaze distant as she followed the railing, her fingers sliding along its polished marble surface. At one side of the stone terrace was a set of stairs that led down to the gardens.

She looked ravishing, her hair tied back loosely to show the curve of her neck. Womanhood suited her well, he mused as he studied the delicate plane of her jaw. He imagined the feel of her soft body against his, and what it would be like to finally deflower her, to make her feel like a woman yet again with his attentions.

Oh, Persephone. Do you not understand how much I need you? How much you need me? I am one of the most powerful gods in existence, yet my heart is yours. I would lay the world at your feet if you would but commit yourself to me. He pressed his hand against the cool translucent crystal of the window as he studied the captive goddess. As if she sensed his gaze, she looked up at the window, and like a love-struck boy, he felt his heart do a quick pitter-patter within his chest.

Chapter XXIV

oOo

Persephone felt his gaze as she stood outside, and turned her head to see his palm pressed against the window, pale fingers stretched across the glass. She could feel him beseeching her silently, his eyes fixed upon her. She rebelled against Fate. The captive goddess did not want yet another person to dictate her destiny. There had to be more than one way out of the Underworld. She remembered the wish that Zeus had offered her all these years ago. If she could contact him, she would wish for her freedom. After all, Zeus was her sire, wasn't he? He had a duty to protect his daughter!

She raised her hand, beckoning to him. The curtain dropped and he slid out from the doorway, his robe slightly open to reveal his upper chest, making for an enticing sight. Was that intentional? She frowned.

"You cannot keep me down here forever," Persephone stated as he closed the distance between them. He stopped a pace away from her, crossing his arms.

"I can. I am the Lord of this realm. None can leave unless I say so. And I say that here with me you shall remain for eternity. This kingdom is timeless. The rules of the other realm do not apply here. Look at yourself, can you honestly say that you wish to leave all of this behind?"

Not forever, Persephone thought. But she was not

willing to admit it. If only she could return to the surface world and enjoy its sunlight and life-energy, then she would not mind visiting this realm, not as long as she had Hades as a host.

"My sire will not approve of this. I am daughter to the King of the Gods, and I will not be prisoner in a dead realm!" She decided to not mention the wish. If Hades knew, he might outright deny her any contact with Zeus or the other gods.

"Your sire? Oh, Persephone." He shook his head slowly. "He gave his blessing for the union."

"...What?" She became still. Surely her own sire, that kind and friendly King of Heaven with his beaming smile, wouldn't... But then, after what he had done to her mother...

"I told him I would have nobody else but you. He said yes."

"But why would he..." She felt the stab of betrayal in her heart, and it was more painful than she would have ever expected. Her own father had given her away, just like that. The man she hadn't seen for a decade, the man who hadn't been a real father to her at all, not even after Iasion had died... How could he have thought so little of her? His other daughters – *her own sisters*! – reigned high on Olympus while she had been cast down here!

"My brother is not without his faults, but he was wise enough to accept my decision. He knew that I would be a good husband. I assured him that you would be well cared for and subject to no mistreatment. He knew you would be better off with me than with any of the other gods or mortals, anyway. As a father, he did not fail in his duty to you, and rest assured, I shall not fail in my own duty as a husband." He sounded smug at this declaration.

Hmph. Stupid male pride. It appeared as if Hades wasn't immune to it despite his differences from the Olympians. She blinked back tears, not wishing for the Lord of the Dead to see her cry. She didn't want him to see just how much Zeus's betrayal had hurt her. He hadn't even thought to warn her about Hades! When Hades drew closer, Persephone whipped away from him.

Mother had been right to raise her to believe that Iasion was her father. Iasion was a good and honest man who had adored his wife and cherished his daughter. While Persephone would have liked to know the truth, she now understood one aspect of the strained relationship between her mother and herself. When put through that, who could blame Mother for this lie?

"And did neither of you think to *talk* to me?" Persephone asked before she spun around, crossing her arms and staring out in the darkness, tears burning behind her eyes.

"When Zeus said yes, that was the end of the matter. He has more children and lovers than he can account for, and of course, your mother prevented you from getting to know the Olympians. He was assured of your safety. As for myself? You cannot tell me that you do not enjoy my company or attention..."

"Damn you, Hades." She jerked away from the hand that reached out to grasp her arm. At her defiant gesture, tendrils of shadows whipped out, wrapping around her legs and effectively halting her progress. Curses! Hades's Gift had more than one practical application, and when she flung her arms at him, trying to claw his face as he closed in on her, the shadows pinned her arms down.

"This is not fair!" Persephone exclaimed with an indignant gasp. She wiggled against her bindings, muttering in frustration at the almost rubber-like pliancy of the shadows, which could effectively solidify themselves to any density at Hades's will.

"I will not let you walk away from me unless you admit it," he replied in a nonchalant manner, leaning against the railing as he observed her struggle against her restraints. The defiant captive stubbornly kept her lips shut, shaking her head.

"So spirited. So defiant. I do enjoy your fire, but there are more productive ways of applying it. Do I need to remind you?" Hades continued on, undeterred. Persephone stilled when she felt a tendril rub against her ankle, slowly working its way upwards, wiggling in a teasing manner as it did so. Oh gods! If it reached its goal, Hades would know...

"Stop! Please!" she begged. It wiggled up her calf to the back of her knee.

"That is not what I want to hear." Hades tutted gently. Now the silky smooth tentacle had reached halfway up her thigh. *Oh gods*. Wait. The gods would not help her...

"You were... are a rather... pleasant suitor." Persephone's gaze was averted, a faint blush on her cheeks. Mercifully, Hades stopped his teasing administrations.

"Was that so difficult to admit, my love?"

"No, my lord." She shuddered as her bindings slid away from her body, caressing her legs as they did so. As soon as she was free of them, she pulled back several paces. "But that doesn't stop me from being angry with you. Or my sire." She spat out the word 'sire' as if it was a curse.

"Do not be so hurt by what he did. My brother might be careless and clumsy at times, but he is not a cruel person. He knows I will take care of you. He personally asked that of me."

"I don't care!" Her eyes glinted fiercely. "As far as I am concerned, the world would be a better place without men in it!"

"Ahh, you sound like Artemis when you say that. She is none too fond of her father, either," Hades shot back with a grin.

"Ugh!" Persephone threw her hands up in the air in frustration, flashing Hades an enticing glimpse of her wrists and forearms. "I cannot believe that I am related to both of you!"

"Surely I am a cherished relation. More so than your sire, at least," the Lord of the Dead shot back smoothly, refusing to be fazed by her temper.

She let out a short shriek of indignation before she darted at him, her small fists pounding against his broad chest. The fact that he merely stood there and let her take blows at him only further roused her ire. How dare he, that self-assured, smug bastard, just standing there and smiling down at her! Suddenly she found her wrists held by his strong hands, effectively

73

preventing her from throwing any more punches. Her body was pulled flush against him when he lifted her wrists, and she glared at him with an angry blush on her cheeks.

"Let me go!"

"Calm yourself, love. I am your Lord and husband-to-be, not something to beat your fists on. Of course, I could always bind you again and have my way with you..."

"Ugh! No!" She squirmed against his grip, catching a whiff of his masculine odor. He relinquished his grip on her wrists, only to wrap his arms around her, muffling her protest against his chest.

"Stop resisting so much," Hades whispered in an avuncular tone, one hand reaching up to stroke her hair, his arms forming a grip she could not escape. "Let go of your sorrow and anger. They have no place down here."

"I cannot! I will not! You do not understand! How could I ever expect a man to understand?"

"I do understand, but what is done is done... Your future lies ahead of you."

Persephone remained silent, pressing her lips together tightly.

"Let me go," she whispered.

"Are you going to try to attack me again?"

"No."

"Good." Slowly, his arms slid from her and he took a step back. Persephone felt her heart pound with anger, but she managed to keep herself collected.

"Is there anything I can do to make you feel better?" Hades asked, surprising her. Was her pain that obvious?

"No." She shook her head sullenly.

"Come now. How about a trip to Elysium? There are many skilled artists and performers, and also pleasant places to walk, though I could give you a chariot ride if you'd prefer that."

"No."

She heard him sigh.

"Then what is it?"

"Not something I wish to talk about." She lifted her chin defiantly, turning away. Fortunately,y he did not follow when she descended the steps to the garden.

Persephone drew her robe over her head, effectively cloaking herself. The air down here was pleasant, but it was missing some of the familiar elements of the night in the mortal world. She heard no sound of insects or small creatures, nor the call of the birds. There was no rustling of grass as the night breeze blew through them. Persephone wished for a moon to light her way – moonlit walks were one of her favorite pleasures. Without these small natural cues, this place didn't feel real. She would have lost touch with this world if it wasn't for the solid tiled marble under her feet, the soft and thick linen clothing that hugged her body, and that musky, shadowy scent that lingered in the air, tingling her nose but offering no definite note or source. When she listened hard, she could sometimes hear a faint ghostly whispering, though she often questioned if this was actually a voice within her own head or not. Dis had a way of teasing and playing with her senses at times, overwhelming her or leaving her unsure, grasping at her perception like she was right now.

This place was alluring, yet unsettling in the dark. She could barely see the pomegranate tree against the sky, and she wasn't sure if the faint iridescent flashes she saw of the flowers were a figment of her own imagination. She stilled, trying to orient herself to her surroundings. *Come now, Persephone! It's the same garden, it's just dark.*

She brought her hands forward, veering off to the left. Cool bark met her palms, and she let out a quiet sigh. What would Tartarus be like in the dark! Ooh! She shivered at the thought.

The Underworld was an unsettling place. Persephone felt like a small child, lost without its mother. She was able to see shadowy outlines, but in a place of darkness, this did not count as much. She wished she was in Mother's arms, wrapped up in a warm and strong grip as Demeter comforted her, soothing away her nightmares and fears. Not even the tree could comfort her because it was not of her own world. On the surface, any tree – whether inhabited by a dryad or not – always had a pulse of life-energy if it wasn't dead or petrified. And despite the hungry rumblings of her stomach, she could not eat the fruit that the branches offered, drooping down as if to entice her, the pomegranates blood-red against the inky darkness that enclosed her.

She reached out for one, feeling its weight in her hand. She lowered her arm, and the fruit came away from the branch easily, surprising her. The pads of her fingers slid along the heavy globe, outlining its faintly hexagonal shape.

Persephone closed her eyes and took a deep breath, allowing herself to relax. She would not allow this realm to overwhelm her. If she could unlock its secrets, who knew what she might accomplish. She was not a child, a sheltered little maiden kept away from the world. No, she was a goddess, one with more Gifts than she was aware of if the Fates were being straightforward about their prophecy for her. Even though her mother had refused to tell her about this bleeding, Persephone sensed that it represented a new stage in her life.

In her mind, she saw the insides of the pomegranate, ruby and violet and deep rose, richly seeded, each plump kernel filled with cool juice and coated with jelly, cradled lovingly in creamy-white flesh. She saw her own blood, imagined her womb filled with these deep colors, surrounded by the pale flesh of her skin. She squeezed the ponderous orb, feeling the temptation of the treat that lay inside and inhaled slowly, trying to not shiver under her warm robe. Her tongue was dry, and she was so thirsty... and these seeds would be filled with soothing pomegranate nectar...

She pressed the pomegranate against her cheek as she felt its cool rind against her flushed face. All she had to do was eat one seed, just *one* seed. It would be sweet and wonderful. And she was alone! Alone to enjoy this succulent treat, and have eternity.

In a different tale that belonged to another race of

people barely known to Hellas, the story was that the serpent convinced the woman to eat the forbidden fruit, and her head became full of the knowledge that had not been intended for her.

Just one seed. What harm of a taste, after all, she had already learned in Khthonios? The other woman had been completely ignorant, and easily charmed by the serpent, but *she* wasn't. After all, one seed could hardly be considered food, could it? It was dark, and she was alone, hidden.

...No, she wasn't. There was that odd prickle at the back of her neck that alerted her that she was being watched. Not by Hades, though. Who could be watching her out here, in the impenetrable shadows? She stilled, rubbing her thumb along the top of the pomegranate. She backed up against the tree, lowering the fruit and holding it against her upper stomach, her eyes trying to see into the darkness and feeling an increasing sense of alarm. When she looked up, she couldn't see the diamonds that had been placed up there! Waving her own hand in front of her eyes, she was almost certain she could see the outline. *Almost.*

Persephone closed her eyes, sitting in the thick grass with her back to the trunk. Her head dropped as she inhaled the clean air, listening to the silence...

She took a step forward, feeling the soft springiness of grass under her feet. Where she expected to come to the path, she found nothing. When she tried to return to the tree, she became even more lost, waving her hand in front of her as she searched for something familiar.

"Hades?" she whispered.

"I thought you were angry with him. So why would you call out for him?"

Persephone stilled, trying to recognize the voice. She had indeed heard it before, but where? The voice was so smooth and velvety, a sleepy caress against her ears. Aha. Was her intruder responsible for the darkness? Doubtless...

"And you would be my rescuer, hm?" Persephone asked.

"It did not sound like you are here willingly. You are a rather articulate young lady." Hypnos appeared before her, his pale features standing out against their surroundings starkly. Persephone realized that she could now see her own hands as clearly as day. The pomegranate she had been holding was gone.

"You were eavesdropping!" she replied with a soft gasp of indignation. He smiled faintly.

"I was merely in the right place at the right time. I sensed that you were unhappy at the banquet, and naturally, I had to wonder. Why should a beautiful Goddess be so sad?"

Persephone shook her head.

"Ahh, no. I saw it in your eyes. After all, eyes are the window to one's soul," the God of Sleep commented with a fluid shrug of his shoulders. He was garbed in deep purple so vibrant it almost hurt her eyes.

"So you sneak around Hades's Palace to eavesdrop, hmm? I doubt he will be pleased to learn of that."

"No, I simply happened to hear that you paid a

visit to Tartarus today, and thought you might be in a mood to receive visitors."

"Who told you?"

"Inquisitive, are you not?" he asked with a slightly amused smile.

"Who told you?" Persephone repeated calmly, glancing at him coolly.

"Even those of the Kingdom of the Dead must sleep sometime."

"You and Hades should get together and tell one another riddles."

"Seems like you are in no mood for riddles," he replied, and Persephone wished his tone wasn't so velvety. In fact, it was *too* velvety. It might be seductive to other women, but she found herself on guard.

"I do not enjoy you eavesdropping on us. I am going to tell Hades you were trespassing."

She was gratified to see a flicker of worry in Hypnos's handsome features.

"Aha," She lifted her chin. "If you knew it was not something you were supposed to do, why risk incurring his wrath? What did you do, hide in the flowers?"

"My hearing just happens to be very good," Hypnos replied. Persephone stared at him, her shoulders squared. He circled around her, reaching out to touch her arm with pale fingers. She growled and jerked back.

"That is funny. Hekate was not much different the first time I met her."

"She is smart. Good for her," Persephone shot

back evenly.

"Come now, you wound me." He placed his hand over his heart. "I was simply thinking that you and I should get to know one another better. After all, you are now part of the Pantheon of Khthonios Would you not agree that it is a good idea to make acquaintance with everybody in your new circle?"

Persephone let out a quiet snort.

"And you consider this..." She waved her hand at the oblivion that surrounded them, "a good way to make acquaintances?"

"This is my domain, or part of it."

"Does not look very interesting," Persephone replied with a shrug.

"Allow me to remedy that." He smiled before lifting his hand. Lush green grass rolled out under their feet and the sky became a startlingly clear shade of blue.

Persephone gasped as she saw the sun hanging high in the sky, illuminating the vast expanse of the field they now stood in. Were they now back on the surface realm? Oh! Her heart pounded as she slowly turned around before facing Hypnos, seeing a small smile on his face.

No. She did not feel the pulse of life-energy, and the sun failed to provide her with its warmth. She frowned, feeling disappointed after experiencing a brief but intense surge of euphoria.

But it was better than the darkness.

"Is there anything else that would interest you? Perhaps flowers? Or animals?"

"None of it is real," she muttered, more to herself

than him.

"I will admit that this is but an illusion. What would you expect from my domain?"

"I suppose. But is it... always so dark?"

"How could there be real light in here? Sleep is merely another form of oblivion, albeit usually a temporary one."

"Certainly," She could agree with him on that. When he started walking, he beckoned to her to join his side. After a moment of hesitation, she joined him, falling in step beside him. It was a slow and pleasant stroll, and even if it was an illusion, Persephone enjoyed the light of the sun and the vivid blue of the sky.

"What about dreams?" Persephone asked. She hadn't yet met Morpheus and wondered why sleep and dreams were ruled by separate gods. After all, didn't these go hand in hand? "It seems to me that dreams should be here." She waved her hands at the pleasant surroundings around them.

"Sleeping people dream. If you are the Lord of Sleep, why not dreams?"

"Ahh, but sleeping and dreaming are not the same thing. Yes, the realms overlap, but sleepers do not always dream, and dreamers do not always sleep."

"I have never had a dream when I was awake." It was an odd thought. "Would it not be confusing? Trying to tell the difference between dreams and reality?"

"Surely you have had daydreams?"

"Yes, but..." She tapped her chin. "Daydreams are a part of the Dreaming?"

"Yes. There are different kinds of dreams, just as there are different kinds of sleep," the God of Sleep explained. Despite her initial irritation with him, she was liking this conversation. His voice was still velvety, but not as much as before.

"I thought there was just one kind of sleep." Of course, she had heard of death being referred to as the long sleep a couple of times when she had still been living in Enna, but she wasn't sure how Hypnos would feel about being compared to death. Even to a god, *thanatos* was a fearsome phenomenon. She hadn't been in the Underworld for too long, but it was clear that the surface gods didn't want to come down here. Hades himself had reinforced that fact.

"What would make you say that?" he was smiling again, in an amused way. Fortunately, it wasn't the kind of smile she found condescending. Rather, it seemed as if he enjoyed her questions, and this reminded her of Hades.

"Well... I mean, sleep is sleep. I close my eyes, and then I wake up. It is the same for gods and mortals, right? Animals too?"

"Yes. All living things require sleep. Even the plants sleep. The sleep that comes with night is the most common one, of course. It is that sleep that helps you to rest and rejuvenate."

"Mhm." She nodded.

"And you have dozed off or taken a nap, yes?"

"Indeed."

"That's another kind of sleep. For everyone, it is different. Some hover close to the surface, ready to act at a moment's notice, like a cat. Others can go in deeper, almost like night-sleep, but for a short time and come out feeling refreshed. Some become half-asleep, often daydreaming."

"Oh. I never thought about that before." She smiled faintly. "What about meditation?"

"Yes. Sleep is a form of oblivion, but a much-needed one in any form. Dreams or not, we all need it for our bodies and just as importantly, our minds."

"Until you mentioned minds, I never thought about how important sleep was. I mean, yes, I would get tired after a long day, but my mind..." Sleep helped her to process things that had happened the day before, or important decisions or the like. Before she fell asleep, she often thought about the new things she had learned in Dis, and the next morning usually felt more clear-headed, better understanding of the sometimes overwhelming new knowledge to be found here. "But what about dreams? That does not seem restful for the mind, especially if you are doing something in the dream or having a nightmare..."

"Good or ordinary dreams are needed for the mind. Nightmares are another thing. If you have more questions about dreams, you can ask Morpheus."

"I have not met him yet. How do I reach him or you?"

"The shades of this place are at your beck and call. After all, you are Queen of the Underworld, my dear."

Persephone looked away. She had seen how responsive the other shades were to the needs of

Hades, and how the shades of Tartarus obeyed Kampe without question. As the daughter of a goddess, the nymphs afforded her a certain level of respect, but there was that gulf between them in age and the standards Demeter set for her attendants. The nymphs were as much her minders as companions.

"We might not always answer your summons, as we all have our duties, and you have the same privilege. The shades are much more efficient and without a question, trustworthy." The pale-haired god stroked his chin as he glanced down at her.

"Thank you for telling me."

"You are more than welcome. Since you asked so many questions, I would like to ask a few," he replied. Persephone glanced at him, raising an eyebrow before she nodded.

"You have not been here a month, and there already is strife between the King and Queen of the Underworld! I cannot help but be curious. He is not mistreating you, is he?"

Persephone crossed her arms, wondering if she could appeal to Hypnos for help. If she said she was being abused...

No. That was a horrible lie. Hades had treated her kindly, and it would be cruel and unfair to make up such a story about him. Angry as she might be with him, she knew he didn't deserve to be slandered. She shook her head in response to his question.

"Then why are you unhappy?"

"That is not something I am going to discuss either." She raised her chin. After all, as Hypnos said, she was Queen of the Underworld. It wasn't a title she wanted, but she saw how important it was to act a certain way. She would keep her secrets close to her heart as she worked her way through her dilemma.

"Then what do we talk about?" Hypnos asked in a light tone.

"You."

"Me?"

"If you are going to ask me personal questions, then you should be ready to talk about yourself."

"Fair enough. But I must be honest, I do wonder about one thing."

Persephone nodded. If she didn't like the question, she wouldn't answer it.

"That you are a goddess I do not doubt. But where do you come from? Who is your father? I know that Rhea has a hair color similar to yours, only hers is a bit less red."

Persephone hesitated. "I... do not wish to speak of my parents."

"... Very well," the pale-eyed God of Sleep replied. "So, what do you think of the Underworld?" Hypnos asked, changing the subject.

"Much better than I had thought it would be."

"I certainly hope so," he replied dryly, winking at her. They continued their walk, talking about Dis for a while before he stopped, turning to her.

"My lady, I fear we must part. It has been a delight talking to you. If you wish to see me again, you have but to summon me." He took her hand before she could react, and raised it to his lips, kissing it.

"I do not think Hades will want you doing that,"

she commented.

"It will be a secret between us," he teased. "But neither of you need worry. I am a gentleman who is merely paying his respects to a lady."

She nodded.

"Until then." The sunny landscape faded away to black, and Hypnos disappeared from sight.

oOo

Persephone gasped softly as she opened her eyes, seeing the garden around her, its colors brilliant despite the gray sky that hung above her head. Wait, gray? Had she been out here all night? From the color of the sky, she calculated it was early morning, and wished that there was a sun down here so she could figure the time more accurately. She loved sunrise and sunset, seeing all the brilliant colors splashed along the heavens.

As she sat there in her ruminations, she slowly realized that there was a tube-shaped pillow behind her neck. When she reached up to touch it, she felt soft velvet under her hand. It was one of Hades's pillows. Had he come down here to ensure that she slept comfortably? She blushed faintly at that thought. He could have easily put her in his bed, though she knew that would have irritated her. In her other hand sat the pomegranate.

She remembered the visions she had. Had all of that been Hypnos's doing, or was the image of the pomegranate of her own imagination? When had she fallen asleep? She remembered being angry with

Hades and coming down here, and taking the pomegranate, feeling its cool weight in her hand. She ran her fingers along the crown, tempted to grab hold of one point and peel it back to reveal the seeds within. Her stomach grumbled, and she shook her head.

She knew that Hades loved this tree. Sometimes he would sit here by himself and think. It was the only tree or fruit within this garden, its branches heavy with the omnipresent ruby-colored fruit.

Persephone picked up the pillow and tucked it under her arm, processing the events of last night. She was fairly certain she had been awake when she had the vision about the pomegranate; it had been in her hand when she woke up.

She climbed up the steps to the terrace. As she entered Hades's chambers, she left the pillow and pomegranate on the table before tiptoeing to the doorway of the bedchamber. He looked so appealing even when he was sleeping, the blankets pulled up to his waist, leaving his arms and chest bare. Despite the issue with her body that she was dealing with, she still felt a warm flutter of arousal within her loins.

It's so easy to be angry with you... yet it's also so easy to appreciate and desire you. She held back a quiet sigh as she retreated to her room.

Cloe appeared, and Persephone slid off her clothing as she did a cursory examination of herself. Nothing seemed worse than last night, and she made note of that. Sleep *did* help to clear the mind.

She donned clothing of deep purple. Cloe arranged her hair in a crown much like her mother often wore, pinning it back with amethyst-studded pins. What would she do today? She had plenty of choices, but there were a couple of things that were on the top of her list. Hmm...

Her thoughts were interrupted as the door opened slowly. She had been seated on her divan, and she glanced up calmly as Hades entered. He was wearing a dark blue tunic that set off the color of his eyes, with a black himation that draped off one shoulder, held by a thick silver pin that matched the silver band that sat atop his head.

"Good morning," Hades said softly as he glanced at her, almost as if he was fearful of her reaction.

"Good morning to you too," Persephone replied. She had no desire to get into another fight, and had decided to make this day as amicable as possible. "Thank you for the pillow. I think that I would have woken up with a sore neck if you had not done that."

She was gratified to see his eyes widen in surprise, and held back an amused smile. Her eyes moved to the pomegranate Hades held in his hand, but she said nothing about it.

"I was thinking we could go for a walk. Would you enjoy that?"

"No breaking the fast?" she asked, wanting to make sure he wouldn't make her sit through another tantalizing meal.

"You brought me my morning meal," he replied with a smile, lifting the pomegranate and admiring it briefly before glancing back at her.

"Oh, good. Enjoy."

"I intend to." He extended his free hand. She rose

off the divan and reached for it, feeling his fingers wrap around her own. Without a word, he led them outside. She found his grip reassuring, even more so when he gave it a gentle squeeze.

Chapter XXV

oOo

Hades didn't seem to have any particular destination in mind. Before, when they had gone down to the Styx, the path had been rather direct. But now as they walked down the same path – at least Persephone was fairly certain this was the same one they had started on before – she wondered if Hades guided her down a turn she had not noticed. Along the path were black and twisted trees with leaves that appeared to be made of pale crystal, and stretching out at either side was a grim landscape of grays that disappeared into infinite blackness. There was not one sound to be heard except for that faint whispering that she sometimes heard if she really strained her ears.

With Hades's arm draped across her shoulders, Persephone felt safe and warm. She appreciated the comfortable silence between them as she ruminated over her own concerns. She still felt hurt by Zeus's compliance with Hades's decree and by his refusal to even include her in the decision. The mighty King of the Gods couldn't even manage a *'Hello, Kora! How are you? It has been so long since I've seen you, what have you been doing? Oh, just so you know, Hades said he wanted your hand in marriage. He is not a bad person, really, and he will be a good husband! By the way, tell your mother I send my kindest regards!'* Would it have been so hard for him to do that? Yes, Mother was fiercely protective of her, but goodness! Zeus was the King of Olympus and the man who had sired her! What if Hades had asked for one of his other daughters? Would Zeus have been so compliant if Hades had asked for Athene or Aphrodite?

She looked up at Hades as he stared forward thoughtfully. Seeing her turn her head, he glanced down at her.

"Hades..... I would like to see Olympus and meet the other gods. After all, they are my family... I mean, I would just like to be able to see them and meet them. You say that knowledge is important. I learn new things here every day. But there are also things up there to know, and you can not learn about everything simply by reading about it or listening to stories." She felt his hand squeeze her shoulder as he stared down at her for several moments. The stark, gray sky above their heads made Hades's skin look nearly white.

"It is not an untoward request you make of me," he finally responded. No impatience, no anger. But he said nothing more. He lifted his arm off her and raised the pomegranate in his other hand. Taking hold of one of the tips of the crown, he pulled it back, revealing seeds that glittered like rubies under the clear sky.

"Eat with me, Persephone. To you, I offer my kingdom and my heart. Be my queen." He fished a seed out of the pomegranate, lifting it to his lips.

"Mmm. Sublime. Like you." He smirked faintly. "You wish to learn more of the world and of the gods? As my consort, you would enjoy the privileges that come with being bound to the Lord of this realm." He lifted the pomegranate again. "Do not see this as some kind of death sentence, love. It is... merely a commitment to a new life, to me. A life that is more glorious than your old one."

She stared down at the fruit, considering her options. Finally, she shook her head slowly.

"No." She looked away.

"Very well. I suppose I will have to eat this pomegranate all by myself, then." Hades ate several more seeds, walking at her side in silence.

"Look, Persephone... I understand that you are hurt by what Zeus did... or did not do. It would have been wise for him to talk to you, but I suspect he did not want to deal with your mother."

"You did not want to deal with Mother, either," Persephone reminded him, wagging her finger.

"I acknowledge that the circumstances were unusual, but I am a loyal mate. It is only you that I desire. I am not like my brothers or nephews. Surely you have seen that?"

"I have not even been here for a moon. What will happen after a year? A century? People change. Look at me!" She gestured to her own body.

"The change in your body does not lessen my desire for you. Your body is growing to match who and what you are inside. You are not a child. You are a goddess, a powerful one. Here I let you do as you please. I love you, you know that. I have told you before and I am happy to say it again. Trust me, Persephone. It is here that you can reach your potential."

"I have no power down here. You know it. I cannot use my Gift." The Fates had told her that she had other Gifts, but she saw no indication of them. *You have but to embrace it,* they said. Did these new abilities come with her womanhood, or from surrendering to Hades and eating his offering?

"You do have power. After all, up there on the surface, you were able to sense me. Nobody else has ever been able to do so, not even your mother. With time, you can discover other facets of your Gift. I am happy to help."

"You will do nothing to hold me back?"

Hades smiled. "I do not want a weak and pampered wife. I want to see you achieve your fullest potential. I would be a rather poor husband if I thought otherwise."

"... I do not know of any other man who would ever say that to me," Persephone responded quietly, looking down at the ground, feeling her cheeks warm further with unexpected pleasure from his words.

"Would I be such a bad husband? I have already committed myself to you, I merely wait for you to do the same."

"The truth..." The young goddess let out a quiet sigh before looking up at him, "I do enjoy your company. I simply cannot bear the thought of binding myself to this place, to cut myself off from the other world. Please do not ask me to cast myself away from the light forever."

Hades nodded, offering no argument.

"I can understand... and respect that," he conceded. "Khthonios is a mysterious, and to many,

94

even the immortals, frightening place. I do hope that you would not be averse to seeing more new places here or giving me a chance to impress you."

"Not at all."

After another companionable silence where Hades finished most of the pomegranate, Persephone spoke again.

"What if I were to wish to do something else now?" she asked.

"You have but to ask."

"I have not yet seen the Judges at work. I would like to observe them. You can keep us invisible, right? I just want to watch quietly."

"Certainly." He bowed his head before draping his arm across her shoulders again. She leaned into him comfortably, feeling him squeeze her.

The path they walked on led them to the large clearing were the souls waited, observing the Judges at work. Nobody looked their way, and Hades guided her over to one side of the podium where the Judges sat, seats forming out of shadow for them.

"Normally, the judging of a soul is a quick process. As the Judges of the Underworld, the three of them share the power, and responsibility, of being able to distinguish between good and evil, to see how much of each lies within the balance of any soul, and the record of their life is written in that very balance."

The soul of a young woman was ushered forward by a shade. As she approached the Judges, she glowed white faintly, standing out amidst the identically-hued souls. Minos glanced at her for a moment before nodding.

"You are a soul worthy of Elysium, but some time in the Asphodel Fields will give you the contemplation you need." She was led away by the shades without protest.

Most souls took on a faintly white or gray tinge as they came forward for judgment as if a light shone upon them. Their judgments were generally brisk, and they would be sent to the Asphodels, whether for a bit of time or indefinitely. Sometimes a soul would glow more brightly and thus be sent directly to Elysium, while a few became dark gray or black as if the light had drained from them, bearing the stigma that would send them to Tartarus despite their pleas.

Of course, there were a few souls who would plead with the Judges to be allowed to go back and take care of their loved ones – such as a mother who had died in childbirth, leaving a newborn and three other children behind. Persephone stirred at that and felt Hades's hand on her shoulder.

"They are already dead. Their bodies lay buried in the earth or lost at sea or burned up. Atropos has cut their threads, and here all must come. If Fate has decreed it, nothing can change it. But see? She shines with righteousness, and a good afterlife awaits her. Do not feel sad about it."

So Persephone watched silently. These people came from all walks of life. She saw types of people that she had never encountered before – sailors, wealthy merchants, royal servants, hunters, priests, warriors and the like – and listened to their commentaries and pleas. After a while, she started to feel restless. She had watched a good amount of people being judged and felt that she had seen enough for the day.

"Thank you for taking me to see this, but I am ready to move on," she whispered. He nodded and took her hand, helping her off her chair.

"Might we go for a ride in your chariot?" she asked. Hades grinned at her.

"Why not?"

oOo

Judging souls was no easy task and had he still been mortal, Minos knew that he would have had a much harder time in his task. Judges in the realm of the living could be bribed or lied to. No matter how good or fair a judge was, there were also skilled liars and manipulators who could worm their way out of a guilty verdict, or those who escaped justice altogether and never came before a judge.

As one of the trifecta of ethereal Judges, Minos had no need to worry about lies, for a soul's sins showed plainly under Justice's divine light, and down here, she was not blind. Those who were unfairly punished in life were assured justice in their death, and those who had been confident that they could escape consequences in death as they had in life were swiftly corrected by judges who could not be bribed or lied to.

Though he would not say it out loud or boast to the ones that he judged, Minos could freely admit to himself that he loved this job.

o0o

The horses sped along the path, their hooves churning up a cloud of dust as the chariot careened along. Persephone was holding onto the rim of the vehicle for dear life and enjoying every moment of it. Hades stood proud and tall, his cloak billowing out behind him, the wind whipping through his hair. The horses moved at a speed that their mortal counterparts were never able to achieve, and still she laughed for more, her grip white-knuckled as she stared up at him.

"Hyah!" Hades carried no whip, but his command was just as effective, and the horses pushed forward. In front of them, several slopes defined the path, and every time the horses sped over one, the chariot was actually up in the air for a couple of moments before landing as the steeds of Hell made their downward descent. At such a dizzying speed, Persephone knew she should feel concerned. Mother would no doubt break into conniptions if she saw her daughter in such a recklessly speeding vehicle!

With one of Hades's arms wrapped around her, the goddess did not feel afraid at all. She found the whole experience to be one exciting thrill ride – literally and figuratively. The path grew more interesting when cliffs appeared at either side, showing off layers of various thickness of mostly gray, but interspersed with a brief flash of black, blue, or purple. One side fell away, revealing a great expanse of blue-black ocean, its waves crashing solidly onto the ebony-and-gray sands.

"The Sea of Eternity," Hades pointed out as the chariot slowed down for a bit so that Persephone could better appreciate the vastness before her.

"Does it really go on forever?"

"Indeed."

Persephone took on a suitably impressed expression as she looked around.

"You can also see the sea from Elysium, though over there, the water is much lighter and bluer than this," Hades explained as Persephone stared out at the shore, where the waves continued to lap at the sand rhythmically.

"It is hard to not stare, is it not?" he asked gently.

"Mhm."

"I find it a good place to meditate. There is a shortcut from the Palace if you would like to try that. I can show you when we get back. Shall we keep going or do you want to stay a bit longer?"

"Keep going."

One moment they were at the bottom of the cliffs, then Persephone found herself on top, speeding along the edge as the ocean spread out below. At her left was a forest of black trees with leaves that looked as if they were made of iron, glinting a dark gray under the light of Dis.

"Faster, please?"

She felt a squeeze around her middle before a loud "Hyah!" boomed from Hades's lips. The chariot jumped forward, making several sharp turns that added to the thrill of the ride. Suddenly, the vehicle approached the edge, and she felt her heart pound. Surely he wasn't going over, was he?

A short shriek escaped her lips as the horses careened over the edge. Their hooves clipped neatly onto the face of the cliff, finding purchase as easily as they had on a horizontal surface. Persephone now stared at the approaching ground with stunned silence, but the horses and chariot righted themselves as soon as they hit the level surface. She jerked backward with a surprised gasp, feeling the adrenaline pounding through her.

Oh, gods! It had been so frightening... but incredible! She offered no objection when the chariot bolted up the cliff and back down before the horses sped across the water, their hooves making small splashes on the Eternal Sea. She kept one hand on the chariot rim with a firm grip and with her other hand, held onto the arm wrapped around her middle.

Persephone had never been on the ocean, having been confined to its shores. The vastness around her impressed her into a respectful silence as the chariot made its way across the waves. The sky brightened, taking on hues of deep golds, reds, and blues filling the sky as if it were sunset. The sea no longer looked so black, and was now more of a deep blue-violet. A glimmer of gold revealed a sandy shore, its grains rich in amber hues. This shore was large but not overly so, providing more than ample space for the chariot and its horses. Persephone glanced up and down the coastline.

The beach was held in by cliffs that appeared to be sandstone, revealing intricate layering of reds, golds, and browns further illuminated by the warm hues of the sky. Within a nook of the cliffs, she spied an opening.

Hades dismounted and she let him help her off. The horses stood where they were as he led her down to the shoreline. The air here was pleasant, with a bare yet enticing hint of warmth.

"Perhaps you would like to go for a swim?" he asked with a fond smile. "I know that ride was thrilling."

"It was!" Persephone nodded eagerly. "But I do not feel like going for a swim."

"No?" He frowned with some concern. "I was so certain that you would enjoy it here."

"Oh, but I do!" She tried to not blush. A swim here with Hades did sound like a wonderful idea, but then he would *know*, and... "I would be happy to swim with you later, I promise." She found herself touched by the sadness she saw in his eyes.

"Something troubles you," he said as he ran his fingers along her arm. She hated the certainty she heard in that soft tone, so she simply looked away at the horizon.

"I would like to know what is wrong, so I can help you feel better," he continued.

"It is nothing you can help me with."

"Are you certain?"

"Very much so." Hades was silent after her response, and she felt his hand slide up to her shoulder before he spoke.

"The opening you saw leads back to my garden. That is the shortcut, whenever you want to come out here..."

"Thank you."

After standing out there for a while, the couple approached the opening while shades attended to the horses, unhitching them from the chariot and leading them back to the stables. As they emerged into his garden, Persephone looked over her shoulder, seeing a doorway that looked no different from the others that led to the other gardens. Oh, this place just got better and better. This was what Hades offered her. All of this, for her commitment to him. Was the rest of the surface world as glorious or enjoyable? As they walked along the path, a shade approached them and said something in that faint, shadowy hissing whisper she sometimes heard.

"The Erinyes are bringing a soul to be judged," Hades explained.

Ooh. She had wanted to see the Furies, and here they were. "Why would they bring a soul themselves?" she inquired.

"Sometimes they drive one to their own end. When the person dies, they grab the soul from the body then and there so that it cannot attempt to escape them."

"And what are you going to do?"

"Go to the Judges and decide his fate."

"I would like to come with you."

"Very well."

The indignant cries of a soul rang through the air of the Underworld, and Persephone heard a brassy, rasping sound. The source of this sound was revealed to be the wings of the three women who had the wailing soul in custody. They were beautiful in a savage, deadly way, their eyes slitted, teeth fanged, hair writhing around their heads like snakes atop a Gorgon's head. Their hair and lips were both the black-red of fresh and deep blood, and shone like it as well.

They were clad in black leather and dark linen, their torsos and bottoms modestly covered while tempting expanses of their arms and legs were visible amidst the straps of material. Their hands and feet were not human, terminating in talons and sharp, curved black claws that appeared capable of tearing through anything.

Despite the lack of density that the soul generally had, the Furies were able to restrain and handle him as easily as if he were solid. The grating beat of their wings quieted down as they steadied themselves on the ground, holding the condemned soul before the Judges. From what Persephone had seen earlier today, she expected the soul's appearance to darken and was not disappointed. She was surprised when the gray became even darker, even more so than she had ever seen. What evil must weigh upon this soul!

"Clytus of Thebes, the suffering you have known at our hands will only become worse. Your sins will be paid in full, over and over. The pain of your victims will be yours. Their screams will come from your throat."

"No! No! Lies, all of it! My neighbors and competitors slander me!"

"You escaped the justice of the mortals. But there is no reprieve from divine justice." Minos stared at him, his face set in a hard scowl. "Your name and crimes are thus recorded here." He tapped the open

103

scroll in front of him. "The only place fit for you is Tartarus." The judges turned to the King of the Dead. "Have you anything to add to our judgment, my lord?" Aeacus asked.

"You have judged ably."

The Judges nodded before the Furies lifted Clytus into the air.

"Off you go," Rhadamanthus stated levelly before he beckoned the next soul forward.

The soul wailed as the Furies carried him off, and Persephone shivered. She offered no protest as Hades led her away.

oOo

Hades took her to the library, where she eagerly listened to more stories and lessons from him. She liked hearing about the other gods, and Hades spoke in a candid manner, sparing no virtue or vice as he spoke about the family from which he had detached himself. It was through the way he spoke of them that Persephone got the impression of how he viewed another god. Many of them, he regarded with disdain. Several he was neutral about, such as Hestia or Poseidon. There were precious few for whom he had a real liking.

He had also been teaching her about the symbols that she saw on maps and scrolls. Each symbol stood for a sound, and strung together, formed words and names. She could not read a scroll yet, but she had learned to write out her name as well as Hades's own and several other words.

"There was once a time where man did not yet draw pictures, much less symbols and words. Life was very different back then. All the stories were passed down orally – and still are – but already man has realized the importance of recording things. They painted pictures of their spirits and gods, of their animals and people inside caves or on animal skins. Now the people of Hellas make statues and paint pictures on their walls and pottery, but as civilization advances, that will not be enough."

"Hellas will... change?" It was hard for her to imagine a different world, one that existed after this one, or before. Painting on cave walls? She had never heard such a thing.

"Not just Hellas – the world. I have seen these changes. Your mother brought secrets of farming to Hellas so they could have crops that they could rely on. She gave them a gift that would help them flourish as a society. Other gods have also given gifts to mortals. Standards of living increase. New problems are created and solved. Change makes gods and humans grow." He sounded so wise.

"And there will come a day when everyone will use this... writing?"

"Yes. It will take a long time for everyone to use language in such a way, but everything must start somewhere. The art will spread to more and more people... knowledge will become widespread through the centuries. Who knows how long it will take. Maybe one thousand. Or five thousand?"

For a young goddess who was barely past a score of years, five thousand years was a stretch.

"If... the world was so much more primitive before, then what will it be like in the future?"

"Only time will tell," Hades replied cheerfully.

o0o

"It would appear that our excursion has left us needing a bath," Hades said with a casual tone. Indeed, there was sand and dust on their sandals as well as the hemlines of their clothing. Persephone paused to wonder. She and Hades had worn such fine clothing, yet he didn't seem to care about what their activities might have done to their garments. She supposed that with a staff of shades at hand to perform any chore needed, Hades would never need to worry about his clothing staying dirty. How nice! She had always disliked doing laundry.

"I will bathe myself in my room," Persephone replied.

"Come. That fountain in your room can hardly be as good as a nice, hot bath... I will rub your back too."

"Not tonight," Persephone demurred, bowing her head shyly.

"Come now. You would not go for a swim with me, and now no bath? Are you loath to have my admiration of your body?"

"Mmm."

"What is with the sudden shyness, my dear? You are not afraid of me, are you?"

"Afraid? Not likely!" Persephone replied in feigned bravado. He grinned at her.

"Then allow me to attend to you, my love. Let me remove these dirty garments of yours and wash your body. And if you like, you can return the favor." The image of his nude body came to the forefront of her mind, as well as the memory of his hands on her flesh.

Damnit, Hades! Why do you have to be so sexy! She was certain that if he tried, he could have anybody he wanted, male or female, god or mortal.

"No, thank you," she replied, trying to keep her expression and face neutral.

"Come now." He took her hand, tugging her into the direction of the washroom.

"No." She was now blushing.

"What is the matter? You do not have to be afraid to tell me."

"I'm not sure you would understand."

Hades was silent for several lingering moments, and she bit back a sigh. "My body, it-" She paused. At her words, his gaze inevitably made its course along her body as he raised his eyebrow.

"Are you in pain? Did something happen?" Hades inquired gently. She gave a brief, hesitant nod.

"It happened the previous eve and I was hoping it might have stopped, but..." Her hands fluttered through the air in embarrassment.

"I grew up with three sisters."

She looked up at him.

"Your mother, she did not speak of this?" Hades sounded somewhat incredulous. She shook her head. He gave out a soft groan, and for a moment, she thought she'd offended him.

"I've managed to take care of myself, but-"

"Hekate will answer your questions." He ran his fingers through his hair, pondering his next words, and she stared at him with nervous expectancy. "If you want to ask her, that is. I am privy to much information but I must admit that as a male, I am ignorant of feminine matters, to an extent."

"You're not upset with me?" she asked. He shook his head.

"You're still welcome to join me in the bath. I am sure you will find it soothing."

"You.... know what's happening. Yet..."

"A hot bath cleanses everything."

"Hmm." She frowned thoughtfully. A quiet sigh escaped her lips. "I would still prefer to bathe alone tonight."

"As much as I would like to have you join me, I would be loath to make you uncomfortable. Will you at least keep me company while I bathe? I will be quick, and then you can have the washroom all to yourself."

"Thank you."

oOo

These words were filled with genuine warmth and appreciation, and Hades basked in that glow. When Persephone sat on a stool near the wall, he smiled before removing his chiton and sandals.

"You do not need to sit all the way over there. I do not bite. Unless you want me to." His eyes twinkled as he said this, and he noticed her efforts to hold back a grin.

He felt her eyes on him as he stripped off his short tunic, and had to resist the urge to strike a pose for her. He was a modest person in both attire and demeanor, but it always gave him a thrill when he knew she was admiring him. Languidly, he stepped into the water, welcoming the heat. As he started scrubbing himself with a sponge, he started talking, asking her questions about what she thought of today's events, so he could keep her engaged. As he had promised Persephone, his bath was quick. Lazily, he dried himself with a towel before donning a robe.

"As I have promised, it is all yours." He bowed his head, making a sweeping gesture towards the inviting bath with his arm.

"Thank you." She was smiling again, apparently having her good humor restored.

oOo

When the door closed after Hades, she slipped off her clothing. Cloe appeared – the little shade always seemed to know when she was changing her clothes – to whisk away her dirty laundry. Cloe disappeared with them and before she could turn towards the tub, the shade appeared with fresh clothing and wool. And then her hair was undone, combed out, and tied her hair back in a loose bun. Oh yes. Being Queen of the Underworld... well, it *did* have its perks. She thought of the pomegranate and Hades's words.

Commitment to him – though it still scared her, part of her thought that it wouldn't be a bad idea. He had proved himself to be a funny, warm, caring man despite his reputation, and he had vowed eternal love. And tonight... his reaction certainly had been much better than she had expected.

The churning water soothed away her discomfort. She closed her eyes and gave out a contented murmur as her head lolled back, the bun at the base of her beck cushioning it against the hard marble.

Why don't I just agree to be your wife, Aidoneus? she asked herself with a feeling of mild amusement. But she already knew the answer.

Clearing her mind and taking a deep breath, Persephone decided to not think about any more unpleasant matters for the night. She quickly lost herself in the calming pleasure of the hot bath.

oOo

While Persephone was taking a bath, Hades reclined on the divan in front of the fireplace, idly munching on some stuffed olives. He had decided to have a quick meal tonight rather than try to entice her with another feast. If he simply eased off with the food for a few days, perhaps that would tempt her. She had a defiant streak deep within her, and he knew she didn't like being pressured. She had enough on her plate as it was and if her anger was focused on Zeus, then all the better for the God of the Underworld.

He picked at his meal, taking his time to finish it as he contemplated the current situation with Persephone.

A couple of hours passed, and he saw no sign of Persephone. When he left his bedroom, he saw that the washroom was still occupied. Stealthily he opened it – not out of a voyeuristic urge, but to make sure she was well – and smiled faintly as he saw her submerged to the top of her breasts, her eyes closed and her lips set in a faint smile. Wait, was she asleep?

He crept over to the bath and knelt down, touching her shoulders lightly. When she did not stir, he held back a quiet chuckle. She wasn't the only one who could be so lulled by the soporific atmosphere of the tub.

"Persephone." He started rubbing her shoulders, hearing her let out a small moan as she stirred from her deep meditative state.

"Mmm... Aidoneus..." The softness of her voice as she murmured his name tugged at his heartstrings.

"I just came in here to see that you were well. It has been... a long while."

"... Mhm." Her head lolled back so she could look up at him, her eyes half-lidded.

"Do you wish to remain longer or would you like to go to bed?"

"I believe I am ready to retire for the night. If you would give me a few moments alone..."

He bit back a comment about unneeded modesty, and retreated to bed, settling in amidst the comfortable blankets. In due time, he heard the rustle of fabric as she slid into the bed. Almost without thinking, he pulled her in for an embrace, and she offered no resistance. His lips met her cheek as he gave her a loving nuzzle, and she giggled softly.

"What is so funny?" he whispered before placing a kiss on her temple.

"Your beard tickles."

"Ahh." He smiled faintly before nuzzling her, causing her to giggle again. "I will keep that in mind the next time I want to see a smile on your face."

"Oh, you! Good night." She rolled over and curled up.

"Mmm. Sleep well."

o0o

Without Hades's attempts to pressure her to eat his food, as well as his taciturn understanding of her condition, Persephone was comfortable in the Underworld for the time being. She was kept happy, warm, entertained, and doted on. The truce that they had silently agreed upon served them well, and the captive goddess felt more on equal footing with her captor.

Despite the lack of physical intimacy, Persephone didn't feel ignored by him, or in disfavor because of her bleeding. They still took walks, talked, and had lessons together in the library or elsewhere. Whenever she expressed a desire to be alone, he would bow out gracefully for his own time or to attend to his duties. As much as she hated to admit it, she was beginning to genuinely care for Hades.

Love? No, she would not use that word. But if she did not feel the binding love that a wife felt, she did feel affection for him as a friend. He was fun to talk with, and his company truly was enjoyable. And whenever he did touch her – with loving kisses or chaste touches – the physical contact warmed her. It was impossible to hate one's kidnapper when he was a loving and generous host.

After several more days, Persephone noticed that the bleeding had stopped, and so had the subtler symptoms. A few more days passed, but the bleeding did not return. As she counted the days that she had had to deal with this, she also counted the ones before that, and realized with a small shock that she had been here for a moon-cycle. Had a month really passed on the surface world? With her grown appearance, Persephone looked as if she had been in the Underworld for years. Nobody could ever mistake her for a child anymore. Her breasts weren't large, but they were full and firm, and the curve of her hips complemented her slim waist. Due to her self-deprivation, her ribs and hipbones were visible against her flesh, but she was still a comely sight. Her face had lost the soft, girlish features that had frustrated her when she had been waiting for puberty to release her from the confines of a small body.

If bleeding was the price of womanhood, then she would be glad to pay in full. She had seen the admiring glances that Hades sneaked her way when he thought she wasn't paying attention. She toyed with some of her clothing and jewelry, admiring the way they looked on her.

She sat on a large rock with a smile on her face, watching as Hades threw a tree branch to Kerberos. The dog was enthusiastic about a chance to play with its master and would cheerfully catch and fetch the stick however far Hades threw it. Sometimes one head would swoop down to claim the branch, or two heads would go for it and have a friendly tug-of-war.

The Lord of the Underworld grinned as he hurled the branch, watching the hellhound bound after it. He took his duties as the god of this place seriously, but it was fun to just let go and... just *play* for a while. Kerberos needed the time too, to frolic and play and bound about as dogs did. Mortals assumed that any god – or creature – spent each and every waking – and sometimes slumbering – moment at their duties, always on hand to answer prayers. To them, the Judges never left their thrones, Kerberos was always a snarling monster, and all Kharon ever did was steer the ferry across the Styx. Nobody else would ever know the Lord of the Dead as a man who would 'play'.

Persephone bit back a giggle as the large dog tackled Hades to the ground. Some mortals said it was giant, and it was indeed large, but Hades was able to handle the dog easily. The top of his head was level to the dog's shoulders, but as he was already a tall man, the creature easily towered over any mortal or god and could intimidate anyone by pointing all of his heads at that person, his three mouths fixed into simultaneous snarls. But right now all he was doing was barking and growling playfully, wrestling with his master just as any ordinary dog. Persephone had to admit that Kerberos was a handsome dog. His heads and body was well-formed. His fur was black and sleek, and around each neck was a thick leather collar studded with short metal spikes.

As Hades growled back and wrestled with the dog, now playing a tug-of-war by taking one end of the branch while Kerberos tugged at the other, Persephone was reminded of Enna and playing with her cousins. Hyalos had had a dog, a handsome black-and-brown creature that guarded the chickens at night and was a good playmate during the day to his master or the other children in the family.

Persephone kept telling herself that this place wasn't her home, but she was happier here than she had been ever since Father had died and Mother had taken her from Enna. She didn't want to admit it, Persephone was realizing that it was possible to find contentment here.

Chapter XXVI

oOo

The tropical garden with the waterfall was one of Persephone's favorites. She visited it often, relishing the golden sky and the lushness of her surroundings. The hue of the sky reminded her of the sun's glow, and the thick foliage and warm air helped this place feel more like the surface world. In here, amongst the exotic flowers and the breathtaking waterfall, it was easy to forget that she was a prisoner in the mighty realm of Khthonios.

But you're not treated like a prisoner, are you? Persephone sniffed a large flower with a shade of pink that she had never seen on the surface world. 'Pink' was the only color to describe it, not rose, magenta, salmon or anything else. It was neon in color, just as all of the other colors here in this particular garden, and she wondered what the mortals above would do with such vivid colors at their disposal. Would Mother enjoy such colors?

She let go of the flower, leaving it where it was to wander ahead, wiggling between the thick foliage. She was now comfortable with leaving the paths in whatever garden she chose to explore, for Cloe was always at her beck and call to lead her back should she get lost.

She was clad in a comfortable pale blue peplos, her feet bare as she had left her sandals on the path to feel the thick grass under her feet. She had used her girdle to gather some of the fabric around her middle so that her lower legs were left bare, and she could feel leaves brush against her calves and arms as she went along. Sometimes she felt a bit bored since she had nobody to play or converse with, but more often than not, she welcomed the silence and solitude.

The distant roar of the waterfall grew louder as she continued her meandering path, and the foliage thinned as she approached the pool. Her mouth felt dry, and she ran her tongue along its roof and her teeth. Water technically wasn't food, Hades argued.

So in a gesture that was almost titanic in its magnanimity, Hades declared that should she thirst, she could drink water at any time, from anywhere, and not be held to the rule about taking nourishment from the food of the dead. So with several mouthfuls of the refreshing water, she was ready to move on.

The water in the pond was so clear and cool, though it felt somewhat empty for the lack of fish or other creatures. She looked down at the stream that flowed from the large pool before she glanced up at the cascading water.

Like in many other parts of this garden, vines grew in profusion along the rock face, and they provided excellent grips for her, making her ascent enjoyable. They emerged from cracks in the rock, snaking along crevices and abutments, and before she knew it, Persephone had reached the top. She took a deep breath, placing her hands on her hips as she surveyed the scene. The waterfall was fed by a large stream, and up here there wasn't as much foliage to fill her view. But the horizon itself looked hazy, the difference between sky and vegetation blurring together.

From the outside, the gardens looked small. One would think that with the gates close together, each garden by itself was no bigger than perhaps a courtyard, or the same size as Hades's personal garden. But once she passed through any of the gates, it was like finding a whole new world. No matter how far she strayed from the path, she never saw any other walls, and then when she wanted to go back, it seemed that it took but a few steps to go back to the gate.

As she stood there at the edge of the cliff, she felt a surge of excitement as she stared down at the pool. She already knew that it was fairly deep, already having swum in it.

Here we go. She took a deep breath and closed her eyes, hurling herself forward. The air surged past her skin before water splashed against her body, droplets shining in the light as they enveloped her rapidly descending form. She went slack, letting the current of the water push her forward, keeping her head submerged. Bubbles escaped from between her lips as she opened her eyes, gazing through the crystal-clear water at the pale sand lining the bottom.

Eventually, she rose to the surface. There was nothing wrong with this pool, but she wondered what it would be like to go swimming in Poseidon's domain and see the various creatures of the sea. It was somewhat disconcerting to go into any of the gardens and not hear the call of birds, or the rustle of a stray breeze, or the various sounds of woodland critters. At least she didn't have to worry about bugs, though she could not help but wonder if there were animals here in Dis somewhere. She had seen meat, milk, eggs, cheese, and honey on various occasions at Hades's table. Did this realm provide these ingredients as they were, or were there ethereal creatures that provided these food items? Hm, she would ask him later.

She climbed out of the water, her damp curls and peplos clinging to her skin. She glanced down at the fabric and shrugged before drawing out the pins and peeling the garment off her flesh. It felt good to be free of the grasping fabric, and to bare her naked flesh to the warm air. She glanced up briefly at the golden sky before she felt a tingle at the back of her neck.

She slowly turned around, seeing nobody. But her senses had never failed her.

"Hades," she called out, placing her hands on her hips. There was a slight rustle to her right in front of her. Demurely, she threw an arm across her chest and shielded her womanhood from his view with her other hand. There was a momentary pause before the rustling came nearer, and she felt hands on her arms, tugging them gently away from her body.

"Still insist on hiding your body from me?" he asked in a light, teasing manner, his voice seeming to come from nowhere.

"Perhaps." She grinned before pulling back.

"Not so fast, love." She felt his hands slide along her middle to form a grip, drawing her into an embrace. She felt a bare chest, but when her hand moved lower, she felt the fabric of a kilt around his hips. It felt a bit strange exploring a man she could not see, but it was still fun. She smirked before she hooked her fingers into the waistband of the kilt where it opened or closed, and gave it a sharp tug, swiftly running the other way with a good-sized rectangle of indigo and black linen that became visible once it broke contact with Hades's body.

"Hey!" She heard his surprised laugh but continued running, disappearing among the foliage. Her mischievous bent compelled her to quickly wrap the fabric around herself. It wrapped easily around her breasts and terminated just above her knees. *Take that, Hades. Sneaking up on me invisible when I'm naked. Naughty boy. But I **do** like that about you...*

She heard rustling and footfalls behind her – the first sound of another being she had ever heard since coming to this garden – and grinned as she darted around trees and ferns.

"You will not escape me, fair maiden!" she heard him growl. She wished she had Hermes' sandals, so she could zip up ahead and elude his grip! This was almost eerily similar to her abduction from the surface world, and she frowned faintly to herself. Did Hades realize the same thing? Her long legs pumped her through what was a seeming maze of plant growth, ducking behind foliage whenever she had the chance, but he remained close at her heels.

"You do not expect me to sit and wait to be taken, do you?" she called back as she navigated her way through the tropical forest.

"It would be nice!" he shot back before reaching out, yanking the fabric from her body and tossing it

120

aside. After a futile attempt to snatch back the fabric, she leaned forward, pumping her legs as quickly as she could. This chase went on for several more minutes before the goddess gave out a startled squeal when she felt an arm wrap around her middle. She was hoisted up in the air before she felt herself slung over his shoulder.

"Let me go!" she cried out, banging her fists against an invisible back, and heard a soft chuckle in response. She continued to wiggle around, but his grip was unshakable, and she felt him nuzzle her hip before placing kisses along it, and she gave out a quiet sigh, her head lolling, her slightly damp locks swinging back and forth.

"You looked like you enjoyed that swim. I was about to join you when you came out of the water," he explained as he squeezed her.

"So you thought you would sneak up on me?" she shot back.

"When you stripped off your clothes, I could not resist."

"Hmph," she replied in feigned irritation. The verdant canopy above them opened up as Hades reached the waterfall, and she found herself deposited gently on the sand at the shore of the pond. A patch of blue on the pale sand drew her attention to her chiton, but before she could reach for it, it was snatched out of sight.

"You have your shadow powers and invisibility. I have nothing. That is hardly a fair battle," Persephone said, raising her chin as she felt fingers stroke the inside of her arm.

121

"Perhaps it is not quite fair, but it is fun. Look at you, all rosy-cheeked," he whispered, sliding a finger along her cheek. She gave out a soft whimper as she shivered slightly, his hand now cupping her face.

oOo

Hades smiled as he looked down at her, drawing her closer with his other arm. Her body was warm against his, and she leaned into his body as he hugged her more tightly. His free hand traveled down her face and along her shoulders. It was interesting to see her respond to his touch when he couldn't even see his own hand stroking her. When he squeezed her breast, he saw the faint, round indentations his fingertips made in her flesh, feeling her erect nipple against his palm. The soft fullness of her tit was a comfortable weight in his grip, and he pressed his palm down, rubbing her breast in a massage that had her arching into his hand.

"Hades..." She placed her hand over his, blushing prettily as she looked down. It appeared as if she was having an inner conflict over what was happening, however minor. *Hmm. Let's remedy that, shall we?*

"Persephone..." He smirked before lowering his head to press his lips to her forehead. She did not pull away as his lips traveled down her face, and when his lips met hers, she reached up, her hand gingerly questing through the air as it sought his face.

oOo

122

All she saw was the foliage, but she felt the definite shape of his brow, and he let her fingers slide down until she was able to cup his cheek. When she felt something warm and wet slide along her lips, she realized it was his tongue, and opened her mouth, feeling his lips press against hers with fierce ardor. Seemingly of its own volition, her other arm snaked around his neck, and with his own arm around her middle, they had each other locked in a firm but loving grip.

As she felt Hades explore her mouth, she returned the favor. The feel of his body against her own reminded her of her arousal and the fact that she had not shared any intimacy with him for nearly a week as she attempted to maintain the upper hand in her captivity. Yes, he valued her thoughts and companionship, but there was no denying the physical reaction that one of them could – and inevitably would – elicit from the other.

Persephone broke the kiss, but slowly, her nose touching his as she felt his hands roam along her body. She knew she ought to say 'no' to any kind of touching from him as long as she remained his prisoner, but at this moment, she didn't have the heart to put up real resistance to something she enjoyed so much. Her grip around his neck loosened so she could lay back, giving him freer access to her body as his hands continued their explorations. When he pressed down or massaged a certain area, she could see the impressions that his fingers made against her skin.

As he touched her, she reached out, groping

blindly until she felt solid flesh under her hands. It was almost like a puzzle, figuring out just what part of Hades she was touching. Her right hand slid along a muscled area that she deduced to be his left upper arm, and squeezed it gently. He flexed his bicep in response, and she giggled softly.

"Mmm," she heard him groan before she felt the light, prickly sensation of his beard against her stomach as he placed kisses around her navel. One hand slid down to squeeze her left buttock, causing her to give out a soft little coo of surprise and pleasure.

"You are a vision of loveliness. Aphrodite herself pales before your beauty," Hades whispered reverently.

"Surely nobody is lovelier than the Goddess of Beauty herself." She had always wondered what Aphrodite looked like in person since the superbly-crafted statue of her in Hades's garden of sculptures couldn't possibly capture and illustrate the full loveliness of the beautiful Goddess.

"Her beauty is superficial. It is beauty for beauty's sake itself. But your beauty... it is vibrant, radiant, alluring. Your eyes hold a glint of wisdom that Aphrodite lacks despite her years. Aphrodite displays her beauty as much and as often as possible. You are more reserved – and modest about it. Your beauty is a rare gift to be cherished."

"You do know how to make a girl feel good," she shot back with a pleased tone. She had learned in her time with him that when he complimented her, it was never flattery. His tone was full of warmth and love, and she found herself with a strange sensation of melting deep within. It was hard to not feel comfortable here. The sky was gold and radiant, the plants lush, the air was warm, the water soothing and refreshing. She heard the dull roar of the water, welcoming the background noise. Hades's touch thrilled and comforted her, and his strong, smooth voice had an almost soporific effect on her.

What was the point of pushing his hands away? She was now aware of the pleasures that one could share with a loved one without having actual intercourse, and while she enjoyed his touches, she was afraid to admit that she wouldn't mind being deflowered by him. What better candidate than a man who had already proven himself to be a skilled lover? Her womanhood tingled warmly at the recollection of these memories with him.

"I would be worried if I did not," he responded with a soft chuckle before she felt his hot breath on her breast. She sighed out his name as he wrapped his lips around the soft pink nipple. Her body squirmed against his, and he relished the feel of her warm skin.

"Yes," she hissed softly as he started to suck, rubbing his tongue against the tip of her nipple. As he lavished his attention upon her breast, he slid his hand along her stomach, pausing only a moment when he came to the edge of the triangle of dark curls that sat above her womanhood.

"You are wet," Hades observed as his fingers slid further south, and she felt a digit part her nether lips, sliding inside.

"So I am." Persephone smiled faintly. When he

wiggled his finger, she squirmed around. When he nudged her knees apart further, she offered no resistance, spreading herself open.

"And what are you going to do?" she asked as she felt his other hand stroke her inner thigh.

"I have not decided yet," Hades replied, lowering his head as he spoke so she could feel his warm breath on her womanhood.

"Do not take too long," she responded impatiently, wiggling around as she felt his hot breath. So that's where he was! She could envision him positioned between her legs, just as he had done several times before. She squinted, hoping to see some sort of outline or hint of his body, but he truly was invisible. Not even the slightest glimmer or distortion of the air betrayed his appearance, though the feel of his hands was clear enough evidence of his proximity.

"I shall not."

"Good." She heard his soft chuckle before he slid in another finger. Even now, after what they had shared, she still found herself surprised at times at the pleasure she felt, or that intimate pleasure existed outside of intercourse. Before she had been carried off by this handsome, dark – and at the moment, unseen – god, she would have never imagined that a man wiggling his fingers into her would excite her so much.

"Hades..." She arched as he pressed his thumb against the hood that concealed her aching bud from his view. He continued his ministrations, coaxing her clit from its hiding place and leaning his head down to flick his tongue over it. Persephone hissed softly in shocked delight, digging her fingers into the sand. He was so gifted with his mouth and tongue... such pleasure promised her even more for when she gave herself to him. What would it be like to be *filled* by him? To have him take her into his arms and make her *his?* Such a thought was thrilling and terrifying.

Her imaginings of future pleasure were interrupted by the ones found in the present as she felt him lap more enthusiastically at her sensitive bud, sending white-hot frissons of joy through her body.

As he proceeded with his tongue and fingers, her breathing became more erratic as she tried to not buckle around so much. Her left hand rose before it reached forward, finally finding the top of his head after several exploratory grasps in the air.

Persephone groaned softly as Hades increased her pace, gasping and crying out encouragingly. It felt almost as of her loins were on fire, sending warm tendrils of heated sensation through her body. She threw her head back, issuing a gasp as she felt Hades push her over the edge, surging into the abyss of orgasmic bliss.

She lay there, trembling slightly as Hades lapped up the reward of her ecstasy. He continued to lick and finger her at a steady, gentle rhythm, sending shivers of post-orgasmic tremors through her flesh.

"Aidon," she sighed, stroking his head, feeling his thick, long hair under her palm.

"Seph..." he replied as he nuzzled her inner thigh. Persephone's head lolled back as he drew his fingers out of her and she considered what he had just called her. It was a nice shortened name. Aidoneus and Persephone. Aidon and Seph. That thought suffused her with such a warm glow of satisfaction.

She felt his head lift under her hand as he sat up, grasping her wrist and kissing the back of her hand. It remained aloft in the air as several more kisses were placed upon it before he lowered it to her stomach.

She reached out again and his hand threaded her fingers before she felt him change position, lifting her leg and shifting so that he now sat next to her. He lowered her leg and she felt hands grasp her sides, pulling her up into his lap. She had but to lift her hand and there his chest was, his heartbeat under her hand. Reaching up, she felt his shoulder and a thick lock of his hair. Further up her fingers explored, tracing along the circle of his beard and detecting a faint smile on his lips. His arms held her in a comforting embrace, and her hand traveled back down. Her fingers slid down the smooth muscles of his chest, noting the faint but defined ridge of his abs. She grazed over his treasure trail before grasping him around the base of his manhood, feeling its hard thickness.

She gave it a gentle but purposeful squeeze before her hand slid up the shaft, feeling his embrace tighten slightly. Again, she thought of coupling with him. Even though he had just pleasured her, her womanhood ached afresh. If she could just lower herself onto him and fulfill her innermost fantasy...

Not yet. She was having a good time, but now wasn't the time for that. As much as she wanted to...

"I... I want you and I should not. You are so wonderful." Her eyes brimmed with unshed tears. "I enjoy being with you and being here... This is such an incredible place. I will never be the same person again."

"Oh, but you are. You are the woman I fell in love with. You have just learned a lot of new things and had wondrous experiences and given the chance to become the Goddess you are. I know you enjoy it here, and I am glad you do," he said as he stroked her cheek.

"When you... were tasting me, I thought of what it would be like if... we had intercourse. It excites me, but it also scares me."

"There is no reason to be afraid. You should know better." He placed a light kiss on her brow, his tone without the slightest note of reproach, yet she could not help but feel just a bit guilty and annoyed, much in the same way she felt when he offered her food. She looked away, still blushing.

"Everything I offer to you wholeheartedly. You are the Queen of my kingdom and my heart." His embrace tightened, drawing her against his chest.

"I know that, Aidon... You know that I still wish to return to the surface world... but I would be happy to come back here so long as you are my host. Truly, I would be happy to be your guest again... and again."

"I will not be a mere host," Hades replied, his voice calm and stern. "I will not have you as my guest, but my bride and lover. I do not take half-measures."

Persephone lowered her head, her thick hair obscuring much of her face from his view. Couldn't he make that compromise, if he cared for her so much? It was reasonable after the fact that she had been kidnapped!

"I will not force you into intimacy or eat my food, but there is no reason you should be afraid. Come now, love. Let us set aside this discussion for later since we were having such a pleasant time."

She was tempted to argue the matter further, but why mar such an enjoyable occasion? What was it Cyane had said? Sometimes if a woman appeared to be especially cooperative, she could charm a man into giving her what she wanted. Hekate had hinted at a similar thing in her bid to try to help the younger Goddess in an attempt to circumvent Hades's order.

So Persephone relented, nodding slowly. If it took a little more time, so be it.

His hand slid down to cover hers, stroking it. His lips pressed against her forehead before he whispered her name, thrusting his hips upward, reminding her of just what they had been doing before their momentary interlude. Her hand slid downward, gently cupping his sac, feeling no small thrill of satisfaction as she felt its warm, comfortable weight in her hand. She was familiar enough to be able to navigate comfortably around his unseen body, and his small sounds of pleasure told her just how comfortably familiar with him she had become. As she stroked and massaged him, his hands moved along her body in a lazy manner as he held her close.

When his lips closed on hers, she forgot their

argument and let herself become lost in Hades's desire and affection for her.

Chapter XXVII

oOo

For once in his life, Hermes was unsure of where he might continue his search, since there had been no hints or even the slightest sign or premonition that might aid his quest. The nymphs had been no more helpful to him than they had been for Demeter. Kora had been there one day, gone the next. He had been searching for over a week now ever since Zeus bade him to aid Demeter in the search of her missing child.

Hermes was a mischievous and energetic individual, but he was not a cruel or malicious person. Had he known that Ares would attempt to rape Kora, there would have been a better chance of him keeping his mouth shut about the discovery of the daughter of the Harvest Goddess. It wouldn't be the first time that Ares had been a brute, but the God of War certainly hadn't counted on his attempted conquest's mother to be a powerful Goddess. And now, to see that Kora was gone!

Ares had been the first suspect to Hermes – and the most obvious. Hermes had done his due diligence, and Ares simply did not have the intelligence to keep Kora concealed from her mother's magic. That aside, the God of War was a terrible liar.

Hermes had gone to several other gods and in his own way – eavesdropping, investigating, or engaging his interrogates with well-placed questions – divulged the fact that none of them had anything to do with Kora's disappearance. Now the quick-footed god had eliminated all of the most obvious suspects from his list. He was determined to do his best and if he wasn't able to bring her back, at least he would know where she was. He did feel somewhat guilty for her disappearance; she was a sweet girl.

He had to admit, he was glad to have been given a mystery to solve, having been bored for a while now. He certainly liked cracking them open like nuts to discover whatever secrets might lay within, and knew that he wasn't the only one anxious to find out Kora's whereabouts. Whenever he came to Demeter with his reports he always felt guilty when he saw the pain and anguish on her face.

o0o

The Lord of the Dead glided through Zeus's grand house, a dark presence casting his shadow among the treasures of the elegant domicile.

"Welcome, welcome!" Zeus greeted him from the divan he was reclining on, gesturing to another one for his elder brother. On the table was set a small feast, but Hades disregarded the meal and the proffered seat. He knew why Zeus wanted to see him, so he would waste no time. Better to be in the Underworld with his love than up here with his brother!

The Lord of the Underworld cut a majestic figure, wrapped in a black cloak that billowed around him and added dimension to his form. A thin golden crown set with onyx graced his head, and his brooch

133

and wristbands were no less elegant. The raven-haired god remained on his feet, staring at Zeus coolly.

"When I received your summons, I knew what it was for, so I am not going to waste my time with pleasantries. I assure you, your daughter is safe," Hades said evenly.

"Very well then," Zeus swallowed.

"Interesting you ask that when you did not even think to grant her the courtesy of notifying her of her betrothal."

Zeus stared for several moments as his brother smirked at him coldly.

"I would think that my guarantee of her safety and well-being would satisfy you. Do you think I would go back on my word? Are you so mistrusting of your own brother?"

Again, an uncomfortable silence hung in the air. Inwardly, Hades relished his brother's discomfort. Was Persephone happy? She had made no demands to leave the Underworld for a while, and he hadn't put food before her in the same span of time. The unspoken truce continued as it had.

Bit by bit she was exploring the Underworld and learning about her new domain. Soon enough, she would be ready to sit beside him as his Queen. His craftsmen had already created a splendid throne for her. Zeus' question was simple enough, but there was no pleasure in responding with a mere 'Yes'.

"You live in a realm that is far different from the other gods. I have seen that place."

"Quite a few times," Hades shot back. With all

the children Zeus had – and that was just counting the divine offspring – that was a good number of trips to the Fates, to ensure that the vicious cycle that his grandfather and father had been trapped in would not ensnare him as well. But Zeus kept his trips as short as possible, knowing only one brief path within the Underworld, and nothing else.

"It is a place that even the gods fear., and for good reason. Kora's just a... little girl!"

Little girl, you say? A maiden of five and twenty years? Hades sneered inwardly. The image of a lithe and curvaceous Persephone, her cheeks rosy from the pleasure he gave her was still enticingly fresh in his mind. Already he missed the feel of her body snuggled up against his. What would Zeus and Demeter say if they could see their daughter right now, clad in finery and adorned in jewels, though the finest of fabrics and the rarest of gems paled before her beauty?

"You do not give your daughter enough credit," the Lord of the Dead replied, waving his arm in a dismissive gesture. "But then, have you ever really known her? As it is, I am a far better judge of what she needs."

"Can you not answer my question without going off on a different tangent?"

"No." *Because it amuses me*, Hades thought dryly. He had told Persephone that Zeus was not without his faults, and that was the truth. Of his faults, there were *plenty* to be had. Zeus might rule Olympus with a firm hand and do his best to arbitrate the various conflicts within his family, but Hades had little respect for his brother on a personal level.

The Lord of the Dead was a reserved man, but he wasn't above sending a barb someone's way or teasing them if he felt it was warranted.

"Is she happy?" Zeus asked, trying to not sound too insistent.

"You should have thought about that before." Hades felt smug as he saw Zeus' face redden almost imperceptibly.

"You are the one who kidnapped her!" Zeus replied quickly, all too eager to shift blame.

"And how many women have you carried off? How many lives were changed forever – and not always for the better – because of you?"

The younger sibling clenched his fist but could offer no swift retort, and Hades crossed his arms.

"What of Demeter?" Hades asked.

"She came to me a while ago."

"And I suppose you plied your usual charm," Hades replied snidely.

"I put Hermes in her service."

"Hmm." Not a bad decision. It would provide a distraction, at least for a while.

"How long should this go on?" Zeus asked with a soft sigh. His brother shrugged.

"Not indefinitely, of course," Hades shook his head. "It is difficult to say though, what a proper frame of time would be."

"Perhaps, if you were to go to her and say that you... found or even *rescued* Kora and that she is safe in your custody..." Zeus suggested.

Hades looked at his brother thoughtfully. *Yes. Not*

a bad idea. Demeter would be so relieved to know that her daughter was safe. But the Goddess would inevitably demand her daughter back. And Hades could only imagine how smothering she might be then. He loved his sister, but he loved Persephone more.

There was no easy solution to this dilemma. Hades shook his head slowly in thought.

"That is a fine suggestion. Nonetheless, she will want her daughter back," he replied. Zeus shrugged helplessly.

"I was trying to help," Zeus replied petulantly. The other god had to bite back a smirk.

"I know," Hades replied in an amicable tone. "That actually is not a bad idea, but I need to think on this some more. Our sister is a force to be reckoned with, and I will not give up my bride."

"I did not think you would."

This time, Hades let a smirk grow on his face. "Good."

Before his brother could say anything, the sunny room suddenly darkened for a moment as the shadows thickened, and then the Dark God was gone.

o0o

Zeus pondered about his son Perseus, relieved that he at least had one less child to worry about. He was now king of a prosperous nation, had a beautiful bride that he saved from a sea-monster, a healthy baby son and another child on the way, and his mother was restored to her royal status.

Doubtless, Danae wouldn't have predicted her life to turn out this way. Yes, becoming with child had led her down a life that was not without hardship. But better that than miserable languishing for who knows how long in that tower, never to see or speak to anyone. And she *had* welcomed his attentions, showing warmth and gratitude and such *enjoyment* of his presence that he had not experienced for a long time.

And now, through Zeus' aid for his son, she had become blessed by him again. She got on well with her daughter-in-law and doted on her grandson. Raising her son in a distant country had matured her, and she no longer needed a man to feel secure, becoming an efficient and competent woman, even in the luxurious and comfortable surroundings as mother to the King. He didn't have to worry about them anymore, which he was thankful for as he now had considerably more pressing matters on his conscience.

He was fully aware that the longer Demeter went on without finding her daughter, the fiercer her wrath was most likely to be. Wishing that situations in the past could be changed made no difference, so he knew it was useless to dwell on what could have been. He had three options regarding his own actions. He could simply keep quiet for as long as he could, letting Demeter find out on her own for however much time it took – which he knew would be cruel – or he could wait for Hades to decide on a certain time. Or encourage Hades to do so.

That left a third option – he could just come clean

about it now and end Demeter's depression and worry. He did not enjoy seeing his sister wander through Hellas, heartbroken for her child. It would be cruel to let her go on any longer, but he feared her wrath. He might be King of the Gods, but they had been sired from the same elder god and delivered from the same womb. She was his older sister and a powerful deity in her own right. Look at what she had done to Ares! Would she seek a similar vengeance against her brother if she found out? Ooh, that was not something he wanted to consider.

So he would maintain his silence.

o0o

Persephone would only have the water, regardless of the wine and nectar that sat in chilled flasks, waiting to be poured down thirsty throats. Hades shook his head as he stared at her. Even now, with all the things she enjoyed in the Underworld, still she feared to eat its food! She took several long gulps from her goblet, but he knew that water was a poor substitute for food. Hunger would maintain its edge, so he felt confident in giving her this small concession.

Even as she drank her water, he saw her eyeing the food. Most of the dishes were hot, steam from the dishes rising into the air in sinuous and thick tendrils, filling the room with the delicious aroma of centuries of culinary experience of his cooks. Everything was cooked and spiced to maximize the smell and flavor, promising an exciting experience to anyone who would explore the food before them. Hades made a small sound of approval as he ate a piece of baklava, honey and nuts pressed between thin layers of flatbread.

He could feel her eyes on him, and he pretended to not see, chewing slowly and savoring the bite. Only when he swallowed his food did his eyes meet hers. She quickly looked away. He thought about the truce that had been drawn between them, but knew that it would not go on indefinitely. One day, she would again ask about the surface world. When he came back from Olympus, he had gently insisted that she sit with him at mealtime, for eating by himself while she hid from him was lonely. He would not try to force her to eat, but he wanted to remind her of what he had to offer.

"Would you like a bite of the bread, my dear? It is fresh from the oven. And there is olive oil to dip it in if you like. Or honey, or fruit. It fills the mouth and stomach with warmth." He smiled. "If you're looking for something sharper and cooler, there are olives stuffed with cheese. They're one of my favorite things to eat.

"Mine too," she replied, then bit her lip, looking down.

"Well, help yourself." He waved her forward, inviting her to sit on his divan – perpendicular to her own so they sat a snug distance from one another – and beckoned with a graceful tilt of the head to let him feed her. She shook her head, staring away resolutely, her hand fluttering to her stomach for a moment before she put it in her lap.

140

Mother, feed me! She let out a low, wavering sigh, trying to rise from her seat.

"The doors are sealed. You will sup here with me," Hades whispered as he stared at her.

"I will not eat."

"You act as if this is torture."

"It is."

"Are you tied to the chair, unable to help yourself to the food? Have I been the one to starve you?"

She looked down sullenly.

"You know that you can have anything you like. Nothing's stopping you, yet you squirm around in hunger. I do not like seeing that."

Persephone continued to ignore him. She thought of the surface world and Mother. Perhaps now that she had grown, Mother would treat her like an adult. After all, hadn't Mother agreed to take her to the autumn festivals and let her participate in the harvest rites of the Goddess? She had often hoped that her mother would treat her as an adult and equal.

Just like Hades does, her inner voice whispered. He was the first person in her life to have ever treated her like an equal. She frowned to herself. But he also wouldn't let her go to the surface world. Hmph. She was only equal to him in *some* ways.

When he coaxed her with a few other items, she shook her head resolutely, even when he joined her on her divan, stroking her arm and waving a plate of various aromatic tidbits under her nose. She turned her face, closing her eyes and resolutely ignoring his offerings as she buried her face in her arms against the arm of the divan, muffling the scent from her nose.

After a while, she felt a faint swoosh move past her and lifted her head to see the shades clearing away the dishes. She sat up but kept her gaze averted, knowing that he was hurt by her refusal of his offering and pleas. She didn't want to admit it, but she was also pained by her own actions, so she remained silent as she felt his eyes on her.

Chapter XVIII

o0o

After a month of being host to his lover, Hades had already planned what to do next to acclimate her to the Underworld. Persephone was familiar with the Underworld, exploring its different realms as well as spending time watching the Judges or Kampe at work, or visiting with Hekate. He was pleased that she did this on her own, for it showed an interest in the workings of the Kingdom of the Dead. She also asked him questions and had also inquired of various matters to the Judges and the Furies, listening with an attentive ear to their stories.

He decided that it was time to take the next step. This was the first occasion where she would formally sit as Queen of the Underworld. Before this, she had been treated more like a guest, given no real responsibilities so that she would become more used to her new home. Still, she refused to eat his food. Hopefully, the weight of a crown would strengthen her bond with him and this realm.

o0o

Persephone gazed in her reflection as Cloe fussed over her hair, its misty fingers arranging several curls in her hair. An intricate crown of platinum, diamond, and black opal graced her head, and a matching set of jewels glittered at her neck, ears, and fingers. Her black silk gown and cowl were woven with silver thread in a detailed, swirling pattern along the hems.

Her calm appearance disguised the nervousness she felt. She knew she could throw herself at his feet and ask him to not do this, and he would acquiesce. But she was curious, and she did want to see how Hades held his Court while she participated. She would be Queen of a kingdom as well, and she felt a small thrill at that thought, even if she hadn't sought the role.

And besides... she had always wondered what it would be like to be worshiped as a Goddess, to sit in a throne and to be acknowledged as a Queen. What did Mother do on her duties as a Goddess? As Thermasia, she was a priestess of the people of Enna, using her Gift to enrich their lives, but it had been a village, and 'Thermasia' was modest. What of the mighty temples built to her in other places, and the festivals and the throngs of people who came to worship her? Persephone had always wanted to see the great city-states, and to see them from Mount Olympus, and never failed to be disappointed whenever Mother left her behind with her father and then the nymphs.

As the Queen of the Underworld contemplated her reflection in the mirror, she recalled a time where she hadn't even had any say over her wardrobe.

She huffed softly as she went through the clothing she had. She wanted garments more like the nymphs wore, and she found her wardrobe choices unsatisfying. She didn't have any jewelry other than a few plain pins to hold up her chitons or hair, and none of her clothing was as fine as the beautiful and ceremonial robes that Mother wore when she left for other parts of Hellas to perform her duties as a Goddess.

Mother was gone again, having left hours ago. Kora had been left under the care of nymphs, under the strict admonishments to be a good girl, mind the nymphs, and to practice her weaving.

Ugh. How she hated it. She had no patience for the work that went into the kind of weaving Mother wanted her to do. Her mind usually wandered to other things, driving her to distraction, especially if she was left alone without Mother looking over her shoulder.

Leave the weaving to Hestia, she often thought as Mother would rap her fingers on the frame to snap her attention back to the task at hand, something Kora always hated. Mother extolled her elder sister's qualities, saying that Hestia was a good woman, a Goddess who did not interfere with the affairs of others and led a quiet, productive life. Such a life did not appeal to the girl.

She was now alone, the nymphs gossiping and frolicking outside. Kora had excused herself, saying she wished to take a nap. Ignoring the looms that sat in the sunny main room, she slid down the hall that led to Mother's bedchamber. The opportunity was golden to explore Mother's wardrobe and try on some of her jewelry, or her fine ceremonial robes.

The Goddess had two large trunks, both made of masterfully carved wood and identical to one another, crafted by Hephaistos himself. One sat at

145

the foot of her bed, containing ordinary and oft-worn clothing. The other one was tucked away in a corner and held all her finer accouterments.

Kora went to this chest, lifting the lid and staring down at fine white linen and cloth dyed with rare and deep hues like ultramarine and purple, or brilliant emerald. There were also a couple of pairs of fine sandals as well as several elegantly-woven cowls and cloaks, gold and silver thread glittering amidst the fabric.

She grinned as she took out the violet peplos and replaced her own with it. Naturally, the garment was too large for her, but she wrapped a deep gold girdle around her narrow hips and folded and rearranged the excess folds before tucking them into the belt. There was a necklace of gold and polished amethyst nuggets, and she placed that around her own neck. Doing the best she could, she pinned up her hair in her mother's style with the gold pins she found within the jewelry box. The arm and waistbands did not fit her slender arms and there was no way to make them fit, so she left them along with the sandals that were too large for her feet.

It had been several years since she had last seen her mother's mirror, but she knew that this trunk also contained said treasure, since Mother rarely looked into it. It was a handheld mirror, its silver surface unblemished and framed in gold wrought in the Harvest Goddess' symbol of bushels of wheat. She propped it up on the platform beneath the window and backed away, seeing the upper half of her body in the reflection. She had never worn such a lovely and deep color, and she smiled at herself, admiring how mature she looked, though keenly aware of the fact that under the generous swaths of her mother's clothing, she had nothing to fill it out with.

She returned to the chest and tried the green outfit. Mother's favorite girdle – the one made by Hephaistos – went twice around her waist, but she admired the design and was determined to try it on.

How nice it would be to have such clothing of her own, and to be seen, and recognized, and praised! She was bored and lonely in this existence despite the attention of Mother and the nymphs. She grinned to herself as she twirled around quickly and did a curtsey to the mirror.

She was careful to put everything back in its proper place and the nymphs were none the wiser. The next day, she decided to try the white robe, the most special item in her mother's wardrobe. It was of snow-white linen and came with a matching cowl, and both were woven with gold thread in an intricate design that like her other accessories, was woven in the shape of wheat, along with several other symbols of fertility and bounty.

Kora was especially careful with these articles of clothing since it was vital that she not get a smudge or dirt on it. Mother kept her house clean, so the floor was well-swept. Even then, Kora took care to not drag the fabric along the floor as she donned the white garb. As with the other clothing she had tried on, she had to fold and tuck the fabric to make it fit. She fastened it with a deep green-and-gold girdle before wrapping the cloak around herself. The cowl

147

itself was of thinner linen than that of the chiton, making her body and hair faintly visible. She studied her reflection in the mirror, arranging the cowl this way and that.

She ran her hand against the gauzy linen, admiring the feel of the fabric under her hands. How exciting it must be to be a Goddess!

"Kora!" The girl whipped around with wide, startled eyes at her mother's furious scream.

Persephone let out a sigh at that memory. Mother had been furious, of course.

And now, the daughter of the Goddess of Bounty was swathed in fabric far finer than her mother had ever possessed in her long lifetime, and the jewels that glittered around her head and neck was wrought with far more valuable gems, the most brilliant of diamonds and black opals and wrought by the finest creative minds in Elysium.

Like her mother, she was a Goddess in her own right, offered the rule over an entire kingdom and the freedom to do as she pleased. Not once since she had been brought here did she have to do a single stitch of weaving.

She looked down at the large diamond that glittered on her finger before eying her reflection. She angled her head to admire the gauzy silk veil that had been pinned to her crown. It was fastened under the sides and back of the crown, and trailing down to her ankles. It added the touch of understated elegance and mystery that her outfit needed.

Satisfied with her reflection, she stalked towards

the door and emerged into the larger room, her veil fluttering around her almost like an aura. The glint of open admiration in Hades's eyes and the smile of appreciation on his lips told her all she needed to know.

Hades himself was garbed in robes of black and dark gray, with a crown and wristbands of silver and onyx. His cloak swept around him in a powerful and graceful manner when he moved, emphasizing his turns and movements as well as billowing out when he strode forward quickly.

She wondered where she might be sitting as she remembered the raised dais with Hades's impressive throne on it. He said that he had set up something special for her. She wondered what that could possibly be, after all the fantastic and splendid things she had already seen in this place.

They emerged into the throne room from a side entrance and her eyes scanned the wide hall before resting on the throne on the dais. She blinked and stared. Had the throne gotten wider?

"Go ahead, look." Hades gently nudged her forward. She approached the steps and saw the distinct form of two separate but identical seats, and her head tilted to one side as the implications sunk in. Upon closer inspection, the throne to the right had a different design than the other one, which she already recognized as Hades's throne. The new throne had a more delicate pattern – resembling vines and spirals in many places – in an organic pattern as opposed to the geometric pattern on Hades's throne. However, in size and stature, it was identical to its mate. The chairs sat close together, but with just enough space between them so that they could both use their own armrests comfortably or touch one another's arm with a slight reach.

The cushion was soft and plush, offering a comfortable place to sit during Court sessions. She circled around the thrones, trailing her fingers along the arms and backs of both pieces of furniture.

"Come sit down." Hades smiled as he climbed up the steps. Persephone slid into her seat, wiggling around on the cushion as she leaned back. The spacious chamber had a slight chill to it, but her cowl kept her warm.

"People from the Asphodels ask me to be allowed to drink the Lethe waters. They come to me with their petitions and I determine whether they have learned enough during their time in the Asphodel Fields to be allowed to drink the Lethe waters. For even as their past lives are forgotten, the lessons they learn remain with them."

"How often do you do this?"

"As often as needed. My Gift connects me to this realm and I can sense its needs." In that aspect, he was no different from Kharon.

Persephone could imagine how such a connection with their kingdom would benefit a king of any realm. Did Zeus and Poseidon share such rapport with their domains?

Several shades floated into the room, followed by a group of several dozen souls. Some of them had sharper outlines while others looked fuzzier in her vision. The group was varied, with old and young men and women. She let her eyes move along the group, making a quick study of each one.

When her eyes fell on the last soul – who had situated himself at the very back of the group – she found herself too stunned to speak or react.

She barely heard the first soul as it floated forward to petition Hades. The words of the man did not register to her as she stared forward.

All these years, she knew where her father was – in the realm of the dead. He was mortal, and not even the love and care of a Goddess kept him safe from the insidious embrace of Death, his life determined by the length of thread that Lakhesis measured for him.

Yet in her time down here, Persephone hadn't asked to see her father. For one thing, she was unsure of how she would handle such a reunion. Iasion had been with her during the happy days of her childhood. He was a man who had loved her truly, and she would always consider him her father, whether he had sired her or not.

The revelation that she was a full-blooded Goddess had placed a whole new dimension on her existence. She was not mortal and would never die. When she had been considering asking Hades if she could see Iasion again, this knowledge had remained firmly ensconced in her head. After contemplating her options, she had decided to leave the entire matter be. Iasion had been a good man, so what was he doing with this group? Had he committed some crime in his life that had downgraded his final destination to the Asphodel Fields?

After her initial shock, she was able to better

listen to the petitions of the souls before her. Since this was her first sitting as Queen, she remained silent and listened to Hades and his subjects while anticipating and dreading her father's turn. She almost felt sick, and her stomach had the sensation of being pulled into a tight knot. As a child, she had always been robust, never falling ill or suffering from any sort of infection. This feeling of lightheadedness combined with the tightness in her stomach was an unwelcome sensation, and she tightened her grip on the armrests.

Only the distraction of the souls asking for another chance at life gave her something else to focus on. As she listened to them, she wondered what her father could have done. Was consorting with a god a crime? She couldn't imagine that the man who had loved and raised her as his own had committed any sort of crime.

Some of the souls were sent back to Asphodel while others were granted permission to go to Lethe. As the group dwindled, her anxiety increased. Iasion didn't seem to recognize her. Naturally, all the souls were interested in their new Queen, and she sat there calmly under their curious glances as they approached the royal couple. But other than that, she didn't see any recognition on his translucent features. Goodness. She wished she had something to fan herself with, and slowly moved her hands to loosen her cowl.

oOo

Hades had been aware of his lover's tension for a while now. Outwardly, she was calm, but he sensed her unease, and his eyes flicked over to her as he saw her loosen her wrap. He glanced over at the remaining souls before his eyes scanned the room. He couldn't see a single reason that she might be upset.

The next soul was dismissed back to the Asphodel Fields, and before the next one was called forth, he turned towards her, squeezing her hand.

"Love, what is the matter?" he whispered.

"Nothing." Her eyes flicked downward and she shifted around in her seat but remained as she was.

"Really?"

"Yes."

"Do you wish to retire from Court?" he asked. Her eyes flicked in his direction, and she stared at him for a moment before shaking her head.

"Very well then." He waved the next soul forward while keeping an eye on her. She remained silent as the next few souls were processed until only one remained. This one was different, though. Souls that came from the Asphodels tended to be a dingy gray in color, signifying their status as souls that were neither especially good or evil. This soul was of a tall and broad-shouldered man, a faint glow emanating from him and marking him as one of Elysium's blessed.

Someone from Elysium wanted to drink the Lethe waters and start over? Such an instance was rare, but not unheard of. He beckoned the soul forward.

"You have seen how the others have petitioned to me. Tell me your case." His voice was stern but calm, as he always addressed his subjects.

"Over ten years ago, I died and came to Elysium. It has been a wonderful place for me, and I have enjoyed my time there."

"Yet here you stand before me," Hades replied. He was fully aware of the fact that Persephone had gone completely still as she looked down at the soul.

"Not because you are an unjust lord." The soul bowed his head. "I am Iasion of Enna. When I was still alive, I loved someone deeply. But she will be unable to join me in Elysium. I cannot be happy if she is not at my side."

"Is she so wicked that you fear she might be sent to Tartarus, or is she already there?"

"No, my lord."

Hades glanced down at the man. *Iasion.* Now, why should this be so significant? He could not be expected to know every soul here, but that name was distinctly familiar to him, and he tried to remember just where he had heard it. A god could hardly be expected to remember every little thing that happened over the centuries.

Then it hit him with the force and totality of a tidal wave. This man had been Demeter's lover and the one that Persephone had believed to be her father all these years.

He slowly glanced over at her and realized with a small shock that she was holding back tears. Was this some kind of cruel trick by Fate, to have such an unlikely person approach him on Persephone's first day as enthroned queen? His mind raced with various options as he barely absorbed the rest of Iasion's words.

"... I am but a humble mortal who was lucky enough to know true love. But I cannot be happy if the one I love can never join me. I only wish for the release from these memories and to start anew."

Hades was a stern man and did not easily let people leave his kingdom via the Lethe waters. Going back to the mortal coil was a privilege, albeit a temporary one. However many times a soul received another chance to go back to the surface world, they would always return. *Thanatos* was inevitable and unstoppable. Iasion was a good man and he could see no reason to deny the man's heartfelt request. As the Lord of the Dead pondered the soul's words, Iasion's attention wandered over to Persephone.

o0o

She glanced back at him, wondering whether she should say something. This was a man she had known and loved through her childhood. She wanted to go forward and take him into her arms – and had to deal with the bitter realization that he was merely a soul, with a body of even less substance than the shades. And she was no longer little Kora anymore.

Growing up was not without its trials, she knew that. Being grown-up meant having responsibility and making difficult decisions, like Grandmother would tell her and her cousins. Right now, all she wanted to do was cry. She was overwhelmed by the intense mix of emotions that churned fiercely within her chest, making her feel almost as if it would burst. She wished she was a little girl again and that her dad was alive again, so he could beam down at her and scoop her up into his arms as he had often done in the past.

"Your petition will be considered," Hades stated.

"Oh." Iasion seemed about to say something further, but apparently had decided against questioning the Lord of the Dead, so he bowed before the shades escorted back to Elysium.

Persephone let out a low, shaky sigh before rising from her feet and climbing down the steps without a single utterance to Hades. The translucent gauze of her veil and the diaphanous silk of her wrap fluttered after her as she strode across the floor, leaving the Lord of the Dead alone in the grand chamber.

Even after she heard Hades calling her name, she continued stalking forward, fighting the tears that were on the verge of breaking out. When she deemed him safely out of earshot, she let out a quiet sob, the tears freely making their way down her cheeks. She was almost surprised that she hadn't burst into tears in front of either man, and continued crying as she roamed the hallways, seeking the quickest way outside.

Had Hades thought to surprise her by bringing her Iasion before her? He had found many ways to entertain and delight her, but she didn't think he would do such a thing like that. He knew she had cared for her father deeply, and still did even after learning that they were not tied by blood.

She lifted the edge of her wrap and wiped her cheeks with it, taking a shaky breath as she collected herself. The tears continued to flow down her face as she slowed her pace, dabbing her cheeks again.

Suddenly, hands slid onto her shoulders and squeezed them as she found herself being pulled back against a warm and hard body. A loose but secure embrace completed his gesture, comforting her without making her feel too restricted.

"Persephone, I did not know he would be there," he whispered.

"I was hoping you were not responsible for that..."

"Requests from Elysium are rare. Never did I think it would be him. I was just as surprised when I realized just who he was. I hope you are not upset with me."

"No." She wiped several more tears with her fingers as she nestled into his embrace. She closed her eyes and let out a deep, slow sigh as Hades waited patiently.

"It is up to you what will happen to him. You can keep him here and spend time with him, if you like. If he cannot have the company his wife, then at least he will have his daughter. I know you care more for Iasion than my brother."

"I could keep him here?" she asked almost incredulously. Her desires would affect a decision he made as King of the Dead? Hades was reputed to be a stern man, moved by no plea or tears, swayed by no lamentation or sad story. Out of all the gods, he was said to be the one with a heart as dark and cold as the realm he ruled. In response to her question, he nodded.

"I only wish to see you happy. I know that having

your father around was some of the happiest times in your life. I only wish that I had a father that cared so much about me."

"He misses my mother. It would be cruel to make him stay here."

"But he would have you."

That was a tempting prospect indeed. Iasion was the only father she had ever known, and perhaps, if he had his daughter, he might be happy.

"Things... are different. I have changed. He should be able to go." She slowly pulled out of his embrace so she could turn around and face him. Hades's words had given her an epiphany. He was willing to share his power with her. She had a chance to do as she pleased. After all, royalty enjoyed certain privileges, didn't they? The same was for gods and goddesses.

If Iasion knew she was Queen of the Dead, he would doubtlessly want to know how that all came about. It was something she didn't want to burden him with.

"He was a wonderful father. I am sorry you didn't have someone like that to look up to." She squeezed his hand as he smiled wistfully. Having grown up with two loving parents made her realize how difficult it must have been for Hades and his siblings. Cast away by their father and out of the reach of their mother, how horrible that must have been for them!

"We made do," Hades replied, warmed by her thoughtful comment.

"Yes, you did not turn out so bad." They both chuckled quietly before he reached out to wipe the remnants of her tears with his thumb. She smiled faintly and touched his hand.

"You can still visit him before he leaves, if you like," he replied.

"Thank you," she whispered, her head resting against his chest.

oOo

Iasion looked around at his surroundings. Being turned away by Hades was disappointing, but at least he hadn't been an Asphodel soul, sent back to a mundane afterlife. There wasn't anything to complain about here. The weather was always pleasant, with a touch of rain here and there for variety. There was no end of things he could amuse himself with whether by himself or with other people, participating in one of the many fun activities to be found around Elysium.

He had never encountered Lord Hades and hadn't been sure of what to expect. The Lord of the Dead had been an impressive figure, garbed in black and sitting proudly in his throne with his Queen at his side. Of course, he had heard about Persephone. Word got around in the Underworld, and the new souls who had seen Persephone praised her beauty, saying that Aphrodite had a rival. He had been skeptical of that until he saw her on her throne, pale and regal. He had never seen the Goddess of Love before, but he would be hard-pressed to imagine anything lovelier than Hades's bride.

There had been something rather familiar about

her. He knew it seemed silly, but she reminded him of his daughter. They had the same hair color and there was something about the curve of her jaw and the shape of her nose that made him think of the daughter he had left behind. Come to think of it, given Kora's current age, she might look a lot like Persephone, except with a darker complexion, of course. The Queen's skin had been very pale, almost like snow.

He remembered her gaze. She had been silent through the entire proceedings, and he would have taken her for a marble statue draped in silk and gems if she hadn't moved on occasion.

He rose from where he had been sitting in the thick grass overlooking the ethereal sea, and startled slightly as he turned around when he noticed that he was not alone.

"Your Majesty." He bowed.

"Greetings." Persephone stood there, clad in a dark blue peplos and wrap, devoid of all jewelry. The blue softened her features a bit, and there was no sharp glitter of diamonds to dazzle him. Even with the warm and bright surroundings, Persephone was still very pale, her hair, eyes, and lips standing out against her fairness. Her hands were folded together neatly, resting against her lower stomach as she regarded him.

"Is there something I can do for you, my lady?"

"Yes. Walk with me."

Perplexed, he followed her nonetheless. Before, she had seemed so cold and regal. Now she was considerably warmer, and he felt that tug of familiarity as he glanced at her face briefly. Yes. This was what Kora might look like right now, he mused as they spent several long moments in silence, strolling along the grass. Finally, he spoke.

"I am honored to be in your presence. But I cannot help but be curious as to why you have come to see me."

"I heard your story in there. You sounded so sad." She sounded concerned.

He stared at her for a moment before averting his eyes, feeling touched by her words. She sounded so kind, and he could not help but wonder how she had become Queen of the Underworld. What kind of Goddess would wish to live down here and be wedded to the Lord of the Dead? Would her story become part of the myths of Hellas?

"Yes." He nodded, encouraged by her apparent concern, "I do not regret my time with Demeter. I never could. And I would never wish death upon her despite my being here, but I still love her. It is hard being here and seeing couples reunited and knowing I cannot expect the same."

"I can only imagine the burden that must be." The regal Queen had a soft expression on her face, making her look almost like a different person than she had been before.

He thought of his daughter, and the happy times he had with her. Demeter would disappear from Enna, whether to Olympus or other parts of Hellas, leaving him alone with Kora, not that he had minded. He loved and cherished his daughter, and treasured the time that the two of them spent with one another.

She had been such a delight to him and the family, and whenever someone had been sad or hurt, she would comfort them. As he noted Persephone's expression, he was rather startled to note that she looked even more like Kora now. There was that soft gaze and sympathetic smile, and the understanding tone that compelled people to pour out their worries to her.

No. It couldn't be. True, there was a strong resemblance, but it was impossible. Surely the Fates wouldn't do such a thing to him. Hadn't cutting his life short been enough for them? He shook his head, pulling himself out of the memories of his past. If he could drink the Lethe waters, he could start anew.

"Do not worry about it," she assured him, seeing the confusion and pondering on his face. "You can go to Lethe soon. You deserve happiness."

"Thank you, my lady." He bowed again. "May I ask something of you?"

"Yes."

"Might we walk together a bit longer?"

"Yes, of course." She actually seemed pleased that he asked that of her. Now, if she were a stranger, he would wonder at why she had been so agreeable to the walk. But if she was indeed Kora, then...

As they walked along the shore, he would steal glances at her. Back then, they had enjoyed taking walks, whether through the village or in the woods. He had been the one to point out various things and what was safe to eat, or not. Since Enna had become fertile, the forests had become a much more pleasant place to explore, rather than the sickly countryside he

162

remembered from his own childhood. Sometimes they would talk, and other times they would enjoy their meanderings in silence.

"When I was still alive, I took walks with my daughter. I miss her too."

"Tell me about her."

"She was a lovely and sweet little thing. She made everyone, including myself, happy. I could not have asked for a better child. She was so full of spirit, and I always liked watching her dance. Every festival, we would go and dance and eat and laugh and just... have fun."

As he talked, recalling happy times with his wife and daughter, he was careful to note her reactions. She appeared very collected, but he did not miss the glimmers of emotion that flashed across her face before, or the sudden wistful expression when he recalled a particularly happy moment he had spent with his daughter. *That's it.*

"I had hoped to see my daughter again, but I did not think she would pretend she was not mine," he finally commented after another short bout of companionable silence.

She stilled for a moment as she looked at him before averting her eyes.

"It was hard to... decide what to say. To be frank, I did not expect to see you, in Hades's court. I thought you were happy in Elysium, but now I feel silly for not thinking about the fact that Mother is a goddess and you are not. I have missed you so much." She blinked back more tears before Iasion closed the short distance between them and pulled her into a hug, his strong arms wrapping around her.

"It is all right, Kora."

oOo

She let out a quiet sob as she leaned into him, burying her face against his shoulder. Ever since Hades had kidnapped her, she didn't feel much like 'Kora' anymore, but when Iasion said it, it made her feel comfortable.

He continued to hold her, stroking her hair just as he had done when she was little. She wrapped her own arms around him, hugging him tightly. After a while, he finally loosened his embrace, and they pulled away to face one another.

"You have grown into such a beautiful woman! Your mother must be proud of you!"

All Persephone could do was nod.

"I... Oh, Kora... Persephone... there are so many things I want to ask you. I barely know where to begin."

"Do not worry about it. You do not have to go to Lethe until you are ready. So take your time."

"Time? There is so much I have missed. Look at you!" His face was full of awe and admiration. She blushed as she smiled at him. He looked just as she remembered him all these years ago since he had died in the prime of his life. That was one thing about dying young – people remembered you in your youth and prime, and you were never old or weak in their memories. She remembered Grandmother very well and had sometimes wondered what Eurycleia had looked like in her youth.

He took her hands and squeezed them, and she smiled and squeezed back.

"But you are so pale." He glanced at her with concern.

"So I am." She glanced down at her hands before shrugging.

"You are not... dead, are you?" he asked, an edge of alarm in his tone. She might be the daughter of a Goddess, but even the mightiest of demigods were still mortal. What could have caused her death? Had Lord Hades taken her in the moment of passing?

"No, no. I am still very much alive," she assured him, her hands moving to his shoulders to squeeze them. Now that she was grown, Iasion definitely didn't seem as tall to her as he did when she was little, but even now he was an impressive sight, frozen in time as a youthful and strong man.

"Oh, thank goodness. Death took me so early, and how cruel it would be if it had taken you as well!"

"He has already taken me." she could not help but reply, thinking of Hades. "The Lord of the Dead is a kind man. You need not worry that I am mistreated."

"How... how did this happen? I never thought that Hades would choose a bride. And my own daughter!"

"Believe me, I was just as surprised as you."

He did not miss her sideways glance, and his curiosity was piqued.

"Is something the matter, daughter?" he queried. She shook her head.

"No. This is a lovely place." In this sunny land, the Eternal Sea was a cheery turquoise-teal color, the sand pale and providing an excellent contrast to these clear depths. It was a stark opposite to the shores of Tartarus, where the Sea was black, with its crests looking much like sharp blades that lapped at a rocky, gray-black beach.

"It is, isn't it? But I still miss home and your mother."

"She misses you too." On this subject, Persephone was happy to discuss. "After you died... well, she had no interest in anyone. She lamented your death and even went to Hades to ask him, but..." She shook her head and sighed softly.

"She still loves me?" The hope in his voice was clear. Persephone nodded in full earnest.

"Oh, yes. She still talks about you, and continues to mourn your absence." She sighed softly. Perhaps, if Iasion was reborn and eventually became reunited with his lover...

"Oh, Demeter..." He stared off wistfully for a moment, clearly grateful for this news. "But what about you? I do not want to just leave you behind, not after being reunited with you such a short time ago!"

"I want what will make you happy. I have missed you dearly, never doubt that. But do not let my presence affect your decision."

"You sound so wise." He smiled at her fondly.

"Come. Let us walk," Persephone said after a couple of moments. He nodded and fell in step, remaining at her side as they continued their stroll. A light breeze blew along the shore, causing the tall grass to rustle and sway, making a pleasant complement to the gently-lapping waves. Most of the

Underworld was silent, but Elysium provided a soothing backdrop of ambient noise, making this place feel a bit more real.

"You are certain I can go to Lethe? I have wanted to be reborn for a long time, but now I want to spend more time with you..."

"You would not remember any of it," she replied lightly.

"Then I would not remember Demeter..." he frowned. She shook her head.

"Lessons learned remain with the soul, and souls meant to be together eventually find their way back to one another." She smiled confidently. "Please, go to Lethe with no regrets. You have my sincerest blessing."

He took her hands again and smiled gently.

"I love you."

"I love you too, Daddy." She blinked back tears as he took her into his arms again.

oOo

Persephone would not tell her father about her true paternity because it wasn't something he needed to know. He loved Demeter, and had raised her daughter as his own, and had been happy. How could she blame Mother for the deception when she had been tricked by Zeus? It didn't change her love for Iasion, so why dwell on harsh truths? They talked of other things before lapsing into a comfortable silence as he showed her some of his favorite spots in Elysium, much as he had pointed out interesting places in the forest and village during their strolls.

Hades took supper without her, not wishing to interrupt her afternoon and evening. He did not begrudge her the time spent with Iasion and bore no jealousy towards either of them.

It was not until very late that evening after he had settled into bed for the night, that Persephone entered his bedchamber. Her hair was pulled back into a loose braid that was draped over her right shoulder. She was wearing a comfortable robe and looking very much relaxed, her face serene as she approached the large bed and climbed into it. He regarded her fondly as she wiggled under the blankets. She looked so satisfied that Hades felt safe asking her a certain question.

"How did it go?" he asked as he reached over to toy with the end of her braid, twirling it between his fingers.

"It was wonderful. We talked about the past and our family. And then he showed me his favorite places." She sounded wistful, even a little sad, but he detected no trace of regret or anger. "I am glad to see that he had such a nice place to be, that all of the good souls gain such rewards. Perhaps you can show me some of your favorite places."

"I would be delighted to." He rolled over onto his side so he could see her better. "Will he be staying here?"

"We spent a lot of time together. I am tempted to have him stay longer, but I told him that he should not let my presence change his decision. Besides, everybody ends up here again, anyway. Life on the surface is wonderful and he should be able to enjoy it." Her tone was relaxed, so her mention of the surface world seemed to be entirely coincidental.

"Let us hope the Fates are kind to him. I wish him the best of luck," he returned easily, drawing her into his arms where she snuggled contentedly.

"Thank you. I appreciate that. Good night." she whispered, and he smiled as she draped an arm across his chest.

"Sweet dreams," he replied. She smiled and rested her head on his shoulder, closing her eyes as she dreamed of past days.

Chapter XXIX

As days turned into weeks, Persephone was no longer as concerned with the passage of time as she had been. She spent most of the last few weeks in a state of serenity, barely noting when the sky above Hades's Palace darkened to mimic the rhythm of the world of the living. She always had plenty to keep her occupied, whether it be time with Hades engaged in various activities, visiting with Hekate, or by herself.

She was content to lay there as she felt the warmth of his body, feeling the gentle rise and fall of his chest against her back. The blanket was pulled up to her chin, and she stared with half-lidded eyes at the muted fire that burnt within the impressive hearth. After sharing the bed of a caring and attentive lover, she knew she would have an impossible time sleeping alone. She loved to snuggle close to him, basking in the heat that came from his form. Down here in the Underworld, Hades was the only other living person she saw on a regular basis. Like any god, he had a steady, warm pulse of life, and that comforted her in this dead place.

She rolled over to face him and snuggled closer, pulling up the blanket further as she inhaled his scent, nuzzling her face against his bare chest.

oOo

"Mmm. Seph." Hades purred softly, pulling her into a tight embrace. He immensely enjoyed her presence and comfort, which was in a way amusing considering the fact that he had spent the last few centuries alone. His hands slid along her face, neck, and shoulders as if he couldn't get enough of the feel of her skin, and she cooed in delight, wiggling against him. Sometimes he was surprised with how much he enjoyed these non-sexual displays of affection, and he smiled faintly before leaning his head down to rain kisses on her face.

Naturally, with such an enjoyable companion and eager lover, he felt his maleness respond. It wouldn't be the first time that they had started off the morning in such a rousing manner, but when she felt the evidence of his desire press against her thigh, she shook her head before pulling away demurely.

"You are just going to leave me like this?" Hades pouted, trying to tug her back. A tempting peek of her breast was visible through the opening of her robe, and he teasingly reached for it, intent on pulling the robe off her body.

Realizing his intent, she scooted away just in the nick of time, climbing off the bed before he could try to ensnare her further.

"You would deny the mighty Lord of the Dead?" Hades demanded as he sat up, the blankets falling to his waist to reveal his sculpted chest and arms.

"It is not my fault you wanted to turn a morning cuddle into something else."

"Can you blame me?" He asked this with a wide grin. She smiled back as she shook her head.

"No, my lord. But I just started... bleeding again."
Her voice was almost inaudible as a faint blush crept
across her cheeks. He stared for a moment before
giving her a brief nod.

o0o

Not surprisingly, a breakfast banquet was set out
on the table when she emerged from her room,
dressed for the day. She ignored it, going over to the
windows and tugging at the golden rope at the side of
the heavy curtains.

"This room needs more light," she declared as
Hades smirked in amusement. After another firm tug,
the curtains finally gave way, bringing clean light
into the chamber and illuminating everything from
the veins in the marble walls and floor to the steam
rising from the dishes.

"You did not seem to mind the darkness before,"
he remarked as she remained where she was, looking
out the window at the terrace and garden.

"I cannot remain in darkness all the time," she
retorted. She looked over her shoulder at him, gazing
at him steadily. While in her room preparing for the
day, she had counted the days she had been here. If
not for her bleeding she would have had a harder
time keeping count since she enjoyed her time so
much here. Today was the fiftieth day since she had
been stolen by the Lord of the Dead to be his bride.
That was almost two moons! It was almost hard to
believe that that much time had really passed. It
would be nearly autumn now on the surface world.

Whenever she asked about Mother, Hades was evasive in his answers. The truce was peaceful, but realizing just how many days had passed gave her pause. She turned to him.

"It has been fifty days."

"Fifty days since when?" Hades asked casually before he picked up a piece of spiced lamb meat, sinking his teeth into the otherworldly food.

"Since you brought me here." She crossed her arms.

"Really?" he asked after he swallowed. "Down here, I do not bother keeping track of the days. After a few decades, you know, counting days loses its meaning." He shrugged. Lacking the rules of Nature above, Dis had no sun or moon, or seasons. Nothing down here changed unless he decreed it. "The days of a god are endless."

"Easy enough to say for someone who has lived as long as you."

"Of course." He shot her a grin before taking another bite of his food.

"Hmph. I want to see my mother. And Zeus."

"Come and eat with me," he replied smoothly.

"No."

"When you eat..." She did not miss the fact that he said *when* and not *if,* "we can talk about it."

"There will be no when. You can tempt me all you want, but it will not work. I want to see Mother!" She stamped her foot. "You say that Zeus is not without his faults. But you have your own, as well."

He placed his hand over his heart, feigning pain as he glanced at her. "Love, you wound me." For a moment, he mimicked a swoon, and if they had been discussing something else, she would have giggled at his theatrics.

"This is not funny. You barely tell me about what is going on in the surface world. Do you think it is right to let my mother worry and look for me?" She could only imagine what was going through her mother's head. Demeter must be fearing the worst after all this time! For all her faults, Mother didn't deserve to be racked with anguish and worry over her child's welfare.

The glimmer of pain in his eyes showed her that her words had found their mark. She would be sure to exploit that to her fullest advantage. He was usually so cool and collected, practically nothing seemed to faze him. She admired that... at times.

"I thought you cared about all of your siblings, even Zeus. I know you have no children of your own, but surely you must feel some sympathy for Mother." On her father's farm, she had cooed over the baby animals, especially the little chicks, savoring the feel of their soft, yellow fuzz against her hands. Goat kids and puppies were also adorable. She always felt sad when one of them was sickly – a rather rare occurrence in lush and healthy Enna – and mourned every time one of the animals died. She had also seen how Ptheia doted on her children, and how Grandmother would fuss over her entire brood – children, grandchildren, and daughters-in-law. There was nothing like the bond between a mother and her child, and despite Mother's protective ways, her love had been strong and true.

174

"Do you really intend to let this go on indefinitely? Will you condemn Mother to wander for eternity?" Her voice was sharper, more penetrating now, and she relished in the fact that he now had his gaze averted as if he was ashamed of himself. Like the legendary Furies, she closed in mercilessly. "You pride yourself on the truth. Yet you will not reveal it."

"I am the hidden one," he replied firmly, returning his gaze to her, refusing to let her see just how guilty he felt. His statement was true – it was even the basis of his name, *Aidon*, or Άΐδης , literally meaning 'the unseen'.

"Is that all you have to say?" she asked coolly, meeting his defiant gaze. Right now he seemed like a child that didn't want to listen to his mother's scolding.

"I have made my decision."

"Ugh!" Persephone threw her arms up in frustration before deciding to express her anger in a more blunt manner. Stalking over to the table, she grabbed the nearest dish and hurled it at him, stuffed olives flying through the air as he quickly dodged her missile, the silver platter bouncing off the cushioned back of the divan before clattering to the floor. Seeing that he had easily dodged her only fueled her wrath, and she grabbed one item after another, hurling them at him as he danced around the room. A bowl of stew disgorged its contents as she hefted it at him, the lid and container separating to shower thick, savory soup against the wall and floor, narrowly missing him. Her aim was improving!

175

Dates and other fruit rained against the divan and floor as she cast the shallow bowl containing them. He looked confused, which pleased her immensely, and she picked up the jug of wine.

"Stop," Hades growled, his hands out as she jiggled the container, getting a feel of its weight as she felt the sloshing inside.

"Or what?" she challenged, raising her chin as she lifted her arm backward. His eyes narrowed, and Persephone felt his shadowy tendrils slide up her feet and legs. Before her arms could be bound, she tossed it at him with as much force as she could manage. He easily dodged the flask, but some of the wine splashed on him as it arced through the air. Immediately after that, her arms were bound, but she smirked at him.

"Are you so defenseless against me that you must resort to using your Gift when I have none of my own to use in this dark place?" she taunted. He did not respond immediately, his gaze moving around the room. She had managed to clear most of the table.

"Am I such a bad host that you must throw food at me?" he retorted.

"Go fuck yourself!" she snarled. It certainly wasn't a phrase her parents had taught her, but she had heard it – and other profanities – shouted by condemned souls after they had been sentenced. It would be directed at the Judges, Kampe, or any of the shades attending to the punishment of various ill-behaved souls.

"Oh, but I thought you were bleeding," he retorted. Her shriek of frustration rivaled the banshee scream of the Furies, and he had to stifle a laugh.

"Let me go right now!" She twisted and struggled against her bonds, knowing it was useless but determined to not just give up.

"Only if you stop throwing things at me," he replied. She nodded tersely.

"Now, unbind me," she demanded in a softer but no less firm voice, chin raised and shoulders squared, appearing dignified despite her predicament. With a flick of his hand, he obeyed her command. She rubbed her arms as she glanced around at the mess she made, biting back a smile of satisfaction. It had felt good to just *hurl* all of these things, and use him as her target.

"If you try to make me eat another meal, I will start throwing things again!" she threatened.

"Then I will simply need to make sure you are bound during our meals," he replied. She exploded with a hiss of frustration, flailing her arms as he gazed at her with an insolent grin.

o0o

Rather than have more food brought up in front of her, he let her leave before the shades were summoned to clean the mess. Good riddance. She had no desire for his company. That insufferable bastard, acting as if what he was doing was just fine, because he was a man! Damn them all to hell. If she could just get her hands on Zeus... or Ares... or even Hermes. *Ugh!*

What I need is some female company. Hekate had

177

a rather sarcastic opinion of men. That was just what she needed. Perhaps she could convince the other goddess to help her out. Fifty days might be nothing to Hades, but she had no doubt that Mother felt each and every one of these days acutely as she searched for her missing child.

"Cloe!" she whispered. Within a moment, the shade coalesced into visibility, hovering there as it waited for her command.

"Take me to Hekate."

The shade floated in front of her, smoothly gliding through the air as she walked down the steps in front of the Palace. She did not even look back as she wrapped her cowl more securely around her shoulders. Without the sun to warm her skin, even the mild atmosphere of the more pleasant parts of the Underworld carried a chill.

She had never been to see Hekate before, even though the Goddess of the Crossroads had visited her several times. She welcomed Hekate's company, for the first time in her life having a real peer, instead of a caretaker like the nymphs. In some ways, Hekate was like Cyane. It was Hekate who had explained to her about bleeding, and how relieved the younger goddess was to learn that it really was nothing to be afraid of, that women the world over – immortal or mortal – shared this same experience.

That came with the knowledge that bleeding meant a woman could have children. It was a rather daunting thought. She knew that some women had children before they reached her age. Auntie Ptheia had only been seventeen when she married – and at

178

this time, Enna had still been a harsh clime – and two years later, her first child had been born into a transformed and peaceful valley. She was a wonderful wife and mother, content with her lot in life with a husband who cared for her, healthy children, and a mother-in-law that she got along with.

Children! What would a child between Hades and herself look like, or be like? What kind of Gifts might the child have? The idea intrigued her because she was curious, and frightened her because bearing and raising a child was daunting. She had gained plenty of maturity and insight in Hades, and it was that insight that also told her she wasn't ready for one. Not for a long while yet.

She was so lost in her thoughts she barely noticed the sky darkening above her head. The path from the Palace led wherever Hades wished, providing long or short routes to whatever location he might desire to go to. The wide path narrowed to a certain extent that it was not wide enough for Hades's chariot, and the sky dimmed further.

Cloe had never failed to lead her to the correct destinations, but it was getting harder to see the shade as the light dimmed. That was a tricky thing about the shades, they all but disappeared from view when it became dark.

As if sensing its mistress' need, the shade extended a tendril backward, wrapping it around her right wrist, the cool wispiness of it causing her palm to tingle a bit.

As her eyes adjusted to the darkness, she made out what looked like a lamp, barely illuminating the person who was holding it. She blinked as she noticed that the path had diverged into several others, spreading out like the spokes of a wheel, beyond the light.

"Hello, Persephone. I have been expecting you," Hekate beckoned for her to walk together. The two women walked down the path that Hekate chose.

"Where are we going?"

"You will see. I think you will like it," Hekate responded. The older Goddess strode forward at a casual pace with Persephone several steps behind her.

oOo

"Do not hide back there. Come walk at my side," she added, looking over her shoulder. Her companion hastened to her side. Persephone was happy to see her, that much was apparent, but the older goddess also sensed worry, irritation, and concealed anger seething under the red-haired goddess' calm visage.

"Did you have an altercation with Hades?" Hekate asked in a friendly tone, inviting Persephone to share her woes.

"Men are absolutely insufferable creatures!" the younger goddess spat out, "We would be better off without them!"

"Spoken like a true woman!" her companion replied with a warm laugh, though inwardly she wondered what the problem might be. What did Hades do to enrage his captive so?

"How do you deal with them when they are being so... dense?" Persephone muttered fiercely.

"Oh, that's easy. I just avoid them. Or when I *have* to deal with them, I just act mysterious and fuck around with them."

"At least your sire did not give you away. Stupid jackass, Mother was right about him."

Hekate continued walking and did not miss a beat, but she found herself turning this new bit of information over in her head. There were quite a few gods who could fit this description...

"Were you not notified of this at all before Hades brought you down here?"

"No. *Nobody* thought to discuss it with me, or even do the basic courtesy of informing me."

Hekate would have done something about Persephone's situation sooner, if not for Hades's gag order. But she couldn't just sit by and let this continue. Hades wasn't a cruel man, but she knew that it was unfair that Persephone had had no say regarding her own fate. Men were rather obnoxious and hard-headed at times.

"Who is your father?"

"He is not my *father*. He is a sire, nothing more."

"Very well then, sire." Hekate could understand that. That was all some men were, really. They took no more responsibility for their children than the animals used for siring.

"I do not wish to be known as his daughter," she replied after several long moments.

"I would not tell anyone."

"It is not that I do not trust you. I just... have no desire to speak his name. I do not want anyone knowing of my association with him!"

181

"No child should be ashamed of his or her parent," Hekate whispered sympathetically. She saw Persephone quickly lift her hand to wipe a stray tear away from her face. She could feel the frustration from the young queen.

"Tell me what happened. Cry if you like, there is nobody else around. What did Hades do?"

"He refuses to let me go to the surface or see Mother or anything like that. And then I ask him if he will let my mother wander around looking for me indefinitely, and he does not care! He demands that I eat the food of the dead, and refuses to even consider anything else!"

Hades goes too far, Hekate thought grimly. "I take it you still refuse the food," she replied gently. Persephone didn't look starved, but there was a certain sort of wanness around her face, and the light tan she had in the beginning was now entirely gone, leaving behind skin that was just a shade darker than snow.

It gave the Queen of the Dead an ethereal sort of beauty, but it also made her seem less... for lack of a better word, *human.*

"I will not let someone else be master of my fate," the younger deity replied grimly.

"Even Fate itself?" Hekate replied dryly. Persephone scowled at the memory of her meeting with the mysterious women who spun and manipulated the threads of life and the cosmos.

"What right do they have to determine the lives of others? They killed the man who raised me, my father," Persephone responded angrily.

Hekate had listened to a couple of Persephone's stories of Iasion while they shared stories about their parents, and he had sounded like such a nice person. Certainly a lot better than her sire. Whomever he might be, she could see none of him in Persephone's features, not even the slightest. As for her mother, there was a minimal amount of resemblance there, though like Hypnos, she noted the partial resemblance between Persephone and her grandmother. It was said that some traits skipped a generation, and this worked to the younger goddess's advantage.

"Nobody can command Fate."

"Where did the Fates come from, anyway? Are they more of Nyx's mysterious children?" Persephone asked Hekate, the two of them wandering along the path.

"They were here before Gaea, and even before Chaos. I get the feeling that what I see, what you see, is merely an image they show us."

"Oh good, I thought I was the only one!" Persephone replied. Hekate paused to stare at her before she nodded.

"That means that you truly belong here. With us. Your senses are more open than the ones above."

"Just because I had that funny feeling about them does not mean that! I miss the surface world."

"I know you did not come down here willingly." Hekate sighed quietly. "But the Lord of the Underworld loves you. I do not deny that he has a funny way of showing it, though... I tried to talk to him about it, but he has forbidden me to help you to

183

the surface world."

"I know." Persephone stared away dejectedly.

"The deities who are part of Dis are few, but we each have a place here. To be among the Olympians is an honor indeed, but it is us who will remain when they are long gone."

"I have no desire to spend eternity in the realm of the dead."

"Lady Persephone, have you not realized that this is much more than a place for housing souls, or to reward the good and punish the wicked?"

Persephone was silent for a moment before she made her response.

"This is not a terrible place. But I miss the surface world. I saw so little of it in my life, and now I wish to see the rest of it. Hades spoke of places outside of Hellas. It is not fair, he gets to see these places and I am stuck down here!" She stuck out her lower lip in a pout.

"I honestly thought that Hades might be better than his brothers regarding that sort of thing," Hekate commented dryly. Hades was no misogynist, but he certainly had his quirks, and once he made a decision, nothing would move him from it. His wrath when Hekate brought up the subject of Persephone's imprisonment evidenced that well enough.

"We are almost there!" she added, giving the other goddess a much-needed distraction from the subject as she pointed in the distance. Previously, the darkness had been stark, like a bottomless pit. But now several stars hung above their heads, and more glittered in front of them as the resemblance to the night sky on the surface world became more apparent.

Last time Persephone had looked at the ground, it was dark gray, but now as she took note of her surroundings, she could not help but be reminded of the Fates' own abode. There were no stars twinkling in the ground, but the surface had taken on an almost velvety feeling, having slight give under her feet as if she was walking on thick grass.

There were several smoky swirls scattered sparsely through the sky, glittering with stardust and stellar vapors, resembling the Milky Way. This cosmic canvas was studded with the shining stars of entire galaxies. Around them, the silence was vast.

Hekate led her on further, walking down a path that was no longer visible.

"How do you know which path to choose, where to go?" the younger deity asked, recalling the identical paths diverging from a single point. "Do you create these paths?" It seemed logical, given that Hekate was the Goddess of the Crossroads.

"Yes and no. All parts of Dis, and the universe itself are connected by paths, literal and figurative. I simply made my own representation of the links between each realm and area. Each of us has our own way of traversing these paths in this world, and on the surface realm as well. Of course, I would be glad to teach you how to make your own. You can imagine it any way you like and create your own

185

network. But we will work on that later since we are now at our destination."

"Greetings, sister Goddesses." Nyx's voice greeted them.

"Hello, Nyx. We thought it would be nice to have a visit." Hekate replied. In front of her, Persephone could almost swear that she saw the darkness rippling before Nyx's dusky face emerged from it.

"But of course. Come, make yourself comfortable." Nyx's voice was deep and smooth and soft, rolling over Persephone and causing her to shiver slightly. *The allure of night...*

"Now it is just us three women. Persephone tires of the antics of menfolk. Something we can all understand, hmm?" Hekate smiled, showing her dimples as she winked at Persephone before turning back to Nyx.

"I would be honored to acquaint myself with you further," the youngest Goddess stated eagerly. She had not seen Nyx since the banquet. A human certainly would have taken notice of the time that passed, but to such a deity as Nyx, that was a mere blink of an eye in the grand scheme of things. Time really was different here.

"As would I, youngest sister."

"Sister? I am sorry, but I am unsure of what you mean by that."

"You are now one of us, a deity of Dis." Persephone had to resist a retort of denial, and nibbled her lower lip as Nyx spoke, *"We of Khthonios are a family of our own, with stronger bonds than that of the many who reside above; you*

are now part of my fold. And you are my twin's great-granddaughter, which also ties us by blood."

Persephone was the granddaughter of Kronos and Rhea through her own parents, and Kronos and Rhea were born of Gaea, the original Hellenic Earth-Goddess, and Ouranos, the Sky. But the overwhelming majority of these gods remained above, many of them living among the mortals. As far as Persephone was concerned, these gods of the other world were far-removed from their Olympian brethren. She hadn't considered her relationship with them. But Nyx and Gaea, *twin sisters*? To her, it seemed like the difference between day and night, which in this case was quite almost literal, when she thought about it.

And here she was in the Underworld, plucked from her parent's world for a greater destiny here – or so the Fates had said – and wondered at the circumstances. Hades had the same parents as his siblings, yet he had left the world above and was happy about it. So had Hekate. This place really wasn't Hell. She could not help but recall Hades's hurt when she would defy him or swear at him.

"Really? I had never contemplated that. So we are all related... in one way or another." The Titans were cousins to the Olympians and in some cases, even brother or sister, or parent. But nobody on the surface seemed to know that even these mighty surface gods might be in some way related to the gods of Dis.

"Relations are different down here. Hades is more closely tied to us than them, as you will be. But do not worry about any of that. Things will happen in

187

due time. Now tell me, Persephone... how is life down here? Are you happy with your Lord?"

"Life here is... interesting." That much was the truth. She was never bored, and found herself mentally stimulated, pondering things she had never thought of before and learning things she had never contemplated. And she liked that. She genuinely enjoyed the locales of the Underworld she had already seen and was eager to explore further, one step at a time.

"Interesting? That's all you have to say?" Nyx sounded almost teasing.

"Yes," Persephone replied quietly, not wanting to get into the specifics.

"There is no need to speak of men here," Hekate interjected as she sensed her companion's discomfort. "I am of the opinion that she would rather hear one of your stories. Perhaps you could tell her the one of how you and Gaea came to Hellas."

"Oh, yes. I love stories!" Persephone stated enthusiastically.

"Sit down and make yourselves comfortable, then."

Persephone was about to point out that there was no furniture before she felt something soft against her back. She relaxed, and felt velvety substance mold itself to her back, legs, and rear end, making for an extremely comfortable seat, indeed. She glanced over, seeing Hekate was similarly accommodated.

"Many thousands of years ago, Hellas was not the lush and civilized land it was. There were no people, and it was a very cold place. However, the

earth started to warm, and the slumbering land came to life. Out of Chaos, I was born, and my sister came soon after. For many, many years it was just the two of us, and we wandered over the world, looking for a place to settle. Much of it was covered in ice, and there were few humans back then, making their living the best they could in such a world, their existence concentrated on their survival and little more than that. They hunted the great big cats with fangs like daggers, and hairy creatures with tusks such as you have never seen before, although neither of them exists anymore.

For a long time, we had no real home. We wandered, seeking purpose in our lives. Unlike the mortals, we could not die, and wondered what our purpose in this world was. Our wanderings brought us to Hellas, where my sister said she wished to remain. The place called to her, she told me. Wearied by our travels I was as well, and chose to remain at her side.

She stayed on the earth and I took to the heavens while she used her gift to shape and mold Hellas into a better place to live. She dug valleys and formed hills, and all the water that had melted from the great ice flowed where she told it to, forming springs, lakes, and rivers. All of this I watched at night while during the day I retreated to the shadows to slumber. She would sleep safely in the darkness while I kept guard over her, The earth was hers to form and shape as she pleased, and it became such a wonderful place that animals came to live there, enjoying the bounty she had to offer them. And then

*humans followed, settling into a place that was far
warmer and hospitable than their ancestors had
known, becoming the ancestors of the civilizations
that worship us."*

oOo

Persephone sat under an olive tree in Elysium,
staring out at the Sea of Eternity as she fiddled with
her bracelet, considering her next course of action.
She had no desire to go back to the Palace, not when
she was still feeling so hostile towards her warden.
She hated the fact that whatever she did – whether it
be calm reasoning, heartfelt pleasing, or just out-and-
out throwing a fit, he remained unmoved in his
decision regarding her life.

It was *her* life! She didn't tell him what to do with
his life!

Down on the beach, she saw several children
laughing and playing, collecting rainbow-hued shells
along the shore or making sand-castles. Of course,
she knew that children died too, but this brought a
fresh surge of resentment against the Fates. Why did
children have to die? They didn't do anything wrong!

She wished her father was here, and for a
moment regretted telling him to go to Lethe. It would
be so nice to have him here to talk with. She was in
desperate need of a hug.

Cloe appeared before her, the clear and warm
light in Elysium causing the shade's wispy form to
look even greener than it usually did. It raised a
smoky arm, making a beckoning gesture. Its meaning

190

was clear – Hades wished for her company.

"No!" was her defiant response.

oOo

"Hades forbids me to get involved in the conflict between Persephone and himself. But it hurts me to see her pain and frustration."

"Her mother is in no less pain," Nyx responded, nodding her head. *"She laments for her child and does not sleep. She has been greatly wronged by the man who sired her child."*

Hekate's eyes widened with surprise. "You know who her father is?"

"I am the Night. I see everything that happens under my cloak, and there are no secrets that can be kept from me."

"Are you telling me that he really is responsible for this?"

"He gave his blessing for it to happen, yet he disregarded the feelings of Demeter and her daughter."

"That's awful!" Hekate exclaimed with righteous indignation. "Who would be so callous and insensitive?"

"A god who has often disregarded the feelings of women in the past and will continue to do so," Nyx replied smoothly. *"He has had more lovers than he can remember, and his children are counted in the hundreds. What are the feelings of one woman and her daughter when he is more interested in being on good terms with his brother?"*

191

"... Zeus?" the younger goddess gasped.

"The one and only."

Hekate's mind was racing with all sorts of possibilities. She could lay a thousand curses on Zeus for all the women he had hurt. Like Hades and Nyx, she had an array of dark Gifts at her disposal.

"The Lord of Dis may forbid you to help Persephone leave his realm, and while cursing Zeus might sound like something that would bring you great amusement, there's a more effective way you can help our friend. After all, knowledge is power." Nyx's smile was mysterious and knowing.

After a moment, a smirk spread across Hekate's face as she realized an option that would circumvent Hades's decree. Knowledge *was* power, and she intended to use it to help her friend and her mother.

Chapter XXX

As the rainbow-hued sky over Elysium darkened to a beautiful blue-purple that glittered with scattered diamonds, Persephone watched a small group of young women walk by, chatting and laughing, all of them rosy-cheeked and wearing finer garments than they had ever worn in their mortal lives. There were flowers in their hair, and their linen tunics and chitons were of light and cheery colors, woven with flowers, patterns, waves, and the like. Persephone remained out of sight, standing under a tree up the hill as she observed the happy scene before her. No matter what anyone was doing, it always looked like fun, and there was never a complaint.

People who died in their old age found that here, they were free of their infirmities and pains. Their eyesight and hearing would better than it had ever been in their mortal lives, their mouths equipped with a full set of healthy teeth, their hands no longer veined and knobbed from years of hard work or arthritis. And if they chose, they could be young again, though some of Elysium's citizens preferred to look middle-aged, enjoying the dignity this appearance gave them.

Orphaned children who had been left to die or been mistreated in their lives by abusive relatives found themselves adopted by – or reunited with – loving parents. And those who had gone through difficult lives – girls married off to cruel husbands, people raised by uncaring guardians, or just people who had led unfortunate lives and were lonely – found new friends and much happier afterlives here in Elysium. Truly, this was a wonderful place for the good of heart.

She had removed all her jewelry and hidden it under her clothing so she could pass as one of the citizens of this dreamy place. Her presence had drawn unwanted attention at first, and she was tired of being approached by people acknowledging her as Queen. She simply wanted to enjoy herself and had done so, going to various amusements. She had watched dancers, musicians, acrobats, and actors. Here, women could act – something that was normally reserved for males above – and there were also singers. Many people discovered or explored talents that they had been unable to in their mortal lives. As long as she kept her cowl over her head and drew no attention to herself, she was regarded as an ordinary citizen in this extraordinary place.

She was determined to stay here for a while, ignoring Hades's summons as she moved from place to place, returning to the locations her father showed her. Here and there she saw people enjoying the food of the dead, and her stomach growled as she watched various food passed around and shared wherever people gathered. It was also offered to her whenever she came near, but she always demurred, however tempted she was to sample the food without Hades watching her. But Hades seemed to know whatever was happening in the Underworld, and she saw shades here as well, though they tended to be tinted

195

in warmer colors to match the climate of this place.

Cloe had been persistent, calling attention to itself several times as it tried to beseech her to answer Hades's summons. But she always turned down its entreaties.

When the sky was dark, people did not automatically go to sleep, though the activity did diminish somewhat. A fair amount of people stayed outside, continuing to enjoy themselves. Despite the happy surroundings, she could not help but feel out of place.

She found a quiet spot in the orchard near the beach, sitting next to a spring that bubbled up cheerily and trickled down the slope to the Sea of Eternity. It was surrounded by more colorful versions of the flowers she was familiar with on the surface world. Idly, she started plucking flowers, braiding them together to make a rope to distract herself. Even though the sky had darkened, she could still see very well.

The silence that surrounded this place was almost eerie. Despite the bubbling of the spring and the gentle crash of the waves, the absence of life remained a constant void in Persephone's consciousness of the world around her.

She looked up quickly as she felt a familiar tingle on the back of her neck, but ignored it as she continued braiding the rope of flowers, choosing various flowers to create a pattern as she fiddled around with the stems, welcoming this distraction of her fingers and mind as she steadfastly refused to acknowledge the presence of her captor. She did not look up or give any indication that she knew he was there, and it took all of her concentration to maintain the even pace she had on her project since she was tempted to just get up and leave.

She heard the rustle of grass as he walked forward, and, though her body tensed, she kept her eyes on her work. She could feel her heart pounding within her chest and swallowed thickly, feeling his presence as he drew near. Out of the corner of her eye, she saw the swish of his black cloak. Dropping the flowers, she bolted off, picking up her skirt so she could run easily. She was as agile as ever, sprinting between the trees, her loose hair flowing behind her, its curls and waves bouncing with each step as she sought to escape her pursuer.

Suddenly, Hades appeared in front of her and before she could swerve around him, his arm wrapped around her middle, scooping her up as she kicked and flailed her arms.

"You should know by now that you cannot hide from me," he chided as he pulled her arms down with his other arm, grimacing as she kicked him. "Now, do not do that, or I will need to bind you again."

"Let me go!"

"I just want to talk."

"No! Let me go!"

"If I set you down, will you listen to me?"

"I don't know." She glared at him hotly.

After several tense moments, he eased her back on the grass but kept a grip on her arm so she could not flee. She kept her face averted, pointedly hiding from his searching gaze.

"My love..."

"Do not call me that!"

Hades stiffened but maintained his grip. "I thought about what you said before. And you are right."

Persephone was silent for several moments, stunned by her captor's frank admission.

"About time you said that," she finally replied, lifting her chin. He smiled ruefully.

"I honestly never had any desire to have your mother wander around indefinitely. I suppose... it was just easy for me to put it off with each day."

"Are you going to tell her now?"

He sighed and did not reply. She glared at him, but before she could make an angry exclamation, he spoke.

"I mean not today. But hear this. She will know by the first day of winter."

"You promise?"

"I swear by the Styx that she will know before the end of that day. I will go to her and explain what has happened. If she promises to not stir up trouble, then she may see you."

"What about me?"

"She will try to take you back to the surface. That I will not allow," he replied, his tone in all seriousness as he regarded her. She did not doubt that he would be able to overcome Demeter if he had to.

"She is my mother, can you blame her?"

"No, but you are no longer a child."

"That is true..." She looked down, relaxing in his grip. When he slowly let go of her arm, she did not bolt. The winter solstice was three months away. Not as soon as she would have liked, but she knew what time was to an old god like Hades, and even Mother. Compared to what he could have decided, three months was a remarkably short period of time.

"Persephone, I do care for your mother. I wish I could have gone about this a different way. But your mother would have rejected me, what else could I do? I love you. I have waited for years. There were so many times that I wanted to snatch you up and carry you away. Out of all the women in the world, I desire only you." He reached out for her again, pulling her closer. "You may consider your abduction a rash or irresponsible act. I will not contest that. I have no desire at all to hurt your mother, and she will know the truth. But I hope you do not think too harshly of me for what I have done." He dropped to his knees, looking up at her as he clasped her hands.

"I cannot live without you," Hades declared as he bowed his head to kiss her hands. "You are the greatest treasure in my Kingdom. My heart is yours." He squeezed her hands. "It is my fondest hope that one day, you will love me as much as I love you. Is that an impossible wish?"

She felt a blush come to her cheeks under his intent, earnest gaze and averted her eyes, her heart pounding. When he wasn't being such a stubborn ass, he certainly could be a sweetheart. She did enjoy his company, in or out of bed. She would be hard-pressed to imagine any man better than Hades, and knew very well that the situation could be a whole lot worse. Look at her life. She was a queen, given the freedom to roam anywhere in the Underworld that she might desire, and allowed to do as she pleased. She missed the surface world, but she didn't want to give this up, either.

"No, it is not an impossible wish. But there is a certain thing that you want me to do, and a certain thing that I want from you. As long as we remain at an impasse regarding that matter..." she trailed off calmly.

"Do not think of eating the food of the dead as a death sentence. Being bound to this realm as its Queen is hardly a dismal fate. And being bound to me... will being freedom."

"No riddles, please."

"It was no riddle." He smiled faintly. "It is a fact."

"How could it be freedom if I am bound?"

"I..." Hades paused, frowning thoughtfully. "I cannot explain it. You have to see for yourself."

She shook her head. "I cannot face what I do not know. I do not wish to lose the things I do know," she replied in an almost inaudible voice.

"Do you trust me?"

"I know you would not try to harm me."

"Then trust me when I ask you to bind yourself to me."

"I cannot."

"Why? Are you afraid of me? Do I overwhelm you?" He glanced up at her with a soft smile.

"Perhaps." She hid the beginning of a smile behind the fingers of her other hand.

"But it is I who am overwhelmed by you. I am Lord of the Dead, but my heart is very much alive.

Only you could ever make me feel like this."

"Oh, Aidon." Her expression softened as she looked down at him. It was so easy to be swayed by that handsome, pleading face, his deep blue eyes seeming fathomless. She blinked and shook her head, refusing to be swayed by his dark charm. Gently pulling her hand out of his grip, she took a step back.

"Love, what can I do?" He rose to his feet, a tall and handsome figure gazing down at her.

"Give me time."

He glanced at her wonderingly for a moment before nodding.

oOo

Sometimes Persephone wondered what it might be like to hop aboard a boat and simply sail into the Sea of Eternity. According to Hades and the maps he had shown her, the mortal world was by no means flat and one could not simply sail on over the edge, but that world was also finite. A sailor or explorer could set out in any one straight line and end up back where he had been, in due time. But Dis had no physical borders. The thought of going forth onto that ocean and following a path into infinity was overwhelming.

Occasionally, when contemplating such things, she would feel unable to articulate her thoughts, unable to put the enormity of this knowledge into simple words. It was awe-inspiring and terrifying. How different this was from what she had known as young Kora, back then in these sheltered, naive days.

She knew she could never be that little girl again. She had learned and understood too much.

There was a rare moment here and there where she missed that innocence. Her old life was of sunlight and Nature, and she knew she was tied to it. Like her mother, she felt a rapport with the earth. With these ties severed... well, not even the most pleasant or intellectually stimulating distractions could make up for the fact that she might be forever cut off from the element that had nurtured her so. However fulfilled she might be here, under Hades's care and attention, he would never be able to satisfy that one raw basic need.

She kept this to herself, allowing Hades to court her and try to win her heart and trust. The Underworld was an enjoyable place to be, and she intended to take full advantage of it, and him. She could see the love and ardor in his eyes, and she hoped that by spending more time with him, she could convince him to give her what she wanted. Cyane and Hekate had spoken of manipulating men, and Persephone knew that there were quite a few ways to challenge or entice Hades, whatever mood she was in. One way or another...

She turned from the shore, walking through the arched doorway to the main garden and seeing the pomegranate tree and darkly iridescent flowers.

Hades sat under the tree, his head leaning against the trunk as he stared off thoughtfully. She stilled and observed him calmly, noting the distant expression on his features. After studying him for several long moments, he turned his head, his gaze resting upon her. A smile crept across his lips as he beckoned her closer.

Persephone moved smoothly across the grass, the pale silvery lilac-colored silk loosely clinging to her curves as she stalked toward him. She had a matching sash holding up her hair, her body devoid of jewelry.

oOo

Hades reached out, grasping her hips as he pulled her down into his lap, smiling contentedly when she snuggled up against him, wrapping her arms around his neck. A week had passed since his promise to her, and for the first time in so long, he was acutely aware of the passage of days. Day by day the deadline approached, and he wished he had the power to put it off even as he knew he would have to face Demeter eventually. But he was content to simply forget that for the time being as he held her close, rubbing her back and nuzzling her face.

"I was sitting out here, wishing you would join me," he whispered, burying her fingers in the thick waves that flowed loosely from behind the sash.

"Join you for what?" she replied with a smug smile, running her hand along his chest.

"A cuddle is just fine, but if you want more..." He smiled back at her, his eyes twinkling with passion and merriment. "Hmm?"

"I may consider it..." Her hand slid lower as she purposefully wiggled against him, pressing her breasts against his chest.

"Is that so? Are you trying to provoke me?" he

asked with a playful growl, wrapping one arm around her tightly.

"Very well, then." She flashed him a brilliant smile. "I do admit, I am in the mood." Her hand slid down his stomach, pressing against his lower abdomen through the himation that was draped over one shoulder.

"Mood for what?" he challenged her, feeling his manhood stir at the pressure her hand applied to his body. Her palm slid several inches lower.

"You, of course." Just as he thought her hand would slide down further, it started upwards, leaving his need aching. His hands maintained their grip on her hips as he maneuvered her in his lap, placing her directly on top of his groin so that she could feel the kind of reaction she was able to elicit from him.

"Ooh." She pressed her pert behind against him, grinding herself on top of him as she kept one arm hooked around his neck. In his embrace, they remained locked together, and she moved against him with ease.

oOo

Persephone had become familiar with the sight and feel of Hades's body and enjoyed teasing him with her hand, much like he liked to touch and titillate her. It gave her such a feeling of empowerment to have the mighty Lord of the Underworld writhing under her attentions. She pressed her hips down, grinning at him when he shuddered, his expression contorting in rapture as she steadily applied that pressure to his aching erection, grinding in a slow and purposeful way.

Her own nether regions had started to throb with that warm, familiar sensation of arousal, and she noticed that her nipples had hardened, pressing against the fabric that covered her chest. As if he had read her mind, his right hand slid up to cup her breast, his thumb rubbing the tit, causing her to mewl softly in delight.

"I have missed touching you," he whispered, burying his face against her throat.

"But missing it makes you appreciate it more," she shot back. One nice thing about her monthly course was that Hades had to rein in his ardor, and it would help him appreciate physical intimacy with her all the more if he were denied the pleasures of her body or touch on a regular basis. She wouldn't let him touch her breasts or most other areas on her body, so Hades could not even have momentary pleasure. Naturally, forcing him to keep it in reserve did cause it to become pent-up, as she was discovering at the moment.

"Mmph. It is hard to think about appreciation when you insist on withholding your feminine charms from me."

"Oh, I am not withholding, at least this time." She batted her eyes at him, smiling coyly.

"I would hope not." His hand massaged her breast, kneading the soft orb as she nodded slowly, giving out a soft groan of enjoyment. She could feel his other hand groping around, trying to work its way under her chiton, but the elusive ankle-length hem proved an effective barrier. As long as she remained seated in his lap, her clothing would be a hindrance, but then so would his own.

However, Hades quickly found his way around this problem by extending his will through several shadowy tendrils that easily slipped under her dress and up her legs, caressing her skin with their silken tongues.

"Yes," she exhaled, closing her eyes. She didn't know why, but she found herself terribly excited by this manifestation of his Gift at times, genuinely enjoying the feel of these ethereal appendages of her lover.

"You like that, hmm?"

"Very much." She squirmed around as she felt the 'tongues' slither and lap up her inner thighs.

"You know, you are the first person who has ever enjoyed the feel of my shadows against their skin," he replied easily as he raised his other hand to caress her unattended breast.

"Mmm..." She sighed softly as the shadows slid between her thighs, caressing her outer labia. "I can see why. But... ah!" she blushed, trying to gather her thoughts as she gazed up at him, "I just like it. I do not know why."

"It does not disturb you in the least?"

"No. It... mmm! Feels so good..." Her head lolled back and she gave out a sudden whimper as the tendrils moved to her inner labia, gently flicking and rubbing against them.

"Then I have a new game for us to play."

"Oh?"

"I cannot tell you everything, that would spoil the surprise. But I will show you just how enjoyable my Gift can be. Interested?"

Persephone's eyes lit up as she nodded eagerly, wondering just what her lover would have in store for her. As his arm slipped around her middle, she wrapped her own around his neck, content to let him pick her up and put her on her feet.

o0o

Hades hit back a predatory smirk as she looked up at him. Little did she know what he really had in store... The idea of what he would do to her had fresh excitement pulsing through his loins, and the mental image aroused him so quickly it was almost painful.

"If you would be so kind as to take these clothes off..." Hades said, his dark eyes glinting with open desire. She was slow and deliberate in her movements as she complied with his request. Her hair came free as she untied the sash.

She shot him a knowing smile before she started to pull out the pins that held up her gown, starting with her left arm. Each time one of the delicate pins was pulled out, several inches of the fabric fell from her body, and he shifted around a bit, feeling his flesh ache in need under the confines of his garb.

When she pulled the final pin on that side, the sinuous material slid down her chest, revealing her left breast. As she stared at him with half-lidded eyes, she reached up to cup her breast delicately, rubbing her erect nipple with her thumb, eliciting a delighted

207

groan from him.

One of his hands balled against his himation in impatience and anticipation. Persephone attended to the remainder of her clothing, pulling out the rest of the pins, stopping at the one holding the chiton up to her shoulder. She stared at him for a moment before reaching up to tug the last pin loose, causing all the silk to fall to her hips. Maintaining her steady, half-lidded gaze, she ran her hands along her breasts and stomach, her palms sliding smoothly against her pale skin before she reached her girdle, her hands wiggling under the material.

As soon as she let go of it, the belt and gown pooled around her ankles, and she stepped out of it, as naked as Hades might ever desire. She stood there calmly and confidently, one hip jutting out as she studied him, and he regarded her just as openly.

"I am naked. But you are still dressed..." Her eyes twinkled as she gazed at him.

"So?" he shot back playfully.

"You are not the only one who enjoys ogling their lover's nakedness, you know."

"That certainly is reassuring to know." He grinned as his eyes ran up and down her body, his need aching afresh as he imagined what he would do to her tonight. In a play of mock modesty, she arranged her hair so that it covered her breasts, and covered her womanhood with her hands.

"Mmm, I think not, my dear," Hades scolded gently as he approached her. She took several steps back, maintaining her modesty as she mirrored his smirk. When he reached for her, she retreated further, darting around the tree.

oOo

Persephone wasn't about to let him enjoy her body as long as he was dressed. She enjoyed the sight of his body, and running her hands along it and feeling it pressed against her. She wanted to see his arousal and enjoy the sight of it as he touched her. When he reached again, she jumped back, a stubborn gleam in her eyes. He laughed, a low, velvety chuckle in the back of his throat as he looked at her.

"Tonight... you are mine," he warned her, his voice taking on the purr he used in their most intimate moments. Before she could retreat further, she felt shadowy binds grip her ankles. A moment later, two more binds reached for her wrists, wrapping around them and pulling them away from her body, raising her hands over her head. She struggled against them as more came up to wrap around her chest and waist, looping around her shoulders as well as her thighs as they lifted her off the grass, the binds around her ankles pulling her legs apart.

The shadows held her at a height that made her gaze level to his, and she dangled against them comfortably as she eyed him defiantly, tugging against her binds.

"No fair." She stuck out her lower lip in a cute pout as Hades regarded her with a satisfied expression, admiring his handiwork. The shadows were distributed evenly along her body, ensuring her

209

comfort as she hung there, wiggling as her legs were tugged even wider apart.

His eyes moved along her body before he reached out, stroking her inner thighs. She stared at him with a coy smile, pushing herself toward his hands. The scent of her arousal became evident to her lover as his fingers slowly caressed their way upwards, and she gave out a soft whimper as he touched her outer lips. As he studied her face, his fingers slid over to her moist inner lips, and she let out another whimper, wiggling under his hand.

"My love..." He leaned in, his nose lightly touching against hers before he pressed his lips against hers. She responded welcomingly, pressing her lips against his own and nuzzling him before he pulled back. He rubbed her right cheek lightly with the back of his fingers as she cooed softly. Letting that hand trail down her face and neck, he squeezed a breast, and she arched against her binds.

"Aidon..." she breathed out, arching against him as he lightly stroked her moist inner area with a finger, rubbing and massaging the slick flesh as he lowered his head to suck on her nipple. She bit her lip, a comely blush becoming evident across her cheeks as he teased her with his finger and tongue. Her head lolled forward as she watched him love up on her body, taking her other nipple into her mouth and massaging the breast he left behind.

As much as she throbbed with arousal, he took his sweet time, exploring her body, his hands sliding along the areas he knew to be most sensitive, listening to her responses as he would press or rub certain areas. Occasionally, he would touch her aching womanhood, but these touches only left her more aroused. However much she wiggled around, her binds remained firm, giving her only just enough leeway to be comfortable.

Finally, he drew away, leaving her as aroused as ever, and she gazed at him pleadingly. Her intimate region was hot and throbbing, causing a warm tingling that emanated from it through her stomach and thighs.

"You liked that," he said softly as he looked at her.

"Yes. Please, come here. Do not leave me like this."

"I would never leave you, love." He caressed her thigh with a hand.

"That is good to know," she whispered in a soft sigh. Hades smiled before flicking his wrist, causing her bonds to shift, her upper half pulled back while her legs were tugged forward, leaving her at an approximately forty-five-degree angle. She gasped softly in surprise, but showed no alarm, and peered at him with curiosity as the shadows lifted her up nearly a couple of feet into the air, bringing her quivering slit level with his face.

Without hesitation, he stood between her legs, lightly running his tongue from her perineum to the tip of her slit, flicking his tongue over her clit, causing her to arch against her binds.

It wasn't the first time she had been restrained by his shadows, but it was the first time she had been suspended in the air, and it was a strange but thrilling experience for her. The shadows melded seamlessly into the semidarkness of the garden, it almost gave her the sensation that she was floating in midair. She looked down at him as he tasted of her with teasing caresses of his tongue, his fingers sliding along her thighs before he slipped one inside of her and wiggled it around. She bit her lower lip, not wanting to make too much noise as he pleasured her, lavishing her womanhood with enthusiastic hunger. As she found herself approaching the brink of orgasm, she whined softly, her limbs trembling against the shadows as she braced herself for white-hot pleasure.

Just before she could reach the apex of pleasure, Hades drew his head back. Instinctively, she thrust her hips forward, but her restraints proved all too effective, and she groaned in frustration as she saw the knowing leer on the Dark God's face.

She was given a welcome distraction to her disappointment when he unclasped the heavy pin that held up his himation, casually discarding the material to the grass before he tugged off his tunic, revealing a view of sculpted chest and stomach that was met with approval. Under her appreciative gaze, he slowly turned around once, flexing his biceps as he did so.

To her dismay, he went back to teasing her, using his mouth and hands to push her to the brink of orgasm again, ignoring her pleas when he drew back again.

"Damn you!" she moaned, straining against her bonds, blushing furiously as she glared at him.

"Tsk, you should not talk to me that way," he

admonished playfully, wagging his finger. She hmphed and glared at him, silently vowing payback as he regarded her. He reached down to caress her foot, feeling it jerk as she tried to tug it away.

"Please, do not tease me so," Persephone begged. She had never been held off from orgasm like this, and she ached for the intense and eventually soothing release of climax.

"Your desire for me is so tangible I can almost taste it," Hades whispered as her binds started to massage her, easing the strain in her muscles as she struggled. With a low moan of surrender, she went limp as the shadows embraced her further, kneading and rolling against her body. Under Hades's control, they wrapped around her entirely, leaving just her head bare.

Persephone could not help but recall the images of the mummies she had seen in Hades's library, the corpses of the kings of Aiegyptos wrapped neatly in bandages of linen, their bodies preserved for the afterlife, waiting while they were housed in their great tombs in the desert. Her arms and legs were not bound together like the entombed pharaohs, but she still felt very snug, and wiggled her fingers and toes. Initially, she thought that this wrapping was innocuous, a brief respite from the merciless sexual teasing he had given her before, but after several moments, she felt a certain pressure around her nipples, and hissed softly as she became aware of a sucking sensation around them, though they lacked the warm wetness of Hades's mouth.

"Hades, please..." She was panting as her arousal

surged anew, and her soft plea was answered when within the cocoon, a shadowy finger started to rub against her slit. "Yes!" she gasped out softly, rolling her hips forward, and he smiled and nodded.

More 'fingers' joined the first – though at the same time, they also felt like velvety tongues – and she squirmed around more frantically as they teased her to the brink again. She tried to count how many of these shadowy tendrils she felt, but they were in constant motion, massaging, stroking, pressing, and she found it impossible to figure out just how many of them they were. Her clit, as well as her inner and outer lips and perineum, were all teased and rubbed, and she whined softly in delight when one of them finally slithered inside of her. She closed her eyes and let her head loll back, ignoring the man in front of her as she lost herself in pleasure, bucking against her binds as he watched, delighted in her reaction to his game.

Just before she could orgasm, the shadowy fingers withdrew, leaving her bereft, and her eyes snapped open as she glared at him. She was about to issue an angry protest when a band of shadow made its way across her mouth, effectively cutting her off. This did not stop her, and Hades smirked as he heard her muffled protests.

He willed the shadows to pull her up to an upright position again, and nuzzled her face affectionately, hearing her muffled whimper.

"Relax. You will not be denied, but it will be worth the wait," he assured her before taking a step back. He stood at full attention, his arousal pointed directly at her.

"See what you do to me, love." He reached down, giving it several strokes. She nodded eagerly. "Good." Under her intense stare, he ran his fingers along the swollen glans, pulling down the foreskin gently. Through the shadows that kept his lovely bride captive, he could feel her arousal spike again, and winked at her as he continued, giving himself languid caresses as his cock quivered slightly. Even though he enjoyed the feel of her pretty little mouth or hands on his manhood, simply having her watch also thrilled him.

She tried to speak, her words lost behind her gag, and he winked at her.

"Fear not, love. I have not forgotten about you." He let go of himself and approached her. Her bindings opened down the front, revealing her chest, stomach, and womanhood, though the rest of her remained wrapped. She wiggled around, her hair cascading from her head down her shoulders and back like a thick waterfall of deep auburn waves, and he smiled as he twirled a lock of her hair between his fingers.

She wiggled furiously, her arousal evident by the sweet musk that emanated from her private area. She gazed at him imploringly, her eyes flush with heat and desire.

She made a lovely captive, bound the way she was, displayed for his eyes alone. Oh gods, he wanted her so badly. He wanted to ravish every inch of her and have her scream his name. He wanted her to take him, to be on top of him, to make him hers as much as she was his. *Patience. She needs to beg for it. She needs to understand how much she needs you.* A strong hand lifted, trailing its fingers along her exposed inner thigh. She rolled her hips forward.

"You enjoy this," he observed as he stroked her outer lips, causing her to tremble. "Despite your protests... you like the struggle. You like being helpless to the pleasures I give you." Hades was no sadist, but he did enjoy seeing his consort defenseless, open to the pleasures he enjoyed giving her. She groaned against her binds, arching when she felt a finger wiggle inside. She was so aroused that her juices had seeped down her inner thighs, signifying that she was ready for the next step in their game.

The binds holding her spread-eagle relaxed, letting her legs drop so that they simply hung from her hips. Only when her legs came to full rest did they firm up again, providing her lower half support and comfort.

Hades pressed his body against hers, the head of his erection nudging against her inner thighs before sliding between them, the slickness of their mutual arousal aiding this cause. He felt her stiffen in surprise, and he shook his head reassuringly.

"You will see. Have no worry." With this, he gently thrust his hips forward, snugly nestling himself between her thighs. Even here her flesh was warm, and he wiggled against her, making it clear

216

that he was not going to penetrate her. The tip of his cock peered out from the back between her legs, and he thrust several times with a slow, relaxed pace. Her eyes widened in understanding, and she nodded slowly. In response, she squeezed her thighs together, and he groaned softly in delight.

She twisted her pelvis, pressing down against him as he increased his pace, whimpers bursting forth from behind her muzzle as one of his hands cupped her face.

Even as her impending climax was vividly apparent to Hades, he simply continued, pushing deep through the hot slickness that her thighs offered, gazing at her intently as she finally achieved her release, grinding herself against him. He felt her spasm atop the length of his manhood and increased his pace, feeling her squirm against him happily.

He groaned her name as he came, coating her inner thighs with his essence as he thrust several more times.

Finally, he pulled back with a quiet grunt of satisfaction. Her head lolled to one side as she hung against her binds.

"How about I let you down, hmm?" he asked gently. She nodded, and he drew forward, reaching out with his arms to wrap them around her middle, one hand on her rear end. Once he had her secure in his grip, the shadows slid away, letting her slump against him as she wrapped her arms around his neck loosely. Even though she was no longer gagged, she remained mute with apparent contentment, resting her head on his shoulder as he rubbed her back.

Chapter XXXI

oOo

The time of harvest drew near. Demeter had always delighted in the fall since it meant that her largest bounty was gathered by mortals, the amber waves of grain a sign of her blessing. She also enjoyed the way the leaves changed color, filling Hellas with a lush palette of everything from rich green to tawny gold and scarlet rust to the deep ocher and browns of the earth itself. Oftentimes she would take her daughter for walks around the island so they could enjoy the beauty of autumn.

This time around, she took no joy in the changing season as she searched for her lost child. However carefully everyone searched, the girl remained missing. Though the nymphs had reported long ago that Kora was to be found nowhere within the confines of Nature, she would not give up. And Hermes – the god that nobody was supposed to be able to keep a secret from – was just as baffled as anybody else.

The Harvest Goddess would not admit it, but she privately enjoyed the mystified expression on his face when he reported to her even as she felt sad and frustrated at his lack of results. It was such a welcome change from his usual mischievous or knowing expressions, and she saw his aid as penance for the chain of events she was certain he was responsible for.

Demeter was becoming frantic. So far, only Zeus

and Hermes knew that Kora was missing, and she was loath to involve the other gods in her affairs. She dreaded the prospect of petitioning the other gods for help. Doubtless the more capricious ones like Aphrodite would laugh at her for being unable to keep track of one child, but certainly, there would be others who would hasten to her aid. Artemis was the protector of virgin girls. Athene was brilliant and probably could come up with a plan or deduction that would help her find her daughter. Hephaistos had a good heart. Poseidon might have a bit of a temper – well, that was an understatement – but he was capable of great kindness. Hera could use her limited clairvoyance to deduce Kora's location. When the gods pulled together – a rare occurrence throughout the long centuries – they *could* accomplish a great deal.

It was a bitter pill to swallow, Demeter had to acknowledge that she might need to take her search a step further.

As the days shortened, the nights grew cooler, and Demeter pulled the cowl of her heavy cloak over her head, the thick black wool insulating her against a brisk wind. She chewed on her lip, pondering what she would say to Zeus. How best to word her request? Zeus would know the search was unfruitful since Hermes also had to report to him.

She was so lost in her thoughts that she did not notice the way the night thickened, seeming to overtake everything as she walked along the path that bordered a grassy meadow. But she became instantly alert as she felt the presence of another person – no, a god – further down the path. She looked up to see a shadowy, cloaked figure, barely visible against the backdrop of night.

Hekate rarely showed herself on the surface world, so she was a goddess that Demeter was not able to instantly recognize.

"Greetings, Bountiful One," the shadowed figure called out in a surprisingly friendly tone. The gods who had encountered her said that she spoke in a low and mysterious voice, often portending doom or misfortune leading from the errors that men made.

"Good evening to you, Hekate," Demeter replied after a moment of collecting herself from the surprise that Hekate's presence and voice gave her.

"I know you are wondering why I am here, so I will not bore you with small talk. You and your daughter have been wronged, and I am here to help you set things right." Her tone sounded helpful, even caring.

Demeter stared at Hekate for several moments, her pulse quickening. *Could it be?* Was her search finally at an end?

"That is the best news I have heard since my daughter disappeared!"

"I thought you might feel that way. I can only imagine the fear you must feel over her safety. You have spared none of your magic or effort in your search. Your nights have been sleepless."

Demeter felt her hands tremble slightly as she balled them into fists. If Kora was hurt in *any* way...

"Where is she?"

"She is unhurt, but she, and you, have been

wronged. I now know the one responsible for this grave injustice. But I do ask one thing of you."

"Yes?"

"Do not tell him who told you. He does not deserve to know where you got your information, and I take personal risk for sharing it.."

"You have my word. Who is it? Tell me!" Though Demeter tried to remain collected, she could not hide the earnestness in her tone.

"Zeus."

The Earth-Goddess staggered back. *Zeus?* Zeus knew? But... what? How?

"But... when I asked him... and he knows that Hermes and I are searching... he sent Hermes to help me!"

"He sent his son as a distraction. He is too afraid to tell you the truth. Ask him."

"How could he..." Demeter felt a painful knot twist through her stomach as she thought of the long days and nights searching, racked with worry, imagining her precious little daughter in the clutches of someone who would abuse and violate her...

"This is Zeus we are talking about," Hekate replied matter-of-factly. Demeter blinked and collected herself, ready to pepper the mysterious goddess with a barrage of new questions. How did Hekate know? Could she relay a message to Kora? Would she...?

When Demeter was about to ask her next questions, the Goddess of the Crossroads was nowhere to be seen. She was almost certain she had imagined it but was brought back to reality by her heart pounding against her chest, her hands shaking from shock.

oOo

Hekate's path took her across the Styx. She did not need Kharon's aid to traverse the realms any more than Hades did, but as always, she asked the Styx permission, to show respect. All she felt was a brief flash of cold before she was home.

She had spent the last few days thinking about what she could do regarding the situation with Demeter and Persephone. She actually thought about taking Persephone to the surface world herself, but the wrath of Hades was to be reckoned with, and a battle between Demeter and her elder brother could only end badly.

She could tell Hera, and let the Queen of the Gods go into a rage against her husband. How often had Hera been wronged by her husband? But in this case... no, it wasn't quite the right time for Hera to become involved, especially when it really was her sister's problem.

However tempted Hekate was to confront Zeus himself and lay a few curses on him, this was not her fight. She would not rob Demeter of the pleasure of confronting the scurrilous deity. Let Zeus be confronted with the consequences of his own stupidity by someone who was a direct victim of said thoughtlessness.

oOo

Mount Olympus was quiet, illuminated by the moon and the ornate lamps that Hephaistos and the Cyclopes had wrought. The bubbling and splashing sounds that came from the fountains and streams scattered around the mountain were almost inaudible, providing a soothing backdrop to the pleasant climate of this haven of the gods.

Demeter strode forward, taking long steps along the walkways that led to the private domiciles of various gods. She did not waver or slow down any time she had to take a turn or climb up a set of steps. The gates to Zeus's domicile opened before she had to lift a hand, such was the power of the wrath that radiated from her. The doors to his palace slammed open to admit her, and she lashed out at various decorations in the grand hall, marble statues of the mighty King of the Gods shattering as they fell prey to the concussive force of her power, and the ornate urns following a similar fate. The mosaic of frolicking nymphs that adorned one wall started to lose its tiles, various stones exploding and snapping out from their fixtures, and the wall hangings started to smoke and catch fire as Demeter stalked towards the carved doors of Zeus's bedchamber.

oOo

The heavy oak door tore itself from its hinges, landing on the marble floor with a deafening thud. Having heard the destruction in the hall, Zeus was already sitting up, prepared to fight. He hadn't been expecting a real problem – perhaps Ares drunk again – but as soon as he eyed his sister's livid countenance, he paled.

The nymph that had been in his bed found herself shoved out of it by an unseen force, scrambling across the floor as she tried to orient herself. She did not need to be told to leave and rushed out of the room without a thought to her discarded clothing.

"You!" Demeter roared. Zeus could actually feel the heat rolling off her body, and scrambled to remedy the situation.

"Sister dearest..."

"Don't try that shit on me!" In the blink of an eye, she was at the foot of his bed, and she tore the blankets from the bed, leaving him naked. Unlike his lovers, Demeter stared at his nude form with open disdain.

"Try what? I was sleeping and then you barge in-"

"Tell me where Kora is!"

"I... what?" he asked, feigning confusion. He had just been woken up, so it was easy enough to accomplish.

"You lumpen jackass! I should have known it was you from the beginning!" She drove her fist down, splintering the thick footboard before she rammed her fist into the post at the left corner of the bed, sending chunks of wood spraying along the bed and floor before the post fell over like a tree that had just been chopped down.

"Sister! Collect yourself! You cannot barge into my home and destroy my possessions!"

This only provoked her further, and she hefted the post over her shoulder, swinging it down on the bed before he realized what she was doing. He gave out a roar of pain when the wood made contact with his stomach, knocking the breath out of his lungs and driving him into the thick woolen mat.

He lay there, unable to breathe as he stared ahead dazedly. He flopped his arms for a moment before starting to lift the post off his body, thankful for the fact that he was not mortal, otherwise his chest would have been literally flattened. A determined woman kept it down, climbing on top of him and straddling the oaken pillar, staring down at him.

"Get off me!" he managed to gasp out, feeling his Gift respond to the danger he was in as he felt the static in the air around him crackle.

"Don't you dare." She reached down, grabbing a good chunk of hair on top of his head and curling her fingers, causing him to wince in pain under her grip. "Now... tell me where in Hades Kora is. Or I will castrate you right here and now."

There was no doubt in Zeus's mind that she would make good on her threat if provoked. After all, look at what she had done to Ares!

"Please... She's safe! I swear!"

"That is not what I was asking." Her voice was level, but her cheeks were still flushed with indignation, and he did not like the dangerous glint in her eyes.

"It is hard... to breathe. And talk. I will tell you, I swear! Just... ah! Let me breathe, for Gaea's sake?"

"You will remain right where you are," she

growled. He nodded.

Demeter stared down at him for a moment before climbing off him, but she remained ever alert, apparently ready to pounce should he try to flee. Wisely, he remained where he was amidst the splinters that littered the bed.

"How could you do this to me? You know how much I love my daughter! She is all I have, and you took her away from me!" She reached out to grab his hair again.

"Now, there is no need for that, please..." Zeus batted at her hand, but she only strengthened her grip.

"*Talk,*" she warned.

"She is in the Underworld," he admitted. He winced, expecting her to abuse him again in some way. To his relief, she simply stared at him, her jaw slack.

o0o

Underworld? No wonder nobody could find her! Even her most powerful magic had no effect in the Underworld! But... what was Kora doing there? What was her beloved child doing in the land of the dead? What possible reason could there be to keep Kora in such a dismal place? And Zeus had known! What part did he have in this?

"Why is she there? In that horrible place? Why would you put her there?"

"I... I did not put her there, I swear. It was Hades."

"... Hades?" Disbelief flashed across her face as

she tried to comprehend the situation. Hades had taken Kora to the Underworld, and for whatever reason, Zeus had been privy to it. What was going on?

"He wanted a bride."

Disbelief was quickly replaced by a fresh surge of fury, and Zeus yelled as his head was roughly yanked in several directions.

"I want her back! Right now!"

"He asked for my blessing, I gave it. Demeter, please be reasonable..."

"You gave away my daughter!" Her cheeks bore their indignant flush even more than before, unsightly red blotches flaring on her cheeks.

"Gave... no, no, *no!*" Zeus raised his hands, "None of this was my idea! Hades demanded her. He told me he wanted her. And only her. What could I do?"

"Say no," came the deadpan reply.

"To Hades?" Zeus asked incredulously.

"Yes!" Demeter snapped, barely biting back her anger. Was her brother *really* this dense?

"If it were any other god, I would have said no. But Hades..." He shook his head, "He is different. His realm has changed him, you know that. Him coming to me? It was a mere formality. He would have taken Kora with or without my blessing. He did not even have to come to me." Zeus sighed heavily and stared up at her pleadingly.

"You knew of this all along. It did not occur to you to warn me after Hades left Olympus? Did you expect me to not notice that Kora was missing!"

"It is not my fault that Hades chose to not notify you of his... decision."

"That is all you can say?" Demeter growled. Zeus was considered the mightiest of gods, but as those closest to him knew, he could be quite a coward at rare moments. Said god looked down, his expression downcast, knowing full well that his excuse was a weak one at best.

"Get off that stupid ass of yours and order Hades to release Kora!"

"Demeter, please calm down. Hades is not a cruel god, and he assured me that she would be taken care of. Certainly, he is a better choice of a groom than Ares. Think about it, she's the Queen of the Underworld! Not bad for our daughter, eh?"

"You spineless-"

"You know Hades as well as I do. Do you honestly think that he would abuse Kora?"

"He kidnapped her!"

"Yes, yes. But be reasonable, you refused to admit any man to your sacred valley. Hades did not have the choice to court her properly. Calm down, and Hades will speak to you."

"Calm? Don't you *dare* tell me to calm down. You and Poseidon and Hades, you gods, you are all the same! Have women come to mean so little to you? You would not let me turn away your advances so you had to resort to trickery, you are ever unfaithful to your loyal wife, you let your brother take your daughter and leave me in the dark about this! What the hell is wrong with you? What have I done to deserve being treated as such?"

"It had nothing to do with you. I did not seduce you to hurt you. And I would not have given my blessing if I did not think that Hades would mistreat Kora," Zeus replied, attempting to use his charm, only achieving the opposite of what he'd intended.

"WHY!" she screamed, and he found his hair yanked in such a way that had he been mortal, his neck would have easily snapped, or even his head ripped from his neck.

"Please. Let me go. It is... hard to talk. When you are ...AH! Jerking around my head like that."

In response, she gave him several especially vicious jerks, ignoring his bellows. Finally, she stopped, and he panted several times before he spoke.

"I swear, this was done in no malice towards you. Demeter, I know you meant best for your daughter. But she is a grown woman now, and Hades is hardly a bad influence on her. She *is* safe, and is that not what you wanted in the first place?"

"I want her back. Or I will go to Hera and let her know what you have done. The other gods as well. I doubt your other daughters will look upon this favorably."

"What can Hera do?" the King of the Gods shrugged, "She has no more power than I do against Hades. And what of my daughters? So I gave my blessing for Kora. What of it? Is it not a father's duty to ensure that his daughters are cared for? I certainly am not the first, nor will I be the last man to give away his daughter!"

Demeter glared at him with a sneer. She knew that her brother thought she was reacting hysterically.

He had grown haughty, practically celebrating his own follies, letting his desires dictate his actions. He thrived off the worship of mortals and demanded their admiration, and his sons and brothers were no different. The mighty gods of Olympus had become lost in their own ennui, pursuing pleasure and entertainment in its myriad forms. They would just laugh at her for her righteous indignation over the situation.

As she glared at Zeus, she realized the perfect way to get her revenge on him for what he had done all these years ago and the fact that with his thoughtless decision, had added egregious insult to injury. Her face went through a startling change, changing from openly livid to cold and calculating, promising something even more terrifying than her immediate wrath.

"You will rue the day that you started this entire mess. You will no longer be a beneficiary of my Gifts. Let us see how high and mighty you are, then."

With that, she was gone, leaving her brother amidst the destruction caused by her ire.

oOo

As King of the Gods, it was a given that Zeus was worshiped throughout Hellas. Destroyer of Kronos, Lord of the Skies, the God of Thunder, the Patriarch and the Wise Leader. And he almost lived for worship. His family knew that all too well, and Demeter intended to use that to her fullest advantage.

Soon enough the mortals would see who held the

231

real power. Demeter was the Giver of Life, and if the Zeus and his brethren did not appreciate it or the vital role that women played in their lives or that they deserved more respect than what was usually given them, well then, why should she share her Gift with them?

Olympia was one of the cities that had Zeus as its main patron deity. Worship of Zeus here was far more prevalent than the worship of any other god, who was lucky to get mention in Olympia outside of sharing the myths. It was Zeus's favorite city, but not even the might of the King of the Gods could save his beloved city from Demeter's cold rage.

o0o

The city was surrounded by farms, ponds, and streams fed by mountain springs, providing ample food and supplies for the needs of the city. Every year, the festivities and ceremonies went in full swing. The gods were celebrated and prayed to, entreated to use their Gifts to benefit mankind, but the name that was uttered or called out most was Zeus.

After all, he was King of the Gods, Lord of Heaven, Patriarch of the Olympians. More than half of the gods of Olympus were descended from him. Eight of his own children made up the Council of the Twelve. He had a beautiful and wise Queen, and his conquests were legendary. He was strong and handsome. Men hoped to be like him in energy and sexual prowess. The priests of the grand temples of

232

Zeus were chosen for their virility and robustness, and the temple maidens were handpicked by these very same priests for their loveliness. In the past, a maiden or two would find themselves visited by Zeus.

Skouros had been the head priest of Olympia for nearly two decades. He had been chosen for the position by his predecessor when he was nearly thirty, in the prime of his life. Even now as he neared fifty, he was still a striking figure, fit and broad-shouldered with a full head of dark brown hair and beard that only recently had started to gray, giving him a dignified appearance.

Like the god he served, he had a large brood, though nowhere near as large as the amount of offspring that Zeus sired. He had been blessed with seven sons and three daughters, and nine of them were alive and healthy. The sole exception had been a toddler son who had wandered too close to a pool and fell in, drowning before his absence was noted. Three of his sons served here in the temple as priests or groundskeepers, and his eldest daughter had been picked as one of the temple maidens to assist in the lavish ceremonies. He had seen poverty before in his life and knew that he was enormously blessed. Zeus was very generous to those who served him well.

He enjoyed walks at night-time because it helped him to think, and gave him a much-needed time of solitude after juggling his duties as priest, father, and husband. Though he would never say it out loud – he was careful to not say anything that might offend his patron deity – when he was in the temple on the hill, he felt like Zeus himself looking down Mount Olympus and even Hellas itself.

Under the light of the waxing moon, he could see the houses below, clean and sun-bleached, clustered closely together around the hills, and more widely spaced as one went on, interspersed by farms, gardens, and orchards. For as long as he remembered, the yearly harvest had always been at least sufficient. Yes, some years were better than others, but this year, the summer harvest had gone on well, and the autumn harvest promised to be especially fruitful. They would have more than enough to last them through spring, and he smiled with satisfaction as he took a deep breath of the fresh night air. He was truly satisfied with his life, and there had been just a few sorrows – like the loss of his son – to make him appreciate his blessings all the more.

His pace was sedate as his sandaled feet padded along the smooth dirt path, glancing up at the olive trees that lined one side of the well-maintained avenue. Skouros looked forward to the olive-harvest time since he was partial to the fruit, and he reached up to gently grasp a low-hanging branch. Most of the olives were nearly ripe, and he quickly scanned the branch, hoping there would be a few ripe ones. He found one that was close enough and plucked it off the branch before he popped it into his mouth, smacking his lips contentedly despite the slightly unripe flavor, careful to not swallow the pit.

Mmm! Most people did not like olives right off the tree and preferred to prepare them in a variety of ways; Skouros was one of the rare few who relished the flavor of them right off the tree, spitting out seeds and enjoying the fruit. Just a few more weeks and the olives would be ready for everyone to enjoy. He looked forward to having new olives with his meals, and freshly pressed olive oil with his wife's flatbread. His reverie was interrupted as he saw a shadowy figure wandering along the path, approaching him. He frowned to himself; this part of the hill was part of the temple grounds, and only people under its employ were supposed to have access to this area unless it was festival, tending, or harvest time. The stranger was wrapped in a cloak that was black or dark brown; it was hard to discern under this light.

"Halt!" he said in a firm voice. The stranger was tall and broad-shouldered, but as he squinted, the drape of the cloak revealed the shape of a woman. It was definitely not one of the nymph-like temple maidens, and he wondered who this woman could possibly be. To his relief, the figure paused but did not speak.

"Who are you?" he asked.

"I am but a visitor. You have no need to worry about assault." Skouros noted that her tone was deeper than the voices of most women, but it still had a warm, feminine feel to it. "I cannot help but notice how happy this place seems. The fields are so fertile. Have you ever known hunger?"

Hunger? What did this woman speak of? "Hunger? Certainly, when I am fasting for my rituals, or when I wake up in the morning and have not yet broken the fast with my family."

"Not that kind of hunger. True hunger, the

emptiness that comes from lack of bounty. When not only is your stomach hollow, but the rest of you." She sounded as if she spoke from experience.

"No, never. I am blessed for that."

"Blessed?" The woman sounded almost amused. "Truly? Why?"

"My life has had few difficulties. I have spent most of my life in the service of great Zeus. He has blessed me greatly, and Olympia as well." Surely this woman would know, if she lived here? Or was she foreign, a visitor from one of the other city-states or any of the villages that dotted Hellas? It might explain why she had traversed into an area reserved for those in Zeus's service. He was a kind man, and quick to forgive. Such a transgression could be overlooked for humble ignorance.

"Him? Just him?"

"This is the city of Zeus! Athene has Athens, Ares has Sparta, Apollo has Delphi, and Aphrodite has Cyprus. Here, Zeus takes care of us all! He truly is a great god!" His voice was passionate, showing affection for the patriarchal deity.

"He can do no wrong?"

"Of course not! He is the mighty king of Heaven and Earth! His wisdom knows no bounds. He is generous."

"And this?" She swept her arm in the direction of the valley beyond the olive trees, where fields and orchards lay within close vicinity.

"More blessings! He sends down the rains to nurture us. What better place to live than here?"

"I see." Her tone was unreadable.

"I invite you to come to the harvest festival. We will celebrate the harvest soon, and thank Zeus for all our blessings. Join us, it is a fun event for everyone. Zeus smiles upon us all."

"I will consider it." She started walking again, circumventing Skouros as he glanced at her wonderingly. He blinked, and when he opened his eyes again, she was gone.

oOo

So Zeus was responsible for the rich harvest that was soon to be gathered? He was the greatest and wisest of the gods? How *presumptuous*. Demeter would be having none of that, and slowly turned around, scanning the valley, seeing the thick rows of grain that stood tall and proud, the symbol that mortals often used to represent her Gift.

The people here believed that their good health and wealth was due to Zeus. That this selfish god was nothing but judicious and generous. Ha! Soon enough, they and the rest of Hellas would know the truth.

"The harvest will fall before any sickle can cut it!" Demeter declared. She raised her sickle, the polished blade glinting in the moonlight as she raised it above her head. The air crackled with heat and power, and she let her wrath pour out of her in rolling waves. She would no longer give. As gods and mortals saw fit to take from her, so she would return the favor a thousandfold.

The life-force that enriched the land around

Olympia burned away before her fury, and she watched with grim satisfaction as the pulse of destruction spread out from her form, increasing its radius as the thick stalks of grain bowed and withered. The fruit on the branches and vines shriveled, and the soil drained the vegetables that had been so lovingly planted and tended throughout the year. Nothing that grew from the earth was spared her wrath, and even the trees dried out and became brittle, leaving a horrible dearth around Olympia that not even Zeus himself would be able to bless.

Chapter XXXII

oOo

"Daddy!" a young girl cried out, and Skouros muttered softly as he came awake, rubbing his eyes as he felt his youngest daughter tug at his sleeve. Normally, his children were not permitted in his bedchamber, and they would not violate this rule of his unless it was an emergency. He groaned and sat up, seeing that he was alone in the bed. Dear gods, had something happened to his wife? Was that why Melissa was so hysterical? Her dark brown eyes were wide and the expression on her young features did not bode well. A little girl of just five should not have such a frightened expression!

"What is it, Melissa?" he asked as he swung his feet over the side of the bed, trying to remain calm. "Has something happened to Mama?"

"No, Daddy. The gardens... And everything!"

"Gardens?" Skouros narrowed his eyes, starting to feel irritated. He would have scolded Melissa, but the fear on her face was so stark that he knew that it must be something serious. And if not, well, she was only a little girl. Sometimes the little ones tended to make a great fuss over things. Melissa was the youngest of his children, and having already raised nine children – some of them still in various stages of childhood – taught him much about being a father and what to expect from his offspring.

"Give me a moment..." he muttered, rising to his feet and feeling the slight ache in his joints. Hm, he was getting old. Oh well. He had had a full life and expected to enjoy many more years before Death came for him. His sandals sat where he had left them near the foot of the bed, and he slipped into them before tossing on a robe over his tunic against the brisk autumn air.

He let his daughter grab his hand and tug her along, leading him through the rooms and out of the house into the courtyard, and his jaw dropped as he saw the dearth around him.

"See, Daddy. I told you."

He had a modest estate with a pleasant inner courtyard and a larger outer yard. The inner yard had a wide open space of grass and a small fountain. The other part of the courtyard was for the gardens, mainly vegetables. The grass was a sickly yellow, and when he stepped onto it, it crunched under his feet with a brittle crackle. The vegetables did not seem to be better off, judging from the wilted leaves. Not wanting to believe what he saw, he leaned down to grab the top of a carrot. The leaves came away without its fruit, and he dug his fingers into the dirt, turning up a shriveled carrot.

Skouros's heart started pounding, and his hands shook slightly.

"And... the farm?" he asked. Melissa looked down, shaking her head. He was afraid to look, but knew he needed to. The outside looked much worse. There were several trees here and there, bearing fruit at different times of the year, as well as bushes. All of the fruit that was to be harvested were now dried-up husks of their former selves, and when he pulled

240

down a branch to examine the damage, it came off with a dry snap.

All the flowers that bloomed at this time of the year were no better off than anything he'd seen so far, many of their petals littering the ground around their parched stems and vines. The priest of Zeus walked as if in a trance, regarding everything with a dazed expression on his face even as his wife rushed towards him, reporting that their neighbors had the same exact problem on their own land. Her voice became a distant echo as he stared down the road. The valley that had been so lush, full of green and patches of other colors, was now all parched of its natural colors, even the large tracts of crops that fed the village. Wheat was by nature yellow and brown mixed into a rich deep gold color, but all he saw was the jaundiced yellow and rotted brown of dead crops. Through the buzzing that filled his ears, he heard the wails of his neighbors.

oOo

Having blighted Olympia, Demeter would not stop there. Zeus was only one god, and there was another that was responsible for the disappearance of her precious child. However, Hades had no city of his own, nor did he have any grand temples attributed to him. Normally, sacrifices to him were private, rather than turned into big festivals. His images were usually to be found within mausoleums and crypts, and rarely, in paintings or pottery. She would have to convey her message to Hades more directly, and she was more than prepared to do that. With the righteous wrath of a mother whose child had literally been stolen away from her, she descended into the dread kingdom of her brother.

oOo

Normally, Kharon had no issue with ferrying a god across the Styx to seek an audience with Hades or the Fates. However, he had explicit orders from his master to not extend this favor to Demeter for the time being, and now it was clear why. The goddess' anger was palpable, and he was relieved to launch himself away from the dock, narrowly missing her swipe as she tried to grab his cloak.

oOo

"Come back here! I will not be defied!" The souls clustered at the shore gave Demeter a wide berth, fearing this mighty deity even in death as her eyes flashed dangerously. How dare he! She felt her heart pound within her chest as the blood pulsed hotly within her veins, causing her to shake almost violently. She raised her arms, determined to reach the other side and rescue her daughter. Like Kora, she sensed the lack of life in this world, and it unnerved her. What could Hades be thinking, keeping her down here?

"You will ferry me across or face my wrath!" she roared. The souls gazed upon her with terror and awe, wondering if the Harvest Goddess was so terrifying, then what must her brother, the God of Death be like?

The ferryman kept his head bowed, pushing his oar through the water as his passengers gazed back at the fuming woman with curiosity. Even though the souls no longer had any flesh to connect them to the physical realm, they could feel the heat of Demeter's anger. As Kharon continued his ferry, Demeter let out an angry shriek, directing her wrath at the insolent boatman with a blast of heat.

Suddenly, there was a bubbling, churning sound, much like one might hear from the ocean, but far more terrifying, echoing against the cavern walls. The waters of the Styx rippled violently with a dull roar, and the souls who had lingered along the edge suddenly pulled back as the river overflowed its banks, sending ice-cold water splashing around her ankles.

A form rose from the churning surface, its body made entirely of the inky water and reflected in flashes against the lamps that stood near the docks, the water gushing and towering over the goddess as the fluid coalesced into a more solid shape.

The form did not limit itself to life-size, and instead assumed Titanic proportions as it grew and molded itself into the upper half of a shapely woman, her long obsidian tresses flowing from the top of her head like a waterfall.

"You would dare harass the Ferryman of Souls?" Styx's voice came from the deep abyss of the river, reverberating off the walls with a frightening cadence in such a profound and terrible tone that it would stop the heart of a mortal as she spoke. The voice washed

over Demeter, wrapping her in a sensation that could only be described as *cold* as if merely listening to it would pull her into the fathomless abyss that lingered just below the river's surface.

However, Demeter refused to be fazed. She had gone against her own sire and his brothers, and would not be cowed by Styx, especially when she had come down here to rescue her child!

"Hades has my daughter, and I will not stand for it!"

"Be as it may, he has ordered that you not be allowed into his realm. You will gain no aid from me or Kharon."

"You would separate a mother from her child?" The heat of her anger rose, but Styx seemed unconcerned.

"Your anger is useless here," she responded calmly, staring down at the Harvest Goddess.

"You will rue the day you defied me!" Demeter responded, though inside Styx's presence and words caused a deep chill to pass through her. On the surface world, she was entirely confident in her power and abilities. Down here, her power was useless. Styx would never allow her to swim across.

"I will have no part in this quarrel. Leave now." Her tone brooked no argument and promised swift retribution for any further attempt on Demeter's part to lash out against the Underworld deities. The air became filled with cold, becoming thick and heavy almost as if it had turned to liquid, and the frigidity seeped into Demeter's veins, filling up her lungs as she tried to breathe.

Demeter strode through the grand hall of the Palace where the Gods held their meetings, her chin raised and shoulders pushed back. She was an imposing sight in her stately garb, her hair braided into a crown around her scalp and held together with golden pins. Her white and green clothing caught the air and billowed around her, adding dimension to her already impressive appearance.

Around the grand marble table were the eleven other gods that made up the ruling council of the Olympians. She did not take the twelfth seat, preferring to remain standing so she could look down at all the others. Her gaze was openly hostile as she fixed them at the head of the table, where the King of the Gods sat.

"Demeter, sit down," Zeus stated calmly, waving his hand as if placating a child.

"Like hell I will." The heat of her gaze could be felt by everyone within the room, and the other gods glanced away, shifting in their seats uncomfortably. *Good*, Demeter thought to herself.

"Sister, be reasonable. Only this morning I have heard the cries and prayers from Olympia. I know you are angry with me, but do not take it out on them. Restore the bounty that you are known for."

"Restore my daughter to me," she retorted evenly.

"We have already discussed this." Zeus said, and she sensed his effort to maintain a calm and commanding tone, "What is done is done. Kora is in

245

good hands."

"Hades refuses to admit me to his realm," she snarled.

"Oh? Well, I will simply have to speak to him about it..."

"Wait, wait." Hermes turned towards his father. "*That* is where Kora is? In the Underworld?"

"And he has known all along, yet he told you to search for her and wasted your time in doing so," the Harvest Goddess said as she stared at her nephew. His lips formed a frown as he glanced at her for a moment before turning back to Zeus.

"You told me to help Demeter search for her daughter, knowing where she was?"

"Well, you needed a distraction, and..."

"Do be quiet, Zeus! I tire of your excuses. You want your people in Olympia fed? Then return Kora to me!" she snarled.

"Father, you had this knowledge all this time? Why would you not tell Demeter?" This came from Artemis, seated near where her aunt was standing.

"Hades wanted Kora as his bride. Demeter would have no husband for her, so Hades was compelled to act-"

"Why do you continue getting in these disasters, dear husband?" Hera spoke up, her voice filled with disdain for her husband's weak defense of his actions. "What gave you the right to do that?"

"I am King of the Gods, and responsible for the welfare of the Olympians. Hades promised to be a good husband, and we all know he is a man of his word."

246

"I never thought Hades would have a bride!" Poseidon stated, flashing his brother a grin. "Oh ho ho!" His laughter boomed through the hall. The silence of Demeter, Hera, and several other gods provided a stark contrast to his mirth. However, a few of the gods – more notably, those of the male sex – joined in the laughter, but were quickly silenced by Demeter's hostile glare.

"You find this amusing? That my only child has been kidnapped and taken to the Underworld as a captive bride, and Zeus knew of this, even gave permission for it, and kept this a secret from me?"

"Father, I am very disappointed with you," Artemis said sourly.

"I have to say that I agree with Artemis," Hephaistos spoke up, glancing at his aunt. "Demeter is a mighty goddess, and it is very clear that she loves and cares for her daughter. I have no child of my own..." this was interrupted by a soft, disdainful snort from Aphrodite, "but I can see the pain and anger in her eyes. No mother should be parted from her child, especially in such a fashion as what happened."

"I have met Kora. She is a sweet person and I bear her no malice. It does not seem proper that she has been snatched to the Underworld. That place makes me... ill at ease." Hermes glanced at Demeter. "If you like, I can go down to Hades and relay a message to him. I am happy to offer my services."

Her expression softened a bit as she studied her nephew and regarded him with an approving nod. "I would appreciate that."

"No, wait..." Zeus said, raising his hand to stay

his son, who was already scrambling out of his seat.

"*Wait*?" Hera asked incredulously. "Let him go, by all means!"

"Hades has made it clear that he will not give up Kora. Hermes will have no more effect on him than a decree from me would."

"So what do you suggest? That I sit around and wait?" Demeter demanded, flinging up her arms in frustration.

"Yes. Calm down. Restore Olympia, and enjoy the fact that your daughter is well-cared for. I do not doubt you will see her soon enough."

"No! Can you not even acknowledge that you have wronged me?"

"Wronged?" Apollo spoke. "A girl has been given to a man of great wealth and respect. Few parents could complain of such a prospect for their child, and Zeus has given his approval." He glanced around the table with warm blue eyes, seeing assenting nods from the majority of the council.

"It would not be the first time a man has kidnapped a woman out of passion," Aphrodite shrugged, flipping her hair over her shoulder. "At least we now know that Hades is not devoid of desire." She let out an airy laugh. Next to her, Ares was silent.

"Passion leads people to do foolish things," Athene tartly reminded her sister, studying the goddess who represented the antithesis of herself as she regarded the Goddess of Love with cool gray eyes.

"Oh, but passion makes life enjoyable,"

Aphrodite replied coquettishly, batting her eyes at her sister.

"We have all seen the consequences of unrestrained passion enough times, I am certain." This jab was directed at Aphrodite and Zeus both, reminding them of all the situations they had found themselves in due to their inability to remain faithful to one lover. "And I would not say that not consulting her mother was an intelligent decision, either."

"Athene..." Zeus sighed. Demeter bit back a smile. It was almost too bad that the eldest child of Zeus did not sit on the High Throne herself.

"Do not tell her to hush," Demeter snapped, cutting Zeus off, "Unlike you, she actually *thinks* before she acts. You – and many others – really should try to emulate her more."

Athene was now smirking openly, and Poseidon frowned. "Now, my brother is a fine King and has served Olympus well. He is such a kind man that not only does he look out for his own daughters, he also cares for his nieces and granddaughters. Demeter, there is no reason to be so upset. Hades is not a bad man. As Zeus said, you will probably be seeing her soon enough. Let us all relax."

"I will not!" Demeter glared at Zeus, "I will not rest until I have my daughter back!"

"What is done is done. Now, restore the crops of Olympia." Zeus sat straight, looking as imperious and commanding as he could. Demeter saw right through this facade, and regarded her brother with a stony frown.

"No."

"There will be consequences."

"Like *what?* My daughter has already been taken from me!"

"If you insist on behaving so rashly, I will have no choice but to remove you from the Dodekatheon."

"Ha!" Demeter sneered at him contemptuously. "Do it. See if I care."

"Now, now." Poseidon shook his head, stroking his thick beard. "I certainly would not want such a thing to happen. Be reasonable."

"Yes. Be reasonable," Apollo piped in, using his voice to its most soothing extent. Not for nothing was he known for being a patron of music. It had the opposite effect, driving the Harvest Goddess' ire further.

"If you are so lonely, why not have another child?" This was put in by Aphrodite, and Artemis stared at her with shock and disgust.

"Let us not quarrel," Hera said with consternation as she regarded her flighty stepdaughter, "Surely we can come to a solution." She looked at her husband, clearly expecting him to agree with his wife, at the very least.

"The only solution is having my daughter back," Demeter growled.

"That cannot be done," Zeus replied. "I am sorry, but I can not take back my blessing, not from Hades."

"Let us have some wine and ambrosia. Surely it will put everybody in a better mood." Dionysus smiled cheerfully, but that smile was quick to wilt under Demeter's angry stare.

"Sounds like a marvelous idea!" Poseidon

clapped his hands. Artemis and Athene shared sideways glances. Hera clenched her jaw.

"Is that how you want it, Zeus? Then your people will go hungry," Demeter reminded him.

"My threat to remove you from the Council is not an idle one," Zeus warned.

"Go ahead. If you truly think so little of me, I have no desire to associate with you, or any god who would disdain me for the pain I feel, or the egregious manner in which I have been wronged." Her hard gaze moved around the table, staring pointedly at the ones who would make light of her predicament. "Hear me, since what is rightfully mine was taken away from me without a second thought, so I will give no more until it is given back."

Before anyone could say anything, she whipped around, stalking out of the room.

oOo

Sparta boasted of the mightiest warriors in all of Hellas. Unlike so many other cities and villages, the girls of Sparta were encouraged to play and exercise, and work outside. Many of the girls might even engage in play combat with their fathers, brothers, or cousins, for there was no shame in having a strong woman at your side, and the contributions of women were valued; if not intellectually, then physically.

From the time they could walk, the sons of Sparta were taught how to fight. They started off with wooden swords, and sometimes a child might get hurt, but it would teach them how to deal with the pain and further refine them into warriors. Nobody could deny the fact that the Spartan lifestyle did breed warriors with prowess that was rarely rivaled by any others.

But no matter how strong, fast, intelligent, or seasoned a warrior might be, one basic fact remained. Warriors needed sustenance.

Demeter did not have a very high opinion of Sparta. She had seen the ravages of war too many times, but she had not taken any action against her nephew's favored city. Until now.

Around Sparta were farms, many of which were run by retired warriors or women whose husbands were on active duty in the army. When not training for battles, warriors often pitched in as well, for farm work was no easy task. While not as glorious as war, it put food in their bellies and built their body and muscles. Spartans had large appetites to match the energy they burned, and the dearth of food would hit them especially hard.

She would never forget Ares's action towards Kora or his attitude in the meeting. He was next on what would become infamously known in a future era as a shit-list.

oOo

Kalia was a young Spartan girl in her prime, having just celebrated her seventeenth birthday. Her father had married late in life, and spent his golden years on his farm, raising his sons and daughter. She was the middle child, with two older brothers and two younger. She had spent much of her childhood playing with her brothers, and though she was not an expert warrior, she was competent enough with the wooden swords her brothers used for practice. Her muscled, wiry body showed others that should it come down to a fight, she would not go down easily. Her older brothers had already joined the ranks of warriors in the city, but her younger brothers still remained, waiting for their turn to prove themselves as mighty warriors that Ares would be proud of.

Sometimes though, she wished for a different life. There had to be more to life than just fighting, and supporting the men who fought, wasn't there? After all, Ares was known as the lover of Aphrodite, Goddess of Love and Beauty. And there was Apollo, the God of Music, and Athene, who rewarded wisdom. And weapons were crafted in the forge, which was Hephaistos's domain. The production and crafting of cloth was also a vital part of their lives, so Hera, Demeter, and Hestia were to be thanked for their part in domesticity. Yet none of the other gods had any grand temples of their own in Sparta and were confined to mere shrines within homes and fields.

Kalia was a comely maiden, and already several young warriors came to her father, seeking permission to court her. However, she didn't find herself attracted to them. She wanted more in her future husband than just strength. She wanted someone she could talk to, someone to share thoughts and observations with. Her father wasn't the talkative type, and he often grunted in response to questions or comments and would look impatient when she tried to share her musings. Her mother wasn't much better, and would sometimes humor her daughter, but Kalia could tell that her mother wasn't really listening. It was not that they were cruel, which she understood, but Kalia could not help but wish things were different.

She gave out an annoyed grumble as she went into the chicken pen, scattering some of their old grain stores to the hens before checking their nests for eggs. She was able and willing to do chores, but the monotony of a Spartan existence was already wearing on her. She had entertained thoughts of running away, but where would she run to, and what could she do? She did not have the talent for dance or song or anything else that might earn her money or a living elsewhere, unless there was someone out there looking for a farmhand or a cook or weaver.

Gods, lead me on a path to a different and more interesting life, she thought as she filled her basket with eggs. The screams of her younger brothers emanated from the other side of the pen, and she saw them wrestling. They were close in age, so one brother did not have an undue advantage over the other, and she stopped to watch, grateful for this momentary amusement. Suddenly, she felt an odd tingle on the back of her neck, a rare occurrence. She had gotten it only a couple of times in the past, such as when her grandfather was about to die. Her heart started pounding. Was someone else in her family about to die? She was about to rush back to the house to warn her parents when her eyes caught a faint wavering on the horizon, almost like a heat-shimmer that she saw only in the hottest days of summer.

The air was mild and crisp, comfortable enough for anyone to work up a sweat and not feel hot, conflicting sharply with whatever it was she was seeing. As she focused on the horizon, she saw an alarming change. The green seemed to be disappearing, and even the vibrant reds and golds that were appearing on the trees around this time also faded away to a dull brown, and a... *bleakness* crept towards them.

"Jason! Ecleus! Get Mother and Father! Now!" Kalia screamed at her brothers. They stopped and looked up at her with curiosity, not comprehending the seriousness of the situation. When their eyes followed her pointed finger, they caught sight of this baffling phenomenon and did as she said. She took a step back as the *thing* approached their farm, oozing over and under the fence and devouring their crops in its fashion, leaving withered growth in its wake.

oOo

Persephone was unable to shake the nagging feeling that there was something wrong, and she put down the tablet and stylus she had been practicing with, her hands shaking slightly. She closed her eyes, trying to collect herself before blurred images flashed through her head – barren fields, starving people fighting one another, emaciated corpses lying about, mothers trying to feed their hungry babes from shriveled breasts, and wails filling the temples as people beseeched their gods to help them. This rapid-fire succession of images had her reeling back, and she opened her eyes.

The more she tried to recall these images, the less distinct they became, but her anxiety remained.

o0o

The afternoon sun shone brightly on Delphi and the people who had come to petition the Oracle to tell them their fates. The waves crashed in the distance as the wind carried with it the scent of the ocean, providing a soothing backdrop to the Oracle's meditation as she went within, doing her best to read the intricate threads that the Fates had woven.

The breeze was cool on her face, but she barely noticed it as she tried to see the future of the young man before her. Her assistants stood nearby, waiting for her to utter the man's destiny before they led him away from the pavilion.

Suddenly, the Oracle's face convulsed in pain, and her entire body stiffened. A strangled moan escaped her throat, and the maidens were immediately at her side, having never seen this before. Sometimes she might twitch a bit, or have an expression of intense concentration, but never pain. She delivered even the direst of prophecies with a calm expression, but the terror had her nearly senseless. The man took a step back when she started shaking.

The Oracle had seen plenty of twisted images in her visions – incest, rape, murder, theft, violence, but the images that were now flashing before her spoke of a dire fate on a much grander scale than she had ever seen before.

People were mobbing the estates of wealthy and the temples of the gods, gaunt-faced and wailing for food, their hands forming claws resembling those of carrion-birds as they descended onto the nobles and priests...

Neighbors fighting one another for scraps of food, friend turning against friend as they abandoned the bonds they shared with others to feed the gnawing emptiness of their stomachs...

Children with swollen and distended stomachs crying for their mothers, gnawing on pieces of leather and even eating dirt as their short lives drew to a close...

Emaciated corpses lying in the beds, slumped against chairs, splayed out on the floors, curled up in fetal positions on the fields that had once nourished them, to be eaten by vermin and flies because there was nobody left to bury them...

Thin, bedraggled priests and priestesses fervently praying to the gods to end their plight even as they cut the throat of undernourished animals, the blood spilling on the ground but offering no sustenance to human or earth...

Wild-eyed people scrambling after things they never would have put on their plates before, seeking out the last of the insects and vermin and whatever else they could get their hands on...

Orphaned waifs wandering the streets, begging alms from people who had nothing left to give...

An epic struggle for existence when there was no nourishment or sustenance, and amidst all these terrifying visions, a great, terrible figure loomed, a sickle in one hand, the other hand empty.

"There will be great famine until the child is returned to her mother!" the Oracle screeched before she fell out of her chair, slumping onto the ground, unresponsive to the frantic attempts of her attendants to revive her.

Chapter XXXIII

oOo

Since Demeter had started scourging various realms of Hellas, spreading her wrath even as Zeus refused to admit that what he had done was wrong, Persephone found herself being visited by disturbing dreams. Being in the Underworld had not completely severed her ties to the world above, and she felt its pain as if it were her own, if only on a subconscious level.

She twitched almost feverishly in her sleep as she dreamed of walking along parched fields, seeing the withered stalks of wheat and feeling their brittle crunch under her feet. What bothered her was that her Gift did not work any better here than it worked in the Underworld. The earth simply did not respond because it had no life-energy of its own for her to manipulate. The evidence of plants here had to mean that at one time, there had been plenty, according to the sheer volume of the dead growth.

The air was dry and carried the scent and taste of dust, and as she walked further, she saw the corpses of dead animals. Here the remains of a cow, desiccated skin stretched across its skeleton, and further, a coop with barely-recognizable hens, their feathers littering the yard and covered with even more dust. To her dismay, she saw tiny little lumps that could only be chicks, and she blinked back tears as she thought about the times she held these little fluffy yellow babies in her hands, cooing at them and stroking their soft fuzz. No matter where she looked or walked, all she saw was desolation.

The sight of the sea brought her relief until she came closer and saw rotting fish along the shore.

Everything felt so real that she wondered if she might be on the surface world again. If not, this had to be some... hellish region of Tartarus that she had never seen! It was as if everything that represented decay – the dried-out fields, the dust-clouds, the dead livestock and seafood, the barren forests and orchards, the houses with corpses lying about – had all been smashed up together to make a terrifying world. Nothing made sense!

She sunk to her knees, letting out a long, loud shriek. She hated this place and wanted to be away from it as far and as soon as possible!

"What are you doing here?" a voice demanded. She whipped around to see a black-garbed man standing there, staring at her with eyes that seemed to bore into her soul. She stared at him for several long moments, thinking about how much he resembled Hypnos. They had the same facial structure and lean build, but where the God of Sleep's eyes and hair were light, this man's hair and eyes were as black as his clothing, and rather than the sleepy, pleasant expression Hypnos often wore, this man's face was the exact opposite, his gaze sharp and penetrating.

"Who are you?" she demanded. He stared at her, and she glared back.

"No god may intrude upon my domain without my leave."

"I was not trying to. Where am I?"

261

"You are in the Dreaming."

Persephone shook her head slowly before gesturing to the desolation around her. "This is the realm of dreams?" she asked with obvious disbelief.

"This is what mortals dream of."

"Every mortal?"

"Of course not. This is only part of it." He sounded condescending, and she bristled, refusing to be talked down to.

"Well, I did not ask to come here or be a part of these dreams. I have not seen anyone. Except for you, of course. Who are you?"

"I am the lord of dreams."

"Aha. Morpheus. Why am I here?"

"I am just as surprised to see you here as you are to be here," he replied.

"There must be some reason I am here. I have seen this over the last few nights. I do not want to be here!"

"Despite that, you find yourself drawn to these particular dreams. This is a troubled place."

"I can tell," she replied dryly.

"Who are you, anyway?"

"Surely... you must know?" How could Morpheus be a chthonic deity and not know who she was? He stared at her blankly.

"Very well. I am Persephone."

"Ah, the bride of Aidoneus. We meet at last." He inclined his head in a slight bow.

"Why would mortals dream of such a horrible place?" she asked.

"Dreams are not always about people's wishes or

fantasies. Dreams also serve as prophecy, and are often a reflection of reality, or the truth that people try to hide from in the waking world."

"Hmm." She frowned thoughtfully. What did that have to do with her? "Is there nothing I can do?"

"You cannot change anything in the Dreaming. This is my domain."

"That is not what I meant. Far be it for me to try to interfere in someone else's realm. I simply meant, how can I stop myself from coming here? It does not make sense that I keep coming back here, and I have no desire to be in this... dreadful place."

"The Dreaming is affected by what happens in reality, and vice-versa. There must be a connection between you and what is happening in reality. Sometimes dreams offer an answer."

Was it just her, or did the chthonic deities enjoy talking in riddles? Before she could ask another question, the visage of Morpheus and this bleak realm wavered for a moment before disappearing and Persephone gasped softly, opening her eyes to find herself in the familiar surroundings of Hades's bedchamber.

She sat up in bed, careful to not rouse the Lord of the Dead as he slept peacefully at her side. As she was about to climb out of bed, a pale, strong arm reached out to pull her back, and she found herself enveloped in a strong embrace.

"Mm, where do you think you are going, my love?"

"I could not sleep," she replied softly.

"Is something the matter?"

"I just.... had a bad dream."

"Oh? Want to tell me about it?"

"No."

"Are you certain?" he asked gently. She nodded, thinking of the horrible desolation in her dreams, and Morpheus's cryptic words.

"Is there anything I can do to make you feel better?"

"I do not know," she muttered. He rubbed her bare arms, nuzzling her shoulder.

"There *must* be something I can do to comfort you."

"Perhaps."

"You know I can do much better than a *perhaps*," he whispered into her ear. She could not help but smile at the obvious concern he was showing, and the affection that he promised. A distraction provided by the skilled and attractive Lord of the Underworld was as good a distraction as any.

"Show me, then."

"Gladly," he replied, pulling her back down as he started to rain kisses along her face.

oOo

Several guards stood around the clearing, watching the four princesses of Eleusis as they relaxed by the well, drawing water from it and cooling themselves on this unusually warm autumn day. Tired of the confinement of the small Palace, the girls had pleaded with their parents to allow them an outing to the hills just outside of the Palace, and with all the worries that had been besieging the family lately, Celeus decided to let them out so they could enjoy themselves. Of course, there were soldiers accompanying them, ready to escort them back at the first sign of danger, but the girls were hardly ones to complain. They had explored the hills, gathering berries and gorging themselves on many of them as they enjoyed the cold water they drew from the well.

Thalassa sat in the grass as her younger sisters played tag, laughing and running around the clearing, forgetting their worries for the time being. The harvest this year promised to be meager, so they would have to ration their food to last through the winter. This meant that they would have very little to try to bribe the warlords with unless they wanted to go hungry. The man who sought her hand was a disgusting man with a scraggly beard, foul body odor, most of his teeth missing from his head, and a leer in his eye that made it clear that he saw women as something to be used as he saw fit, so she could not expect to have a husband who treated her like Father treated Mother. Demophon drew closer to death, becoming paler and thinner every day at an age where he should be learning how to walk. All their prayers and sacrifices had been for naught. Why did the gods ignore their pleas?

"Halt!" she heard one of the men shout. Her head whipped up to see a solitary figure meander through the trees along the thin path. It appeared to be an old woman, slow of step and stooped over.

"Stand down," Thalassa said, raising her hand. The guard remained where he was, his spear raised, but he made no move towards the newcomer. The woman – at least, Thalassa was certain it was a she – was wrapped in a worn dark gray cloak.

"Who might you be?" Thalassa asked as her sisters stopped their playing to stare at the visitor.

"Ahh, child. You may call me Doso."

"Doso, you look so tired. Come and sit down." Thalassa had removed her cloak because it was so warm, and folded it to make a comfortable seat. She guided the old woman to it and helped her sit down.

"Would you like some water?" Eirene, the youngest of the girls, asked.

"Oh, that would be so nice. Thank you!" she said, lifting her face, showing a network of wrinkles around a pair of bright, yellow-green eyes. Eirene quickly hastened to draw up another bucket of water, carrying it to Doso and scooping out a cupful with the ladle they had brought with them. The old woman gulped up the contents of the ladle, and Eirene was quick to refill it.

After Doso was sated, she beamed at the girls cheerfully. "Thank you for such kindness to a little old woman."

"It would be very rude of us to not offer hospitality," Thalassa replied matter-of-factly. "But what were you doing alone? Do you live in the city?"

"Oh, I am afraid not, dear. Pirates raided my village and killed so many men, and took the rest as slaves. I managed to escape, and have been wandering for days. I cannot return to my village, it is in ruins and I have no more family."

The four girls stared at her in shock and

sympathy.

"Would you like to come home with us?" Thalassa offered.

"You would take in an old woman?"

"Of course. Come with us, please."

"You are too kind!" Doso beamed at them, feeling warmed by their generosity towards a stranger. "Oh, I do not know your names!"

"I am Thalassa. This is Melinoe..." She gestured to the girl who was a couple of years younger than herself, "and Aethra..." She pointed at the next younger girl, "And Eirene." The youngest sister waved at Doso.

"Would you like some berries too? We have been gathering them." She gestured to several baskets, and the old woman nodded. After eating a handful, she glanced at the girls. Thalassa remained near while the other girls went back to playing.

"How do you feel?" Thalassa asked, her brown eyes twinkling warmly.

"The water and berries were good for my body, but the kindness you have shown nourishes my soul," she replied. Thalassa draped her arm across Doso's shoulders companionably, giving the old woman a gentle squeeze.

o0o

Demeter was silent as the girls led her into the Palace. She was even more impressed by their hospitality when they revealed that they were princesses. They could have just turned her loose in

267

the city, but no, they were actually inviting her into the Palace! She could see that they had good hearts, and for the first time in so long, felt her heart warmed. So many of the mortals she had encountered would ignore her, or act inappropriately, especially when she was in the guise of an old woman. It disgusted her that people would ignore the laws of hospitality, but she felt all the more justified for spreading the famine. These girls would certainly be shocked if they knew that hunger and misery followed her step!

However, her wrath was mollified by the kindness of these girls, and she maintained her guise as Thalassa led her through the courtyard. She glanced at the garden, her eyes meeting the insolent stare of a young man that to her resembled vermin, with his beady eyes and pointed nose.

"Oh, that is Abas, the gardener. Ignore him," Thalassa whispered as she helped the old woman up the steps. The cries of a baby broke the silence, but the wail was thin and reedy, and died away with a gasp. Demeter did not miss the stiffening of the maiden's shoulders at the cry.

They entered a spacious chamber that had a weaving loom at one end, and a table at the other. Near the window, a middle-aged but modestly attractive woman sat, cradling a baby against her chest, trying to comfort it. She looked up as the girls entered with their companion.

"Greetings, Mother. This is Doso. She came to us when we were at the well. Her family and village were destroyed by pirates, but she managed to escape

268

and has been wandering for days. I told her she could stay in Eleusis if that pleases you."

"Oh, of course. Pirates, what a dreadful thing! Why must people turn to such evil these days?" the older woman replied. "Welcome to Eleusis, Doso. I am Queen Metaniera. We might not have much to offer, but you are welcome to rest here until you find a place of your own to stay."

"Your hospitality is much appreciated." Demeter took several steps forward, eying the bundle in the Queen's arms. "When I was outside, I heard a cry. Was that from this baby?" she asked. Metaniera sighed softly and nodded, sadness written clearly on her face as she glanced down at the child. As if on cue, the baby started crying again, and like before, his wails were lacking the robustness that a healthy child possessed.

"Might I see him? I am good with children, and I can try to comfort him."

oOo

Normally, Metaniera was wary of anyone else handling her child, but Doso's eyes were filled with such warmth and kindness that she could not help but feel a bond with the old woman. She nodded and gently deposited Demophon into Doso's waiting arms.

"Oh, look at you," the old woman clucked gently, rocking Demophon gently as the child squirmed and cried.

"We have tried everything. But no matter what

269

we do..." Metaniera shook her head.

"Oh, I know. This child is not sick for lack of love or care, I can see that. At least the Fates have been kind enough to give him a mother who loves him." Doso's tone was understanding, and Metaniera found herself liking this woman more and more. As she watched, Doso crooned to Demophon as she rocked him, and the child's fitful crying ceased.

"I can see that his sickness has taken a toll on you. Would you let me earn my keep by taking care of him when you have other matters to attend to? Even mothers need rest."

Metaniera glanced at the wizened crone thoughtfully, seeing how peaceful Demophon looked in her arms. It was a given that Demophon would die soon, but if this woman could offer some comfort to him in the final days of his short life, then so be it. Perhaps Fate had brought her here for a reason.

oOo

Persephone stared up as the sky above Hades's garden started to darken, tightening her wrap against the cool air, thinking about her dreams and the unsettling visions she had. Mother was angry, that much was starkly clear. What exactly was she angry about? Had she finally learned where her daughter was? She wondered if her mother would ever accept the fact that her daughter was no longer a little girl.

She would never be Kora again. That girl was dead in a sense, lost to the inevitable march of Time. Persephone had to admit that while she missed her mother, part of her was actually afraid of facing the woman who had given birth to her. What if Mother tried to change her back to a girl? Doubtless Mother would try to prevent her from ever seeing Hades again.

If she was ever to have a relationship with her mother again, things would have to be different, because there was simply no way that things would go back to the way they had once been. Nor did she wish to return to Mother's custody, with Demeter breathing down her back whenever she wasn't off performing her duties as a Goddess. Persephone looked down at her hands. What kind of Gifts did she have other than making things grow? What could she be a Goddess of? What were the abilities that the Fates claimed she had?

She closed her eyes, dozing off lightly as she sat there, meditating.

"Surely you would be more comfortable in my bed rather than under the tree." Hades's playful voice broke through her reverie, and she opened her eyes, seeing him standing there with an open pomegranate in one hand.

"Hmm... oh! I just dozed off when I was meditating," she replied. He shrugged and smiled, sitting with her as he popped several seeds into his mouth. Persephone had adjusted to the lack of sunlight, so in the darkness, she wasn't blind. The seeds glistened wetly amidst the pale flesh of the fruit, and she stared at it for several moments, wondering what it would taste like.

Almost as if he sensed her thoughts, he extended

271

his hand in offering, and she fought the urge to lick her lips. The seeds shone like polished garnets, promising a juicy reward to whoever ate it. It was forbidden fruit, so why did she want it so much? She longed to pluck a seed and pop it into her mouth and just bite down on it, and suck down the sweet jelly...

"Please share this with me, love," Hades whispered, his voice both pleading and seductive.

"You just love tempting me, do you not?"

"Temptation implies that I am trying to get you to do something naughty," he shot back lightly.

"You certainly have tempted me often enough." She smirked, her eyes twinkling at the memories of shared pleasure.

"Very well then," he shot back just as playfully, "But you must admit, being naughty is fun."

"I do not know about that..." She batted her eyes at him.

"You do not know? Mmm, let me remind you." He leaned in, pulling her in for a kiss. She parted her lips eagerly, glad for a distraction from that damned fruit. She ran her tongue against his lips and jerked back violently as she tasted the sweet, lingering flavor of pomegranate. Hades blinked and frowned with concern, staring down at her intently.

"What is the matter?"

"Your lips... I could taste the pomegranate." The taste still lingered in her mouth, tart and sweet and rich. She actually wanted more!

"Oh." He touched his lips with his fingers. Persephone felt light-headed. What if that taste forever condemned her to the Underworld, to never see the surface again? She felt his hands on her shoulders.

"Do not look so frightened, Seph. A kiss does not count as food of the dead." He lightly pressed his fingers under her chin, tilting her face up to look at him.

"Really?"

"Certainly. I have no desire to trick you. You can enjoy my kisses all you want."

"Promise?"

"Promise." He smiled before he lowered his head to kiss her again. She kissed him hungrily, relishing the lingering flavor of the fruit.

"Aidon..." she sighed softly as he broke the kiss to nuzzle her throat, peppering it with even more kisses. Suddenly, he lifted his head, and she looked at him quizzically before following his gaze, seeing a shade hover several feet away. The shade spoke in its odd, almost inaudible whisper-hiss, and Hades nodded, rising to his feet. He turned back to her, offering his hand and helping her to her feet.

"Get ready for bed, love. I will join you shortly."

"Where are you going?"

"I am needed urgently."

Before she could ask him to be more specific, he ushered her up the stairs firmly.

"Is something the matter? What is going on?"

"Just something I need to do as Lord of the Underworld," he replied evasively before disappearing. When she tried to leave the lavish apartment, she discovered that the door was sealed, much to her irritation.

273

oOo

Hades's dark robes billowed around him as he appeared on his throne, startling Hermes and causing him to flinch back.

"Hey, warn people when you do that!" the younger god muttered. His uncle merely smirked coldly at him.

"Tell me why you are here." the Lord of the Dead stated. "I assume you have a message from Zeus." He sounded almost bored as if what Zeus or anyone else might say was of no concern to him.

"Demeter is angry. Please, return Kora to her!"

This news did not surprise him. He knew of what had happened with Styx. How had his sister found out? Had Zeus finally confessed to her?

"No."

"Demeter is ravaging Hellas and says she will not stop unless she has Kora back. Zeus has commanded that she stop what she is doing, but she refuses. And now, nobody can find her!"

"My sister does have a flair for the melodramatic at times. But the same can be said for my brother..." Hades stroked his chin.

"She will stop if you let her see her daughter."

"She will just take Persephone away from me."

"... Persephone?"

"Kora is an unsuitable name for her. She is no longer a little girl."

"... Oh. But what about the mortals above? Demeter has said she will not restore the harvest until

274

her daughter is returned to her."

"That is out of the question. Once she accepts the fact that her daughter is no longer a child, then I will consider allowing them to see one another. Besides, I know that it is Zeus who triggered her wrath." He smiled thinly. "I know my brother too well."

"That is what you want me to tell her?"

"Certainly. Feel free to assure her that Persephone is safe and well. Doubtless she has feared abuse or violation, but you can also tell her there has been no such thing."

Hermes looked at Hades with curiosity. "No violation? But, you kidnapped her and..."

Hades's expression hardened. "I am not a brute like Ares."

"Very well, then. So I am supposed to tell Demeter that her daughter is safe, but you still will not let her see her. That is not going to help."

"You can tell my sister that I never had any intention to hurt her. I do care for her. I did not do this to spite or worry her, but she would not have allowed me to court Persephone. You have seen what happened with other men. I saw no other recourse, though I sincerely wish things could have worked out better."

"What if Demeter still refuses?"

"Then I have no choice but to keep Persephone down here." The Dark God's tone was calm but carried an undertone of iron-hard certainty. Hermes swallowed and nodded.

o0o

The threads of the cosmic tapestry that the Fates wove resembled a spider web in a way and often manifested itself as such to the mortal eye. In mortal art and visions, Fate took many different forms, and to some, she – or they – was a spider that forever spun the threads of life, designing a web far more intricate than anyone – mortal or god – could ever imagine.

As ordered as the universe was, chaos also existed. Balance could not exist without two opposing forces, and Fate was no exception. Sometimes, the cosmic threads that guided destiny moved on their own, turning into a different direction than had been laid out for it, much like a vine that did not wish to grow in the path that its gardener had established for it despite careful guidance and pruning.

"Look at that," Klotho whispered, pointing to a thin, almost invisible thread. It was barely noticeable amidst the glittering and multi-colored strands that surrounded it or the blue thread that it was already attached to, and was little more than a wisp as if it were but the phantom image of a thread. Many such threads existed, appearing briefly on the tapestry before disappearing, having no effect on the other strands within the web. The only thing that set this one apart from many of its ilk was the longer, stronger thread that clung to it tenaciously. Such instances had happened in the past, but these thin wisps of threads always slipped away, no matter what was there to hold onto them. This particular thread was about to break away and fade into nothingness. But now, a bright, shining golden-green thread was also intertwined with this little strand. Such a thread was not mortal in origin, and clearly belonged to a goddess, for the threads of the gods were always far longer and radiant than anybody else's.

"Fascinating," Lakhesis murmured, gazing intently at the configuration of threads that surrounded it.

As this shining cord wrapped around the other two threads, an extraordinary thing happened. This little wisp of a strand – a short and weak life indeed – actually started to lengthen, and its end – the part of life that had not been lived yet – became thicker, taking on a faint green hue, safely nestled between the green-gold of the new thread, and the soft blue thread that it was attached to.

"The loss of one child has saved the life of another," Atropos stated. She made no move to cut the newly grown thread, and let it be, leaving it to find its place within the cosmic web.

Chapter XXXIV

o0o

Metaniera smiled wistfully as she stood in the doorway, watching as Doso sang softly to Demophon. The baby was quiet, nestled against his nurse's chest. It had just been a couple of days, and already Demophon was a calmer baby. Knowing that her child was under the care of a competent and caring individual allowed her to relax somewhat and to be able to better concentrate on the rest of her family and kingdom. Just now, she had been able to enjoy supper with her family, and talk about various matters uninterrupted by the pained wails of her son.

Doso looked up, a smile on her wrinkled features.

"He has been a good boy. A bit of fussing, but nothing that some singing cannot take care of."

"How are you able to manage so well?" Metaniera asked.

"Oh, you raise enough children and grandchildren, you learn a thing or two. They always responded well to my voice, so I saw no reason to not try singing to Demophon."

"I wish I could sing as well."

"Oh, my lady, everyone has their own talents. It does not mean you are any less of a mother. Is that right, Demophon? You know your mother loves you very much?"

To Metaniera's surprise, she actually heard a soft giggle from the child. It was a small sound, barely two gurgling laughs, but she found herself floored.

She had never heard her baby laugh!

"He looks about ready to settle down for the night," Doso stated.

"I think I will spend some time with my daughters. It has been a while since I sat down with them."

"Certainly. We will be waiting here. Go, enjoy yourselves."

Metaniera smiled before disappearing from the doorway. Demophon was quiet for several moments, and his nurse was about to put him back in the cradle when he started fussing again.

oOo

"Hmm, what's wrong?" Demeter asked, drawing the child back to her bosom. "Are you hungry?"

She shifted around, adjusting her cowl and chiton. With a deft movement, she exposed a breast that contrasted sharply with her wrinkled face. The infant latched onto a full and plump tit, pressing his little face against the warm mound and sucking the nourishing milk that issued from it.

Demeter let out a low sigh of satisfaction. Since she was the Goddess of Bounty, she could produce any kind of bounty upon command, and for Demophon, her breast-milk flowed afresh. It comforted her immensely to feel that small suction on her breast, and she relaxed, letting the babe have his fill. She cooed softly as she stroked his hair, cradling him close to keep him warm as she stared distantly at the small fire that danced in the hearth.

The baby smacked his lips contentedly after he had his fill. Demeter smiled as she covered herself up before lightly poking the baby's arms. He giggled and waved his arms – something he had not done in a long time – and she continued, letting him grab her fingers on occasion. His grip was weak, but at least he was trying to hold onto her. Before, he had not had the strength to even reach for anything.

Carefully, she unwrapped him and tickled his feet. There was not much movement, but he did giggle and squirm around. This activity tired him quickly, and Demeter wrapped him up again, placing him in the cradle as she sang to him. He slept soundly, his breathing slightly shallow but otherwise steady.

She moved to the loom, resuming her work. Though she wasn't quite as proficient as her elder or younger sisters at the art of the loom, she was still very skilled at the craft and often used weaving as a distraction. She would sit at the loom and simply let her fingers dance along the threads. Kora had never cared much for weaving, and would often sneak away when she had been left alone to weave. And when she did weave, she made her fabric as plain as possible, not wishing to spend the extra time in weaving patterns, so as to complete her task more quickly. No matter how many times Demeter had tried to encourage or scold her daughter, Kora never showed any passion or affection for the craft, which was disappointing because women should learn how to weave. The domestic arts were indispensable!

But oh, if she could see her daughter again, she

would just hug her close! The Underworld was a terrifying place, and she dreaded to imagine what her poor baby must be going through. It was simply unfair that Zeus and Hades had conspired against her over the welfare of her own daughter! What was this world coming to if a mother was not allowed to care for her own child?

She started working the loom more furiously, pouring her frustrations into the process, her hands moving rapidly across the fabric as she worked row after row.

"Doso? *Doso!*" she heard Metaniera say, and looked up, snapped out of her furious reverie.

"Pardon me, my lady. I was so intent on my work." It felt odd to speak to a mortal this way, but Demeter was intent on keeping her guise.

"There is no need for pardons, Doso. I am just here to take Demophon. Please, weave for as long as you like. We have more material in the storeroom if you like. Enjoy your evening."

"I will." Demeter nodded slowly, gazing at Metaniera as she scooped her slumbering child from the cradle.

oOo

Demophon barely stirred in her arms, but his breathing was even, much to her relief. Metaniera glanced down at him as she retired to the bedchamber she shared with her husband. Celeus stood by the window, wearing a warm robe over his tunic. As she entered, he glanced at her, and she was warmed by the affection in his eyes.

Rarely did happy marriages last, especially royal ones, but she was lucky. Even now, twenty-five years after she married the then-Prince of Eleusis, he looked at her with the same affection that he had on their wedding night. His eyes never strayed to a servant girl or city maiden, and he was also an attentive father to their children, sons and daughters alike. When it was discovered that Demophon was sickly, he hadn't made the decision to leave him outside to die, as the Spartans would have.

oOo

"How is he?" Celeus whispered as Metaniera set him down in the carved wooden cradle.

"Quiet and sleeping well. I do not know how Doso does it, but he actually looks content," Metaniera said. Celeus walked over to the bundled-up baby, noting the placid expression on Demophon's face. His cheeks were still hollow, but he was no longer so pale.

"That he does." He stared down at Demophon for a moment, wondering if this meant that perhaps, just perhaps, his son might get better. Children died every day, that was a fact of life, but that didn't mean he liked it or wanted to accept it. No child should die. He gently tucked the blankets under his son's chin, a fond smile flashing for a moment on his face. Certainly, he had been surprised when his daughters brought home an old woman, but the laws of hospitality were to be honored, and it looked as if

282

their kindness was being repaid. Metaniera liked Doso, and he saw no reason to not let the old woman stay. She had a kind appearance, though he found himself slightly unnerved by her vivid green eyes.

"The baby is getting his rest. We should, as well," Celeus whispered, cupping his wife's cheek with a hand, giving her a loving smile. The kingdom was beleaguered with many worries, among these the meager harvest. Already the family was rationing their own food, and Metaniera had plans to hide some of this year's harvest in their storeroom. Hopefully, he could find a way to budget the food for the city and see if they could reach some sort of compromise with the bandits outside the city. Only recently, he had been hearing that other cities were having disastrous harvests. When he was nestled in bed with his wife, he could allow himself to set aside his worries for a while.

"Yes." Her eyes gleamed in the firelight, and he smiled. Even now, with crow's feet around her eyes and gray in her black hair, she was still beautiful to him. She touched her hand to his own and returned his smile.

oOo

Abas slunk around the Palace grounds. It was easy to do so, since most of the soldiers were stationed around the perimeter of the Palace walls, leaving the rest of the Palace less guarded. He was familiar with the layout, having grown up here with his father as the former gardener.

He didn't like it here. The guards looked down at him, and the princesses would not give him any notice. He was the kind of person who was perpetually unhappy with his lot, and always found something to complain about. It mattered not that he had three square meals a day, a roof over his head, walls to be safe behind, and a steady job that had been handed to him for the virtue of being the son of the former holder of the job. He often entertained fantasies of being rich and powerful, of telling others what to do instead of being told what to do. He would have girls finer than the snaggle-toothed kitchen maid who had laughed him out of the pile of straw she slept on because he hadn't been well-endowed, and had 'ended' so quickly.

Of course, if he hadn't been such a self-centered person, he might have realized that Caliroe would have been considerably more forgiving of his physical shortcomings if he had been an attentive lover and had listened to her instead of focusing on his own pleasure. But because he believed that nothing that happened was ever his fault, he had convinced himself that it was because Caliroe was an uppity little bitch. Just like Celeus's daughters.

He groused to himself silently as he crept around the pillars, thinking about the small stash of treasure he had managed to steal over the last few years. The Royal Family of Eleusis was by no means immensely wealthy, especially compared to other city-states such as Thebes or Sparta. Their income was modest, and most of it went back out to various things needed for the city, including its army. But once in a while, he was able to pilfer a coin and even had a couple of earrings and necklaces among other trinkets. He had gained no small amount of pleasure from overhearing Thalassa lamenting the loss of her pearl necklace the other day. He had carefully buried his stash throughout the garden; the last place he was certain anyone would look.

He knew that it was a risk. If he had been caught stealing anything, it could and would warrant an execution, or if he was lucky, exile or some kind of disfigurement. But he enjoyed the thrill and the perverse pleasure to be gained from lashing out at the royal family in this way. He felt no sympathy at all to Metaniera for having a sickly baby. He didn't understand why she had to cry over it. He had seen Demophon a couple of times and didn't see why anyone should make such a fuss over a baby that was going to die anyway.

After stealing some dates from the kitchen storeroom – something that was frowned upon because Celeus insisted that everybody within the household ration their food – he slid out to the large inner courtyard. The fountain no longer spouted water, but the pool was still almost full. He drew from it to water the gardens and was glad for that convenience. He hated doing any more work than was absolutely necessary.

As he casually munched on one of the dates, Abas noticed a cloaked figure slowly moving along the edge of the courtyard almost like a ghost. The crescent moon above offered limited light, but he had been lurking around in the darkness long enough to be able to see adequately. Oh, it was that old woman that Thalassa had brought in. What was the point in letting her take care of that stupid sick baby, and feeding her when they were already on rations? Celeus was a daft old fool. Had Abas been king, he would have left the baby to die and kicked the old woman out. Bah. People were so stupid.

"What are you doing out here?" Abas asked, barely holding back the contempt in his tone.

"You are the gardener, are you not?" the old woman replied. Before Abas could answer, she continued, "I am merely out for a little stroll. Have no mind of me."

"Out for a stroll? This is not your place. I thought you were here to take care of Demophon." He crossed his arms.

"Certainly, but he is with his mother now, and I do need to stretch out my legs. Not my place, you say? Big words from a lowly gardener."

"Lowly?" Abas spat out, "My father and grandfather were gardeners here. You are just a useless old woman that Thalassa picked up from outside. You are lucky that the King and Queen let you stay here!"

"You have quite a mouth on you, hmm?"

"I will not stand here and let an old lady scold me," he retorted hotly.

"I suppose you were never taught to respect your elders."

"What is it to you?" Abas didn't know why, but something about the old lady unnerved him. He felt a sudden urge to strike Doso, or chase her away with a rake.

"I am shocked that such kind people like Celeus and Metaniera have a person such as you in their midst. You do not seem like a happy or grateful person to me."

"Mind your tongue."

"Ha! This coming from the man who has the temerity to look at the royal family the way he does! You do not care about anybody but yourself. That family has been through a lot, yet they have such kindness in their hearts as to put themselves on rations when they ask it of their servants, or welcome a poor woman who lost her child, into their home."

"Oh, boohoo, who cares about your child? Your kid probably deserved to die, anyway!" he replied contemptuously. Suddenly, the old woman seemed to almost explode, her cloak billowing around her. Abas gasped and jerked back, trying to convince himself that it had been a mere illusion, a trick of the light, but Doso now suddenly towered over him, broad-shouldered, her eyes almost glowing as the hood fell away to reveal the visage of a much younger-looking woman.

"You refuse to see how fortunate you are, and you take your unhappiness out on everybody else, Abas. Since this life dissatisfies you so, I will remedy that for you! You should be so fortunate that the Goddess of the Harvest is so willing to help you!"

Abas felt a tight, constricting feeling around his chest, and feared for a moment that she meant to take his life away in a literal sense. But suddenly, she was even taller than before, towering over him much like the Titans of old when they had terrorized the mortals. He saw her lift her sandaled foot, and how *huge* it was!

Run, run, run, he thought, snapping into panic mode as he turned and fled. Goddess of the Harvest! Gods above, he had enraged *Demeter!* Already he was regretting his actions – not because he had hurt her feelings or offended her, but because she was angry with him and he feared punishment above all else, especially from such a powerful deity.

Everything seemed so enormous! The plants towered over him, and there were walls where there shouldn't have been. He tried to comprehend just what exactly had happened, why everything had changed, why even his own vision seemed different. The colors and focus were different, and he no longer ran on two legs, but four.

He only barely registered all of this as he was so intent on fleeing the wrathful deity. His tiny heart beat at a pace far faster than that of any human being, and the capacity of his brain was focused entirely on his survival. He barely noticed when he was able to climb up the wall, and skittered up it, feeling the cool air on his scaly flesh as he reached the top. He took no time to appreciate the view that lay before him, especially since he no longer had the human capacity to see all of this clearly.

He sped along the edge of the wall, frantically wondering what he should do, his human soul conflicting with the constraints of his new body. However, he was able to collect himself for a moment, trying to ponder his next choice of action.

He needed to hide from the wrathful goddess, but where?

A sudden screech broke the silence, and he instinctively darted forward again, his instincts telling him to *hide*, to duck for cover because that screech certainly meant *death!*

Abas was about to scamper down the wall when a sharp, searing pain tore through his side, knocking the wind out of his lungs. He found himself torn away from his foothold and lifted through the air, flailing his small arms and legs, his tail whipping around furiously before his struggles ceased.

oOo

In the Underworld, Persephone usually wore ankle-length clothing since it was so cool here, but today, she was clad in a chiton that ended just below her knees, and the wrap she wore terminated below her hips. She felt a bit under-dressed, but Hades had wanted her to dress this way for what he said was a surprise. Since his surprises were always fun even if some of them might be unusual, she was eager to see what it might be.

She waited patiently in the garden, lifting her head when she heard the clip-clop of hooves. Did he mean to take her on another chariot ride? Hades came into view riding his own horse, looking striking and regal atop the intimidating creature. Even though she admired the beautiful steeds of Hades, she was also a bit frightened by them. They were the first horses she had ever seen before in her life, and if she had seen

289

horses on the surface world, she would have noted that these hell-horses were larger and stronger than their mortal counterparts. She had never seen Hades riding a horse, and gazed up at him as the horse trotted gracefully towards her, lacking the chariot she usually saw behind it.

"I thought that we might go for a ride," Hades stated as he looked down at her. He looked relaxed in a knee-length dark blue tunic, his hair pulled back in a loose ponytail.

"Where do I sit?" she shot back, though she already had a good idea of just where she would be sitting. He grinned and reached down, pulling her up onto the horse. She sat in front of him, her back against his chest as she felt his thighs squeeze her hips gently. The horse had no reins, but Hades controlled it effectively by holding onto the mane with one hand as the other arm wrapped around her middle. She felt tall at this height and looked down at the ground.

"Do mortals really ride horses like this?" she asked.

"Indeed, though one has to be careful how he does it." He smiled at her.

The horse started off at an easy trot, and Persephone instinctively allowed her body to sway slightly with it, feeling safe in Hades's embrace as he led the creature through one of the garden gates. The vista that opened up before them was a grassy meadow, the sky bright and blue as an ethereal breeze blew across the blades, causing them to sway in gentle waves. As he urged the steed on faster, the wind whipped through her hair, and she gave out a delighted laugh.

o0o

Hades smiled and gave her a squeeze before he pushed his horse even faster, knowing how much she enjoyed speed – their rides in his chariot evidenced that.

It was the first time he had ever had anyone with him when he went horseback riding, and he enjoyed the sound of her laugh and the way she squeezed his arm, her warm body pressed against his. Though his steed was fast – much faster than a mortal horse – he was agile and graceful, so the ride itself was pleasant and enjoyable with a minimal amount of bouncing. It was this bit of being jolted around that added thrill to the ride, and he let out a whoop of his own that was quickly accompanied by her shriek of delight as the ebony steed bounded over a small knoll, soaring gracefully through the air.

o0o

Persephone's heart was still pounding as the horse slowed down, and she eyed the sparkle of light reflected off waves as they came up to the shores of the Sea of Eternity. She found herself scooped up in his arms as he slid off the stallion before he spun her around, causing her loose braid to swing around.

To her surprise, the grass was not as coarse as one might expect, but felt rather soft. The blades gave

291

away easily when she sat down, but were also amazingly springy, making for a comfortable seat. Hades sprawled out next to her, his arms bare as he carried no cloak, and he glanced up at her fondly. She smiled back. Several meters away, the horse lowered his head to eat, casually munching on the grass as his onyx coat gleamed under the light that filled the sky despite the lack of a sun.

As her pulse slowed to its regular pace, she tightened her wrap. The atmosphere was pleasant and the breeze was mild, but without the natural warmth that sunlight brought, this place – just like any other place in the Underworld – carried an undeniable touch of cold. When his arms wrapped around her, she leaned against him, closing her eyes.

They did not speak, and she simply relished his presence, snuggling against him as she felt a light kiss on her temple. His scent enveloped her – faintly earthy, though quite different from her mother's bountiful-earth smell – along with that subtle musky odor that was uniquely male. There were traces of other things she could not quite identify, things she wanted to describe but couldn't find just the right words to do so. She might describe one of these odors as an underground pool, and another trace made her think of the night air mixed with a hint of smoke. A note of sharp rawness would have been identified as ash. Hades truly was a complex and fascinating man, though she did know what he liked, and would sometimes use her knowledge to manipulate him into doing what she wanted. Although she had not yet discovered the key to him allowing her to go to the surface world... *Yet.*

But of course, she was not going to give up. As much as she enjoyed Hades's company, she had other needs. The Lord of the Underworld was just as adept at getting her to forget these needs as she was at manipulating him, and she gave out a soft sigh as he squeezed her more tightly. She had fantasized about what it would be like to have coitus with him, to lay back and spread herself for him and let him take her properly. How would it feel to be filled up by him, to feel his heated flesh deep within hers? There were times when she was tempted to just give herself up on the spot and just let Hades ravish her – and based on previous intimate experiences with him, he could do a *very* thorough job. Had she had her choice of any man she wanted, would she ever experience such emotion and passion with anyone else?

"Aidon?" she whispered.

"Hmm?"

"I... there is something I would like to ask you."

"Certainly."

She opened her eyes and craned her neck to look up at him.

"Nothing actually *grows* down here, right?"

"Correct."

"Would a child grow?" she asked. Hades glanced at her, furrowing his eyebrows in curiosity.

"Do you mean the children in Elysium? They can have the form of adults if they want to."

"No, not that. I mean, the laws of nature... well, I mean, Underworld nature, they are different from those of the mortal world and I understand that,

293

but..." She closed her eyes for a moment, trying to gather her thoughts and word them in a way that made sense, "If I tried to plant a seed here, it would not grow. If you planted a seed, would it grow?"

"I might be Lord of the Underworld, but even I cannot command things to grow," he replied lightly. She shook her head.

"No. I mean, *your* seed."

"My seed? Hmm? *Oh!*" His eyes widened in understanding.

"Yes."

"No." His voice was calm.

"Hmm." She couldn't say she was disappointed. It wasn't that she was averse to the idea of children, but she knew she wasn't ready to be a mother. And goodness, how Mother might react to her own child having a child!

"Life cannot begin in the Underworld. It never has. The food of the dead would never nourish a child, even in your belly. Being the Lord of the Dead requires sacrifice on my part."

She looked down, nodding.

"I am sorry, Persephone."

"Do not be. I was just... curious." She looked back up at him before squeezing his hand reassuringly. "I will admit that I have been thinking of... intimacy with you. But I know what that leads to, so I just wanted to clarify, you know..."

"I suppose we would have had to talk about this sooner or later, hmm?"

o0o

"Yes." She stared off at the vista for several moments, and Hades watched her. She didn't seem sad or angry, but she didn't look happy, either. Not having children didn't bother him the least, but he hadn't considered how she might feel about the subject until she had brought it up just now.

"Does that knowledge bother you?" he asked. He wondered if she would plead with him now to be allowed to return to the surface world.

"No. I suppose I should not be surprised, given this place..." She took a slow breath. "Hey, let's go for a swim!" she said, looking at him. She had noticed the sad expression on his face, surmising that he would feel sorrowful for not having children. She would have been surprised and flattered if she had known that he was thinking of her request to go to the surface world at that moment, and was actually considering it.

Fortunately for him, she did not know. The change of subject surprised him, but he welcomed the distraction, and smiled at her as she rose to her feet before he chased after her.

Chapter XXXV

oOo

The Sea of Eternity turned from a dark black-blue shade into cheery degrees of bright teal and turquoise, its waves crashing on a shore of golden-silver sand that shone white under a clear sky. The horses easily sped across the water and landed on the shore, waves lapping around their hooves as they took a momentary pause. Persephone lifted her hands from the mane of the horse she was riding and stretched her arms above her head. It had been a bit scary riding her own horse, but it was already well-trained, and merely had to follow the lead of the other horse, allowing her to ride it comfortably without having to worry about steering. She was happy to simply ride wherever Hades led her, gripping the mane of her steed as the two of them went for a delightful ride.

In the distance, she could see other islands that were as lovely as this one. According to Hades, these islands sat at the fringes of Elysium and held strange and wonderful secrets. Not even the residents of Elysium could come here.

"I have not been to the Blessed Isles in many years," Hades said as he nudged his horse into a casual pace, and Persephone's horse followed. "Long ago, I had a palace built here for my use, and I thought you would like to see it."

Lush palm trees gave way to a low whitewashed wall that revealed to be the first of several terraces that climbed up to a palatial structure of clean white stone. It was considerably smaller than the one they lived in, but no less beautiful. At the bottom of the terraces was a beach with perfectly clear waters partially enclosed by a gently curving lagoon and sandbar. Here and there on the sand, exotic shells gleamed with the sheen of jewels.

Hades dismounted his horse before helping Persephone off hers, pressing her to his body for a moment. The horses were left on the beach as he led her up the stairs, coming to the highest terrace. The terraces were filled with a lush variety of flowers and plants. There was a hot spring to the left, surrounded by multicolored tiles and making for an inviting scene, steam rising gently off its surface. At the other side, there was a comfortable divan and a low table, so one could dine outside.

The small Palace was airy, with high ceilings and an open layout. The back of the Palace revealed a garden that was almost like a jungle, and rather than being decorated with murals or frescoes, the walls of the interior and exterior were plain, giving the rooms a clean and open quality. The floors were tiled with different kinds of marble, some of them varying shades of cool blue with green and purple veins while others were tawny or rust with ochre and golden streaks. All of the rooms afforded splendid views of their tropical surroundings.

A grand staircase led them up to the second floor, which offered even better vistas. A solarium – the title ironic here in a sunless land – was filled with books and comfortable furniture. Unlike the walls on the first floor, the walls up here were covered in frescoes of sea-creatures, many of which had been extinct in the mortal world for eons. The bedchamber featured a grand four-poster bed directly in the middle of the room, sheer curtains of rich red silk hanging from all four sides to make a closed space that light would shine through to create a red aura within. Pulled off to the side were heavier velvet drapes of a darker shade.

"You are the first person I have ever brought here," Hades whispered into her ear, his hand on her back.

"Mmm. I am very flattered." The bed looked so inviting, but she also wanted to sit in that hot spring... and take a swim in the sea, and ride her horse down the beach... oh! There was so much to do!

oOo

"You should be," he joked. She looked ravishing in a dark blue satin chiton that terminated halfway up her calves, her hair tied by a ribbon of the same color. Her cheeks were faintly rosy from the ride on the horses. On her feet were sandals with elegant thin black straps that complemented her slender ankles. The overall image she projected was that of an elegant, relaxed, happy woman who was enjoying her time with him. Doubtless he would be sharing pleasant memories with her here...

oOo

Persephone certainly enjoyed the luxury Hades kept her in, and the shades were efficient and quiet. Having been raised amidst others – first her family and then the nymphs – it had taken her a while to get used to all the solitude that could be gained here. There was nobody to disturb her – or Hades – and that added to the unrealness of this place. Oh, she knew very well that the Underworld was a real place, with its own tastes, aromas, and textures, but the lack of people other than Hades and herself in his house reminded her all the more that this was not a place for life to flourish. She appreciated the privacy, but sometimes she wished she could be surrounded by chattering, living souls.

She stroked the velvety ebony coat of the horse beside her, resting her cheek against his shoulder. She let out a quiet sigh before she leaned her face against the steed. This was a wonderful place indeed, but it was lacking in a vital aspect.

Would Hades ever consider letting her go back to the other world? Why did he find the possibility of her returning to the surface world so distasteful? She had already made it clear that she would be happy to return to him and spend time with him. Now, how many kidnapped maidens were willing to make such concessions to their captor?

As she stroked the horse's coat, she was reminded of the thrill of freedom she felt when riding a horse, with or without Hades. She glanced over her shoulder back at the small palace. Hades was nowhere to be seen, so on impulse, she grabbed the mane of the noble creature and hoisted herself atop it.

She closed her eyes for a moment, feeling the air rush against her face and hair as the horse shot forward. Soon enough she grew used to the rhythm, and relaxed slightly, letting her hips sway back and forth as she lightly bounced on the horse's back, her fingers forming a tight grip on the mane. There were other islands visible on the horizon and she was tempted to lead the horse over the water, but she managed to restrain herself. Hades had given her a gentle admonition to remain on this island and to not go off it without him. She was curious, but Hades would not give her a warning without reason.

The island had a nice variety of shoreline. There was plenty of beach, but also rocky inlets and tide pools. She would stop every once in a while to examine the iridescent shells, plucking up a couple that she especially liked and tucking them into her girdle. She knelt down to pick up a spiky murex shell, its points stretching out from the body and making for an eerie and fascinating sight. As she turned it over in her hands, examining it, she sensed Hades's presence.

"Thought you could sneak off?" he asked, hands on his hips.

"You did not say anything other than to not leave the island," she replied defiantly. He smirked faintly.

"Relax, love. I am not angry with you."

"I would certainly hope not."

"Such a mouth on you. That could be put to better use." His smirk widened, and she blushed.

o0o

The swirling waters of the hot spring kneaded and soothed her flesh as she sat there, the bubbling liquid reaching her chin. She had only been sitting here several minutes, and already she felt sleepy. Ever since she had come to the Underworld, she had discovered an immense love for hot baths and springs. There was nothing quite like the hard churning of heated water against one's body. Of course, it didn't hurt that Hades was also stroking her hand, and she found sweet comfort in that gesture.

As she opened her eyes again, she saw shades moving about silently, setting down a small feast before them. The dishes were positioned so that they could eat comfortably off the ledge while sitting in the tub. Demurely, she turned her face away. The Isle of the Blessed was a lovely place, but she would not be swayed from her resolution.

"Come, have something to eat, love. You look so pale."

"Lack of sunlight will do that to a person," she replied pertly.

"I am pale too, and you do not seem to be bothered by it," he retorted, refusing to be put down. "But you do need to eat. You need color in those cheeks."

"I am not hungry."

"Tsk. So stubborn." He popped an olive into his mouth.

"Would you expect otherwise?"

"Of course not, but there *is* such a thing as *too* stubborn."

"For you, perhaps," she shot back evenly. Hades chuckled softly and shook his head.

"I will admit, I do admire your strength of will. Very few women, or even men, have that strength."

"Then you simply will have to continue admiring me." She raised her chin haughtily.

"Ahh, but I would admire you even more once you give in to me good and proper." He ate another olive, making a small smacking sound of approval.

"Where would the challenge be then, after giving in to you? You want me to taste the food of the dead, and you also desire my maidenhead. If you had them, then what?"

Hades stared at her in genuine surprise, and she blinked and stared back at him. Why should he be surprised? Hadn't she stated what he had been trying to gain all along?

"Persephone, is that what you think? That I merely want to... take your maidenhead?"

She stared at him, neither denying nor confirming it.

"Of course, I would love to be with you in that way. Have no doubt of that. But it is not about your maidenhead. Why would you think that?"

Persephone quickly looked away, watching the waves crash on the sand below them. She felt his hand on her shoulder as he drew closer to her.

"You are not a conquest. Sometimes, surrender is, in fact, a victory, and you would have much to gain. What I want, *need*, is you. I ache for you. It matters not whether you have your virginity. Never think that such a trifle is what I value, my dear. You are what I want, completely. The more of you I have, the more I will desire." His voice was a velvety whisper.

With that, Persephone felt a certain burden lifted off her shoulders. "Really? I could always expect the same passion you show me now?" she asked as she felt his lips kiss along her earlobe.

"Forever."

She let out a slow exhale as he wrapped an arm around her middle, pulling her into a loose embrace. He reached with his other hand and took a silver goblet, taking several gulps from it before looking back at his lover. When he pressed his lips to her own, she tasted pomegranates. She gasped softly and started kissing him more fiercely, feeling his hands on her sides. When the taste disappeared, she quickly pulled back, blushing.

"These kisses of yours are a powerful temptation," she whispered.

"Then give in," he responded cheerfully. She grinned before scooting back, sitting at the other side of the small pool. He slid forward, about to close in on her before she darted to the left, eluding him.

"You should know better than to try to elude me, Persephone." His dark eyes twinkled as he reached for her. This time, he managed to grab her arm, and pulled her close, wrapping his arms around her tightly.

"All I ask is for you to trust me. I love you," Hades whispered fiercely, burying the side of his face against her hair. She closed her eyes and remained silent, letting him hold her.

"I have not seen Abas in several days," the royal cook informed Metaniera. It had always been one of Abas's jobs to deliver the vegetables he grew to the kitchen so the servants there could prepare them. Doso sat quietly in a corner, spinning some wool as Demophon dozed comfortably in his crib nearby. As she overheard this exchange, she had to bite back a smile.

"Come to think of it, I did not see him, and the gardens have not been harvested yet. Hmm." Metaniera frowned and rose to her seat before stalking out the room, followed by the cook. Doso chuckled softly to herself as she glanced over at Demophon.

The Queen strode outside before going down to the courtyard. Many of the servants slept near the kitchens or dyeing room, but Abas had been given the room adjacent to the courtyard after his father's passing. It opened into a secluded corner of the courtyard and gave Abas one of his few delights in life due to its privacy. Of course, Metaniera could not know just how much Abas had enjoyed this little out-of-the-way chamber. She knocked firmly on its door. When no answer came, she knocked again. "Abas! Are you ill?"

"Perhaps he is..." The cook wrinkled his face, sticking out his tongue.

"Do not joke about such matters!" Metaniera replied firmly, though she didn't want to admit that such a matter was a possibility. Raising the lamp with one hand, she used the other to push open the door. Within, the small, windowless chamber was messy but showed no signs of its occupant. The musty straw was piled in one corner with a couple of blankets tossed over it. The few pieces of clothing Abas owned lay on the floor or tossed across the stool that sat in another corner of the room. Metaniera frowned as she noticed remnants of food and wine, and picked up a bottle to hear the sloshing sound inside. She sniffed the mouth of the container, dismayed to recognize the scent as one of their quality wines, reserved for banquets and other nice occasions.

"You are certain nobody has seen him in two days?" Metaniera asked, still holding the half-full flask.

"I asked the other kitchen servants and the guards," the cook replied.

"What could have happened to him?" she asked.

"Only the gods know," he shrugged.

oOo

By the time Metaniera returned to her baby's side, Doso was staring into the fire, meditating while she lightly stroked the hair of her infant charge as he slept in her lap, loosely curled up.

"Did you find the gardener?" the nursemaid asked, not skipping a beat as she continued staring into the flames.

"Unfortunately, no. Nobody has seen him, and his room is empty."

"Whenever I saw him, he always seemed

305

unhappy."

"There is nothing I can do about that. His father was a loyal servant and wonderful gardener, and his mother was one of my personal servants when I was young. She always cheered me up with her stories and was a good friend. She died shortly after giving birth to Abas. I have always tried to be kind to him, but..." She shook her head.

"Some people are simply never happy with their lot. There was nothing you could have done for him. It is possible he ran away, but who knows," Doso replied calmly, remembering the contemptuous gleam in his eye as he had mocked her.

"He was our gardener. He was at least competent in his job, and the kitchen staff already have much to do."

"Would you let me take care of the garden? When I was not taking care of my family, I would be out on the land. I just loved it."

"You are certain?" Metaniera found it hard to imagine this little, wrinkled old woman kneeling in the dirt and digging out vegetables.

"I have been taking good care of your baby, haven't I? Really, do not worry about little old me." Doso beamed up at the Queen, her smile causing more wrinkles to stretch across her face for an almost comical appearance.

oOo

Demeter hummed to herself quietly as she knelt next to one of the patches of vegetation, ready to

306

harvest the ripe vegetables. It was gratifying to dig her hands into the dirt and pull up what the earth had to offer. Thanks to her blessing the earth, the vegetables were more robust than they would have been if she had not come to live here. She turned the carrot around in her hand, weighing it in her hands before nodding with approval. The farmers and gardeners of Eleusis would enjoy similar results. Though she would lay low for the time being, she had plans for this city.

She filled her basket several times, depositing surprisingly fine specimen of various vegetables into the waiting hands of the kitchen staff. There was something else that Demeter wanted to dig, but she would have to wait until the Palace had turned in for the night.

After spending some more time with Demophon before handing him to his mother, she slipped outside, moving smoothly along the pathways until she came to a corner of one of the plots. Carefully slipping between two unharvested rows, she stooped down and started digging. Her Gift, being connected to the earth, allowed her to sense the presence of buried objects. She had sensed it even before she started collecting the vegetables.

She felt leather come in contact with her fingers and quickly grasped it, pulling it up to reveal a small bag. With a curious frown, she quickly shook the dirt off the bag before opening it. Her fingers slid into it before feeling something round and smooth, and she pulled out the mysterious object to reveal the soft gleam of pearls under the moonlight. What other treasures were buried in this garden?

Abas had been clever enough to split up his cache, but Demeter located them all and came up with several more pieces of jewelry and several pieces of gold and silver. The bags were simply made and not of the tightest stitch, but they had served well enough to store these treasures.

She fingered the pearl necklace, seeing that it was an antique due to the tarnished gold. Still, it was a fine piece of jewelry, well-made, and the dark gold helped to make the pearls seem brighter. As she was a goddess, she had nothing to gain from keeping these items. Doubtless they belonged to other people, though she wondered if perhaps any of this had belonged to Abas's mother. But such an article was too fine to belong to a maidservant. Could it be a royal treasure? It was worth asking.

oOo

Metaniera was in a particularly cheerful mood. She had dipped into their store of pigments though there wasn't that much left, and used it to dye most of the wool and raw linen they had. Her son had been quiet and happy today, reaching out for the sunlight with his little hands when she had let him sit outside in the courtyard for a while. Last night's supper and this morning's breakfast were especially scrumptious, due to the unexpected quality of their produce. Demophon was napping, and she was in fine humor, wanting to spend the day with her daughters as she had not done often enough as of late. Her daughters didn't have an equal level of skill in spinning or weaving, but it wasn't to see who could do better. She just wanted her daughters around her, to talk with and laugh and share stories with, as she had done with her own mother and sisters before marrying Celeus. Sometimes a servant might even join them and sing or play an instrument for them. Eirene had shown a talent for the pipes, so Celeus had given her a set as a gift and she might play while the others weaved.

They sat in the solarium spinning wool into yarn and trying different color combinations with the colors that Metaniera had dyed them with. Already Eirene was fiddling with the distaff, obviously disinterested in the rough wool in her lap, but Metaniera would have her work just a bit longer. Eirene did need to learn patience, and how to be at least competent in this household craft.

She heard a soft clearing of the throat and turned around to see Doso at the doorway.

"Might I have a word with you alone, my lady?"

The Queen nodded, setting down her distaff and yarn. She quickly turned towards her daughters. "Continue what you were doing. And that includes you, Eirene. Eyes on the wool!"

The youngest Princess stuck out her tongue at her mother's back as Metaniera left the chamber.

The pair of women walked down the hall, Doso taking slow steps much as any old woman would. Metaniera maintained the nurse's pace.

"When I was in the garden yesterday and digging around, I found several things," the crone said. Metaniera raised her eyebrow.

309

"I do not know whom they belong to, so I thought it best to come to you privately."

"Certainly. I appreciate your prudence," the Queen replied with a nod. The old woman reached into her sleeve and pulled out an object that Metaniera instantly recognized.

"Thalassa's necklace!"

"What?" Doso glanced up at her.

"Months ago, Thalassa came to me in a panic. She was unable to find her pearl necklace. She said that she put it away properly as she should, but the next time she went to get it, it was gone."

"Hmm." Doso frowned, shaking her head slowly. "Then you should recognize the rest of these." She pulled out several different pins and an armband.

"Yes. These pins are mine, and the armband belongs to Triptolemus!"

"And this?" Doso pulled out the gold and silver.

"Celeus would know more about that than I. He did say something about some gold and silver being missing a while ago, I believe." She held out her hand, and Doso obediently gave her the treasures.

"Thank you for returning this to us. These pins were a wedding gift from Celeus, and I have always cherished them. I was so dismayed when I could not find them!" Metaniera's affection for her husband was clear in her voice. "Would you like to sit with us? You must have some good stories to tell, and we do enjoy your company."

oOo

"Certainly, my lady." Demeter smiled to herself as they returned to the solarium, where she was treated with more camaraderie and respect than she got from members of her own family.

Chapter XXXVI

oOo

After being subject to the searing pain in his sides, Abas had lost consciousness and known oblivion. When he was conscious again, he found himself flying over the earth, pulled in one direction by some unseen force. The journey was but a few moments. Below the earth he went, and came to a stop as soon as he was placed near the banks of a river.

Where am I? he asked himself. All around him were what seemed to be people, only they did not appear to be flesh and blood at all. He saw them in varying states – some peaceful and calm, others wailing or hysterical. To one side was the river, the other revealed a cavern wall. In the wall he could see a crack in the rock, admitting a sliver of natural light. *There we go.* He had no intention of staying in this strange place.

The crack revealed itself to be a staircase upon closer inspection, and he started to climb it, but there was the mysterious force again, pulling him back. As much as he struggled against it, he could advance no further. He reached for the light, and saw it glow through his fingers.

What? Abas stopped his struggles and stood on the bottom step, lifting his other hand and slowly rotating them. His fingers were translucent and gray.

"Where am I? What is this place?" he asked, spinning around wide-eyed. Many souls nearby ignored him, too preoccupied with dealing with their own recent deaths. He shoved through them and ran to the banks of the river. The surface was quiet, and he was barely aware of the ferryman in the distance. However, when he tested the water with one foot, the cold seared through it just as if he was still flesh and blood, and he jerked back with a sudden cry.

"The little one thinks to attempt to swim across the Styx!" he heard someone laugh. He turned around to see a fairly young woman, her features smooth and her garb plain.

Little? He *hated* being called little and became so incensed over it that he completely missed the mention of the river before them. Even as a grown man of nearly thirty, he had resembled a scrawny teenager, right down to the occasional outbreak of acne. Despite his long days of tending the Palace grounds, his exercises had failed to give him the ideal physique he had always wished he had. His muscles were wiry and covered by pale flesh that sunburned. Unfortunately for him, he did not have a warm or charming personality to make up for his flaws.

"Little?" Abas asked outraged, stalking towards the woman. He did not know or care who she was, but he wouldn't stand for it! However, before he could close in on her, several others shoved him back.

"You have to wait your turn, just like everybody else here!" someone else informed him.

"Wait my turn for what? Nobody told me there was a line!" There was a quiet mishmash of several voices.

"You do not know, do you?" the woman who called him 'little' asked.

"Know what?"

"You are dead. Otherwise, you would not be here. You will cross the Styx with Kharon soon enough."

Dead? If Abas had still been a mortal creature, he would have felt the thudding of his heart against his chest as he hyperventilated and felt light-headed. Without these cues to alert him to his state of anxiety, he could only stare at her with numb shock.

"Oh dear. I take it your death was sudden. No wonder you were trying to swim across the Styx! I was confused at first, too."

Abas stood there mutely, processing the events that led up to his death. He remembered the taste of dates pilfered from the larder, and slinking outside for some fresh air. That stupid old nurse had been strolling around as if she owned the place. And such a rude little old woman she was! He had been sorely tempted to kick her. And then she mentioned her lost child and he had mocked her.

"No!" Abas jerked back. He remembered the constriction around his body, and how everything had changed. Out of the constraints of his brief incarnation as a lizard, Abas was able to process things normally again. He remembered scuttling along on four legs and climbing up a wall before being swept up into the air by something with claws...

That woman he had angered... she was a goddess! The Goddess of the Harvest. He didn't worship her, but her name was familiar enough to him. He started pacing back and forth by the bank of the Styx, thinking about what had happened and silently cursing Demeter for her actions. How dare she? These gods thought they were so high and mighty, and then to wander around in disguise like smelly old women! As far as he was concerned, *he* was the wronged party. He had been here far longer than she, and did an actual job. All she – Doso, Demeter, whatever the fuck – did was show up in front of Thalassa and play on the girl's kindness, and be a nurse to a baby that was just going to die anyway.

Why did his life – and death – have to be so unfortunate?

oOo

Metaniera only lowered her arms when Demophon turned his head away from her breast. He did not cry or fuss as he had before, and now drank her milk with a fairly healthy appetite. When she held him up and patted his back, he no longer vomited his meal like he had been so prone to. He might burp up a bit, but no more than an average baby. He had even started to crawl, though he still had a ways to go before he could walk. At first, the changes had been subtle, but there was no denying them now. Demophon was getting better, and it couldn't have just been Doso's singing.

Even his siblings remarked how much better he looked. His cheeks were now faintly rosy, and though he was still pale, he no longer had a gray pallor.

Metaniera was determined to find out what was

happening with her son. Did Doso know some sort of secret – herbs, maybe, or a spell? What with the improved harvest in Eleusis and the fact that the warlords had been struck with a plague that tore through their numbers like wildfire, the Queen was more inclined to believe that Doso was a sorceress. Thank goodness she appeared to be a good one. The only odd thing was Abas's disappearance, but after the old woman had uncovered the stolen cache of money and jewels, she realized that Abas would have never been happy here, and more things would have gone missing before the gardener might abscond with these items in the pursuit of a new life. She had never seen a smile on the gangly young man's face, and even though he was a competent enough gardener, it was clear that he took no pleasure in his tasks. And Doso was even better than Abas at maintaining the gardens.

The Queen of Eleusis could not help but wonder, why was Doso here? She was doing all of this kindness for them, surely she must want something in exchange. She frowned at this thought. What if Doso would demand more of them than the warlords had ever done?

She would see what Doso did to Demophon to get a better understanding of what the old woman did. She entered the chamber where the nursemaid now resided, seeing a half-finished project stretched across the loom. Rows of herbs and other plants drying along strings were tied to yarn strung across one corner of the ceiling. She glanced down at her son, brushing back a loose black curl from his face, sending out a silent prayer to the gods and hoping that they might at last hear her silent plea.

As the old woman sat on a comfortable stool, her gnarled but nimble fingers twisting wool into yarn with her distaff, she looked up and regarded the Queen and Prince with a warm smile. As always, Doso treated the baby gently, and Metaniera could feel the care as their arms touched. Surely this woman had no evil intentions?

The crone started humming softly to the infant and continued doing so as Metaniera retreated from the room. So that the crone wouldn't have any reason to not believe she was gone, the Queen moved from the doorway and walked along the hall, taking a leisurely stroll around the edge of the courtyard. After doing a complete circuit, she stealthily crept back to Doso's room. She peeked through the slight gap in the door, seeing the light of a flame flicker along the walls. She heard Doso singing in an almost inaudible voice, and the baby cooing quietly.

Still, her curiosity spurred her on. She inched the door open and slid within the shadows, stifling a scream at what she saw. Metaniera stared in horror at the scene before her. Demophon was atop the hot coals in the hearth while his nurse – the woman who the queen had trusted – simply sat next to the fire, idly poking the child in his stomach. The child's mother was about to move forward with maternal indignation, but the baby laughed. *Laughed.* It was a healthy, full-bodied laugh, the sound of delight from a truly happy and comforted baby.

He lifted his arms, clapping his fat little hands as

317

his nurse tickled him, cooing at him softly. He was naked, his skin orange and gold amidst the flames. She narrowed her eyes, thinking of her son's appearance ever since Doso had come here. Hadn't he slept more soundly? Didn't he cry less? Wasn't he drinking her breast-milk with a healthy appetite? If this woman had enough power to place Demophon within fire without harming him, then what else was she capable of?

oOo

Demeter smiled as she touched the baby's chest, feeling how warm it was from the flames. She still possessed some ambrosia and was now using that to ensure the child's survival and health. She had smeared the substance onto his body before placing him into the fire. The bad parts of him would be burned away, and he would be a healthy and happy little boy. The traces of ambrosia in his blood would add extra robustness to ensure his vitality. And never before in his short life had Demophon ever been so warm! The flames licked at his skin without burning him, and as the sickly parts of him burned away, he felt free. He had been just a little baby, unable to put into words what pained him so, but now that pain was gone. As Demeter tickled him under his chin, he laughed again.

"There there now, is that wonderful? All nice and warm, no?" The hardened ambrosia was now starting to chip off him, falling down in little iridescent flakes and hitting the embers before filling the room with a faintly sweet and invigorating scent.

o0o

Metaniera felt her nose and lungs filling with that scent, feeling a rejuvenating burst of energy. She was unable to hold back a gasp, and Doso's head snapped up as she glanced at Metaniera.

Immediately, the mother sprung forward, snatching her child from the coals and wincing as she felt the heat on her arms, clutching him tightly, staring at the nursemaid with wide eyes.

"What were you doing?" Metaniera asked. She was surprised that her question didn't come out in a panicked scream, for inside her heart was pounding.

"Simply making him healthy," Doso replied.

"What kind of witch are you? What is your price for all of this?" She backed away with the baby as the old woman rose from her stool, growing larger, her back straightening and shoulders widening.

"Did I ever ask for anything more than a roof over my head and food in my belly?" Doso asked, her voice deep and firm, echoing off the walls. Metaniera fell to her knees, quaking in terror as she imagined what sorts of things this woman was capable of.

"Please forgive me, my lady. I meant no offense. I simply wanted to ensure I understood what you might ask of me. You have protected us from our enemies, blessed our harvest, found what was stolen from us, and gave my dying son a new life. These are all great gifts, and I only wished to-"

"You are a prudent woman. You recognized all

the gifts I have given and acknowledged that you might be asked to recompense me. This is the first time anyone has ever asked to do so. Rest assured, my intentions have been nothing but good. I simply needed a place to... get away, and your family freely offered me refuge and comfort. You and Celeus care for your people and want your children to be happy. I only wish that I knew that my own child is happy, but she has been stolen from me, and her father has no concern for my feelings."

"Oh, how dreadful!" Metaniera's trembling ceased, and she approached Doso. "Please, you are welcome to stay here for as long as you need to. I will tell nobody about your secret. If I had one of my own children stolen away from me, I would be miserable! How could such a thing have happened?" She slid Demophon back into Doso's arms, dusting off the glitter of dried ambrosia from her chiton.

"Such things happen because so many men are insensitive and thoughtless. The father of my child seduced me through trickery. I had been raising her by myself when her father agreed to a marriage, and my daughter is kidnapped by the man chosen to be her husband! And I had no say or even knowledge of the matter! Only after several moons passed in my worrying and grief did I finally discover where she is, from another source because her father was too much of a coward to be honest with me! Only my poor child is trapped in a realm I cannot enter. In my anger and grief, I have turned away from my family, to give no more to them until my child is returned to me."

"Abominable!" Metaniera frowned, appalled at

such carelessness. Even though Celeus knew that it would make her unhappy when the bandits had started asking for their daughters, he still wouldn't hide it from his wife. They talked about everything, especially the welfare of their children. Her beloved husband would never think of giving one of their daughters away and trying to hide it from her. "Is there any way we can help you?"

"Nobody can enter his realm but for the dead and the few alive he gives permission to. And I am not one of them." Doso explained dejectedly.

Nobody but the dead? But only one dreadful place fit that description... If it was that realm, then no wonder this woman was so unhappy!

"I am always here if you need to talk to me. And anything we can do..." Metaniera responded compassionately. She glanced at the infant, now curled up happily against Doso's breast.

"Yes, Metaniera. There is something you can do for me. The city temple – it is old and decrepit. Your prayers to Zeus have gone unheeded."

It would seem so, Metaniera thought as she bowed her head. An ancestor of Celeus – one of Zeus's many illegitimate children – had dedicated the temple to Zeus, and he had been their main deity, though not to exclusivity as he had been in Olympia. But Zeus had remained first and foremost, and the Eleusinians had appealed to him to help them with their woes, which always came to naught in the end. Ares had also ignored their prayers since war always amused him and he enjoyed the increasing energy and blood-lust of the rogue warriors outside the city.

"You have called his name the loudest, but does he ever answer? My name has barely been uttered, and I am unable to hear it amidst the louder cries from other cities."

Metaniera felt her cheeks burning. This woman... she was a *Goddess?*

"Strip the temple and restore it in my name. The other gods will know that I am to be reckoned with." Her cowl fell away, revealing a braided crown of dark golden tresses atop a strong and broad face with a straight nose and smooth cheeks. "To the faithful, I will bring bounty. The Harvest is mine, and mine alone."

oOo

Since Demeter could detect metal and minerals within the earth as part of her Gift, she pointed out a quarry that revealed beautiful marble. The workers and artisans were imbued with bountiful life-energy that kept them moving and working quickly, keeping them nourished and healthy at the same time. The harvest had gone so well that it was not hard to believe that Demeter had answered their prayers, and with the construction of the new and beautiful temple, the city experienced a rejuvenation. The disease that had decimated the army outside the city hadn't infected one resident.

Demeter approved of the temple, but even having a grand and beautiful place of worship in her name did not ameliorate the pain she felt at the loss of her daughter or the anger she felt towards her family.

Kalia stared at the chickens with a steady eye, gripping a knife. Their food stores were soon to run out since the harvest had been completely destroyed. The ground had dried up and the plants withered at an appalling rate, shriveling up before anyone could get a chance to eat them.

Rather than waste what little was left of their stores, they had decided to eat several of the chickens. This meant more food for them now, and less wheat to expend in the future on their fowl. Ever prudent and efficient, they had had enough food to ration at a reasonable level ever since that disastrous day. But now, as it started getting colder and colder – rather prematurely for this time of the year – they could not deny that their stores would barely last through another month, and only if they rationed the food very, *very* strictly.

More and more she was discontented. Mother kept her busy with weaving, a simple and efficient art for Spartan women – after all, did warriors and their women alike not need material for clothing, bedding, and warmth? But soon enough their wool ran out, as they were not willing to trade any of their food to their neighbor for wool from Nikos's dwindling herd of sheep. Kalia went foraging for food, and through this way had gotten to know more about the world she lived in. Other Spartans were not much better off than herself. The men got a slightly bigger ration of food, but her father was losing weight like she was.

She looked down at her slender arm and the wrist-bone that was starting to protrude at an alarming angle. How much longer would this go on? The Spartan Oracle could only say that unless a stolen child was returned, people would starve. Several children within the city had been returned to their parents after being stolen by family members. Still, there was no change in the increasingly antagonistic clime of Hellas.

She was increasingly unhappy at home, even more so because everyone else was. The environment was hostile, filled with desperation and negativity, and she had no desire to be part of it anymore.

oOo

"Daddy, I am hungry," Melissa whined. Her rosy cheeks had lost their plumpness, but she was none the worse for wear. However, having been indulged before with food since it was so plentiful, she was unused to being told 'no' when it came to having a treat. Because there was no harvest to be had, there was nothing fresh to eat.

Skouros let out a heavy sigh. This year's harvest had been looking so promising that a couple of weeks before harvest time, they had decided to go ahead and partake of their old stores to make room for the harvest. People were having banquets and picnics, using up most of what had been left of their stock before the harvest suddenly soured. Suddenly, there was strict rationing. Nobody was satisfied with the portions he gave them, but his wife and himself kept the larder under strict guard so that nobody would pilfer their meager provisions – not that he could blame them for wanting to. He himself had to fight the temptation to eat what was left of the preserved fruit.

"We are all hungry, but we have to persevere." He let out a weary groan. The two cities nearest them would not trade with them for food, being in equally dire straits. All the messengers sent out from Olympia returned with bad news.

"I cannot even have a date?" Melissa inquired, her dark eyes widening in an effort to sway her father. She was cute and could bat her eyes or widen them for appropriate effect to get what she wanted. However, the hungry rumble in Skouros's stomach reminded him that now was not the time to indulge his children.

"No." His voice was unintentionally gruff, and he practically barked at her. "Do not ask for any more food. Your mother and I will give you the rations you need, but this is not a time for whining or indulgence. Now, stop it."

The girl's eyes widened, but for a different reason, and she ran out of the room before he could see her tears.

o0o

"Damnit!" Zeus roared as he spun around, walking back and forth. The prayers from Olympia became more and more pressing by the day. They had eaten what was left of their stores from last year

325

and were now starting to go hungry. Everywhere, disastrous harvests brought about fervent prayers to Olympus, but nothing anybody did could undo the damage Demeter did. Let the clouds pour rain and the sun shine its warm light onto the barren earth, they could not coax any growth. A few cities or villages still had stores, but many were depleting their storehouses, and an unfortunate amount had already done so.

Demeter continued to hide, knowing full well the consequences of her actions! He had never seen a woman act so unreasonable! He wanted to shake some sense into his sister. Some of the other gods had already come to him, pleading with him to find Demeter and just do what she wanted. The warriors of Sparta had nothing to eat. Thebes, having already had a difficult harvest the year before, was starting to starve, seeking to trade with other cities and offering plenty of gold, only the neighboring cities had no spare food to offer. It had only been a month since Demeter stood up to him before the Council. How could things have gotten so bad?

As he groused about the situation down in Hellas, he took a piece of ambrosia from the plate that the nymph held for him. Demeter had made good on her threat, and even though he was angry with her, he did not want to admit that he was also beginning to feel panic. Suppose Demeter never restored the harvest? Then Hellas would be devoid of people! Where would they go if there was nobody to worship them! The people to the south worshiped the gods with animal heads, and further south were deities with skin as dark as night. To the north were wild, nameless gods that protected the various tribes. The eastern lands held gods of their own, just as old and sometimes older than the Hellenic deities. The gods of Hellas could take what people were left and move them to the west, where there were still lush forests and valleys. But Demeter was certain to follow them and spread her dearth.

Even with what was going on in Hellas, Hades still refused to give up his bride. His Kingdom would grow greatly in due time to all the people who would die from this famine. No amount of pleading, cajoling, and even threatening would sway the Dark God.

Between his sister and brother, he felt helpless, even impotent. The lovely nymphs who surrounded him didn't amuse him as much as they usually did – nor did they even want to. Being Nature deities, they shared Demeter's anger and were affected by her wrath. He could use all of his Gifts, and it still wouldn't bring forth the harvest. He was King of the Gods, yet he could not give the mortals the one thing they needed to survive.

"Father!" Zeus heard one of his sons call out. He looked up, seeing the lanky figure of Hermes descend from the sky, landing several paces away.

"I have news for you. The people of Eleusis have been building a grand temple for Demeter, and their harvest has been good. I was not able to confirm that Demeter herself was there, but there was a definite trace of her presence," Hermes stated.

"Hmm." Zeus stroked his beard as he pondered

just what to do with this bit of information.

oOo

Before the Queen of the Dead was spread a feast that any mortal in Hellas would have readily pounced at. Odors of various spices and delectable ingredients filled the air, dancing along in soft wisps of steam. Yet she would look at none of it, and kept her gaze fixed on the floor, her hands folded neatly in her lap.

She wondered how her mother was doing, and the rest of her family. Hades remained sketchy and evasive, even at times outright refusing to speak of it, whenever she brought up the goings-on of the surface world. *It was not important enough for you to know*, he'd say. Or, *There's so much to enjoy here in the Underworld! Why concern yourself with the other world!*

For over one season, she had been trapped in the Realm of the Dead. There were very few things to complain about. Hades was a warm and generous host. Her comfort and enjoyment were always seen to, whether he was with her or not. Yet she sometimes felt intimidated by him and his sheer power. His gaze could feel as if it was penetrating into her soul. She was afraid of the unknown. She knew that Hades wouldn't lie to her, but she simply couldn't... just cross the line. There was no going back if she did.

Part of her felt collected during these meals with him, sitting there calmly and ignoring the food while making pleasant talk with him. But she also wanted to swipe something from the table and just plunge it into her mouth and bite down and taste that flavor. If it tasted even half as good as it smelled...

Out of the corner of her eye, she saw Hades rise from his divan and sit next to her. She gazed at him languidly. In his hand was a pomegranate, cut neatly into half and revealing clusters of the seeds. He was silent, offering her the fruit. She stared down at it, remembering well the tart sweetness of Hades's lips.

oOo

Hades ran a finger along the slick interior of the fruit before bringing it up to her face, gently dabbing her lower lip with it. It left an enticing stain on her pale flesh, and he lightly smeared it from side to side. She sat there, unmoving as he spread it to her upper lip, giving her lips that were startlingly dark against her white skin.

oOo

Persephone felt the moisture and darted out her tongue to flick at it. She trembled slightly. Her eyes met his for a moment before looking down at the fruit.

Flashes of a starving world caused her to gasp softly and pull back. She quickly rose from her seat, wiping her lips with the back of her hand.

oOo

Hades scowled. He loved her and wanted her to be happy, and yes, he was willing to be patient. But damnit, a man could only be patient for so long! He was tempted to bind her and force food into her mouth, but such a deed would forever taint their relationship. It was clear that she enjoyed his company and wanted to be here. Why must she be so frightened of the food? What was it that kept her from taking his offering? Quickly, he collected himself, setting the pomegranate aside.

"What is the matter?" he asked, reaching to place a hand on her shoulder.

"I... I have these dreams... and I see them even when I am awake."

"The nightmares?" he asked. She still wouldn't tell him what her occasional nightmares were about. Her response was a soft sigh.

"Persephone, how can I help you if you will not tell me what is wrong?" he asked. "Let me use my magic to keep you safe from these nightmares."

"You can really do that?"

"And more." He smiled faintly. She paused, wondering.

"Think about it?" he asked, seeing the indecision in her features. "For now, let us just forget supper. There are plenty of things we could do..." He raised his eyebrow, a clear implication of just what he had in mind.

"You are right. There are plenty of things to do. We could watch the Judges, or go to Tartarus... or you could take me to your library for a lesson. Of course, there is always going out for a ride, on your

330

chariot or the horses..." She batted her eyelids at him. "Nice things like that."

"Do not play 'nice' with me," he shot back. "I have seen what you can do."

"Then be a dear and humor me, will you?"

"Yes... my dear," he replied dryly, but not without humor.

Chapter XXXVII

oOo

"I have had enough of this!" Aphrodite cried out with a dramatic wail. "The people of Cyprus are starving! My temples are filled with my worshipers, and they are dying! People have turned away from me, thinking that I care nothing for them! But I cannot command the earth!" She threw up her slender arms, aquamarine-studded gold bands glinting in the sunlight as she did so.

"My Oracle predicts disaster, and her prophecies are always about Demeter and her daughter," Apollo said. "She is unable to prophesy anything else. The only way to resolve this is to return Kora to her mother. Simple as that. Even Hades must bow down to your order, Father, for you are High King of the Gods, and your brothers and sisters agreed on that, did they not?" he asked, his voice firm and reasonable as he spoke, though no one knew that the normally self-collected god was hiding his anxiety.

"Athens has a limited food supply, and it is being threatened by Sparta. They claim they want to share, but they just want to steal it for themselves!" Athene's eyes flashed angrily as she regarded her warmongering brother.

"Zeus, this really is becoming wearisome. I thought that my Kingdom would be safe from her wrath. Alas!" Poseidon shook his head. At first, the coastal villages had been able to support themselves, but after time, even they started to feel the wrath of the scorned goddess. Demeter's fury had wormed its way under the ground that the waves crashed upon, first killing off the seaweed and other plant life on the shore before extending further. People had to go out further and further to fish, and the fish had also started dying, coming up with huge clusters of pungent and festering seaweed. This dead ocean debris washed up on the shores, and the starving and desperate people would take what they could off the dead aquatic creatures even if it was rotting. "She is angry with you, and she definitely let us all know it!"

Hephaistos remained silent. Because he had spoken in Demeter's favor, the harvest in Lemnos had been decent enough to last its occupants through the winter. However, to make it on the meager stores, they couldn't trade or sell it to anyone else. An insidiously clever move on Demeter's part to ensure nobody circumvented her will. He wasn't about to let Ares know, otherwise his older and often abusive brother would doubtlessly try to wrest food from Hephaistos's people. Blacksmiths might make armor and weapons, but that did not mean they could wield them well.

"Zeus, you cannot sit around any longer and wait for Demeter to get over her anger. She is determined to see this through the end," Hera commented snappishly.

"Hermes just told me a bit of news that I think you would all be interested in. The people of Eleusis have built a grand temple to Demeter. Their harvest has been blessed, and their people are secure and happy. Her magic is there. She is out to spite me, we

333

all know that, but perhaps listening to pleas from any of you might soften her heart."

"It is worth a try," Dionysus stated. The harvest had been dismal, and his worshipers were not only out of wine; they were also out of food. The wild Maenads had tried fermenting beverages from preserved fruit or vegetables, but the results had been barely satisfactory. The nymphs were feeling the pinch of Demeter's choke-hold of Hellas's life-energy. The myriad minor deities of Hellas no longer found enjoyment in Nature. Rivers and forests alike dried up, leaving the mortals in more dire straits than before. Demeter certainly was thorough in her wrath, and the scale of destruction spoke of the immense power she wielded.

"Then we will need someone who she is not angry with. Someone she will welcome and actually listen to," Hera said. This, of course, excluded Zeus from the list of candidates to make contact with her, and nobody needed to mention this.

"I will do it," Athene said.

"If anyone can do it, she can," Hephaistos stated, showing full confidence in his sister's abilities. Yes, Athene was aloof and could come across as blunt or even bitchy at times, but there was no denying her sharp mind. Diplomacy had always been a forte of hers, and her arguments could be persuasive, indeed. Zeus nodded. He wisely saw that a woman's touch might serve better in this situation.

"I doubt that any of us could disagree with Hephaistos. The situation down on Hellas is critical. I am certain you know the importance of your words,"

Hera said. Athene nodded solemnly.

"So I will not waste my time on useless chatter. Go now with my blessing, with *our* blessing."

oOo

Eleusis was a stark contrast to the other cities in Hellas. Though it was a bit small, it was still a good-sized city, and even though the fields were now harvested, Athene could see that they were healthy and the soil dark and rich. The few people she saw outside working all looked content. She crossed a bridge that ran over a stream, seeing how clean and fresh the water looked.

The gates to the city were open, well-fed guards standing at alert. After a mere few questions, they let her pass. Her guise as a middle-aged woman was serving her well. She was clad in a plain brown chiton and matching cowl, with a straw basket folded at her side. As she lifted her head, she felt it. There was no denying Demeter's presence here. Outside among the fields, she could feel the goddess' power sustaining the land. But now, the goddess was *here,* somewhere in Eleusis, probably in disguise.

Athene had plenty of experience fitting in with the mortals, and was inconspicuous as she wandered through the marketplace. One thing she had noticed about Eleusis was that it was warm. It was late autumn, yet the weather was pleasantly cool and mild. People went about in sandals or bare feet, and nobody was wearing anything heavier than a light cloak or cowl. Here and there, along the paths and in front of the buildings, plants were growing from the dirt and from between bricks or slabs in buildings or paved walkways.

It wasn't hard to find Demeter's temple. Many cities in Hellas had similar points they used in city planning, such as the location of temples, wells, and the like. When one understood the criteria, it became easier for a stranger to find his way through a city.

The temple before her was indeed grand. The marble was like nothing she had ever seen before, with a particular color in its background and veins that was entirely unique to the regions around the city. Several different marbles had been used, but the most prominent one was beautiful pale green with veins of gold. The people treated the temple with reverence, keeping the grounds around it maintained and swept, the lush moat of grass surrounding the building clear proof of the temple's blessing. The sun shone on the marble, bringing vibrancy to the verdant marble that was reminiscent of the thick grass.

There appeared to be nobody guarding the temple, nor were there any priests to come out and shoo her away when she approached the gap in the grass. There was some quiet singing and chanting coming from within the temple, but they seemed to be from solitary worshipers rather than a group ritual. The place gave her a feeling of serenity, and she gazed around calmly. As she entered the main chamber, she was awed by the sight before her. A life-size statue of Demeter dominated the room. It was carved from white marble and stood atop a matching dais. In her right hand, she held a large sheaf of wheat wrought of gold and brass. In her other hand was a sickle made of silver.

A couple of women were kneeling before it, praying quietly. A girl in her mid-teens approached her, garbed in an immaculate green and white chiton. She was a fairly attractive young woman with dark eyes and hair, and she smiled at Athene welcomingly.

"Have you come to pray before the statue, or would you like to meditate in the garden?" she asked.

"Whatever gives me more privacy," Athene responded neutrally.

"Come with me."

The priestess looked a bit thin as if she had gone hungry lately. This caused her to stand out in contrast to the well-fed people of Eleusis. Was she fasting?

The inner courtyard was more verdant than she had expected. It seemed that anything and everything that bloomed or grew during this time of the year was all here, fully – and lushly – represented. Though there was a clear-cut path that led from one end of the yard to the other, there were plenty of little nooks and crannies where one could sit and meditate. A natural spring bubbled from the ground, creating several small streams that crisscrossed the garden. There was a bench here and there, nearly hidden out of sight by the shrubbery. Athene saw a couple of people sitting in the nooks created by the careful planting and configuration of bushes and trees, and could not help but marvel at this place.

To Athene's surprise, there was a tree heavy with ripe olives.

"May I?" she asked, gesturing towards a low-hanging branch. The priestess nodded, so Athene plucked an olive. It was just the perfect level of ripeness, juicy and firm.

How could this be? The time to harvest olives had been over a month ago. Any olives left on the trees would have been overripe at this point. Seeing the surprise on the visitor's face, the priestess smiled.

"Demeter's blessing allows us to enjoy the fruits of our work longer. Feel free to eat anything you see here, we only ask that you do not harvest here for your home. This is for the worshipers to enjoy."

Athene could not help but think of the marginal harvest in Athens. The olives there had been nowhere near as delicious as this. She reached out to take a few more olives as the priestess watched, and the girl did not object when Athene placed the seeds in her pocket.

"What is your name?" the priestess asked.

"Aegea," Athene responded smoothly. "And you?"

"Kalia."

"Well, thank you for showing me here. I would like to be alone now."

"Certainly." Kalia inclined her head in a slight bow before cheerfully wandering off, checking on the others in the garden. Athene glanced at the tree again. What had the Eleusinians done to gain the Harvest Goddess' favor? She remembered the dearth she saw in Sparta and Olympia, where the people who were still alive barely had any strength to bury their dead.

Near the tree was a small clearing, and she sat down in the grass. It was soft and springy – even more so than some beds. She wondered if people ever fell asleep here, especially after eating the robust fruit she saw on the trees. The place certainly was picturesque, and she could feel the rich abundance of life-energy here, though unlike Demeter, she lacked the Gift to manipulate it.

She let out a slow exhale.

Demeter, I need to talk to you. Athene said, concentrating on the message and sending it out, knowing that her aunt would sense her presence, wherever she was.

There was a ripple in the air around her, as if the life-energy around here was pulsing with the beat of a human heart.

"I knew that the other gods would come sniffing around here, eventually," the voice of the Harvest Goddess whispered from around her as if coming from the plants and grass themselves.

"You would not expect us to not come to you as soon as we learned of your location? This place is beautiful and the people are so happy."

"Naturally. But why have you, of all people, come to me? I have ensured that your city had a harvest ample enough for its needs."

"Please do not think that I am ungrateful for it, aunt. But so many others suffer needlessly. They are not even aware of our conflict. They pray and plead to you, but you ignore them."

"They prayed to me only when the other gods failed to give them what they needed."

"Hm." Athene couldn't argue about that. She usually didn't find herself outsmarted in conversation,

339

but Demeter had done so with a simple truth. A logical argument came quickly to her mind.

"If there is one thing that can be said, it is now the gods and mortals alike are fully aware of your Gift and what a lack of it can do. You made your point. Can anyone deny your power now?"

"Yet that alone cannot bring back my daughter."

"How we all know that. Out of all the people that had to take her, it was the one god we all do not dare to challenge openly for we know his power. Ill luck, indeed. And of course, there's Zeus's part in all this. You would think he would have become a bit wiser over the centuries." A depreciation of Zeus would give them common ground, and Athene intended to take advantage of that in her argument.

"Loathsome oaf," Demeter agreed heartily, the leaves on the trees rippling furiously. Athene had to bite back a smile.

"You certainly have made him aware of your displeasure. His favored priest just lost his youngest daughter."

"Ah, I remember him well. Saying that Zeus was the greatest god of all," Demeter said snidely. Athene frowned. She had been hoping that the mention of someone else losing their child would evoke sympathy in Demeter's heart. Skouros was anguished over the loss of his little daughter, and his others hovered near death. The man himself was little more than skin and bones. Everything that could be eaten was gone, and the children gnawed on leather straps or ate dirt in frustration, trying to appease their hunger however fleetingly.

340

Demeter had every right to be angry with Zeus, but it wasn't right to spread this kind of misery. Wrath truly was clouding her judgment as a testament of just how deeply angered Zeus had caused her to be.

"The mortals are as varied as the gods are. How can sailors not worship Poseidon? How can the blacksmiths not acknowledge Hephaistos? Wives and mothers need the knowledge of Hera and her strength. That man did not worship Zeus to spite you."

"So am I to sit back and let Zeus commit a wrong against me? Despite all that is happening, he still refuses to make reparations!" Demeter retorted coolly.

"You know the pain of losing your daughter. Yet when people lose their children, you do not let up on your curse. Mothers have to bury their children every day, and the little children watch their mothers lowered into the ground. Your suffering has become a thousandfold, a hundred thousandfold. No one can deny the wrong that Zeus has committed upon you, but your vengeance has gotten out of hand. I am on your side, well and truly. You know that. But the mortals need you more than Zeus. Would you deny them simply because it was their lot to worship the ones who have angered you?"

"Zeus and the others know exactly what they can do to appease me. They have only to do so, and all of this suffering they complain about will end. That is all." The life-energy stopped pulsating and went back to a smooth, quiet flow, and Athene knew she was alone. She let out a defeated sigh.

oOo

Aegea slid through the cool temple past two priestesses. The shorter one turned her head as the woman passed them, getting the same faint tingling sensation that she always did around Doso. The first time she had felt such a tingle, she had been alarmed, unaware of her latent talent.

Just in the way that every god had some kind of unique ability – or combination of talents – to make up their Gift, a few mortals were lucky enough to have a Gift of their own. In Melinoe's case, it was the ability to sense divine energy. Eleusis had been absent of it for as long as she had known. Though their temple had been dedicated to Zeus since her distant grandsire's time, the mighty god had paid little if any notice to the city. But in time she had come to recognize Doso's energy as positive, especially after seeing how her baby brother thrived under her care. The little boy was now walking, and his eyes sparkled. She felt better and healthier as if Doso had somehow added vitality to the food she gardened and cooked for them.

The energy from Aegea felt different, however. It was more crisp and clear as if it was tightly restrained and given one definite direction.

"Melinoe, is something wrong?" the taller girl asked. She shook her head and turned back to Kalia. She didn't know how to explain these feelings that she had, so she kept them a secret.

342

"Oh, I was just wondering if I had ever seen her before. She looked new."

"She wanted to worship in private, so I led her to the garden," Kalia replied. Melinoe nodded approvingly. They were the two youngest priestesses of the temple. As soon as plans for the temple had been announced, a search had been announced for potential temple priestesses to come to the Palace. Doso was the one to decide who would serve the temple.

Not long after that, Kalia had come to Eleusis. It was clear that she had gone hungry for a while, and it was almost amazing that she had walked all the way here from Sparta. Under the care of the priestesses and a friendship formed with Melinoe, Kalia had offered herself to the service of Demeter. It made Melinoe happy to have a companion her age, since the others were older and more matronly, like the goddess herself. If it wasn't for Kalia's initial gaunt appearance, Melinoe wouldn't have believed her tales of a starving and ravaged Sparta. She had stolen a loaf of stale bread made from the very last of her family's wheat stores – hidden from the Spartan soldiers that had confiscated most of the farmer's dwindling stores – and a slice of goat cheese. On the road, a starving man had overwhelmed her and stolen her pack, leaving her deprived of everything but the clothes on her back.

She had been nursed back to health after using the last of her strength to get to Eleusis, though she still looked a bit gaunt. After growing close to Melinoe, Kalia had confided how she had been unhappy in

Sparta and how she had always wanted something more, to serve a greater purpose in life.

o0o

"Doso, there is someone here to see you," Metaniera said, moving to the side to reveal another old woman wearing a brown cloak that had deer woven along the hems in silver. Artemis did not miss the recognition in Demeter's eyes.

Artemis bowed her head slightly to the queen, thanking her graciously for her assistance before the mortal woman retreated from the room.

The younger goddess regarded the old woman sitting before a loom in front of her, weaving a vibrant scene with two females dancing in the grass. One Artemis recognized immediately as Demeter herself, and the other – and smaller – figure had to be her lost daughter.

"Greetings, dear aunt."

"Hello, Artemis. How nice to see you," the old woman replied, continuing to weave. Artemis's cloak slid away, revealing her true form.

The Goddess of the Hunt was a tall and graceful woman, wild hair tied back though several thick waves were loose, framing her face in a way that made her lovely in a way she didn't intend. She was clad in a plain cream-colored tunic and brown linen leggings. Her lower legs were wrapped in leather straps that connected with comfortable sandals.

"It is so nice and warm here. No wonder the Eleusinians bask in your glory." Artemis's tone had a

344

touch of flattery in it, but also admiration. She paused. "Am I welcome here?"

"You may approach," Demeter replied regally. Artemis approached her, her head held high, the sunlight catching in her dark brown hair and bringing out auburn highlights. Her eyes were tawny brown, with flecks of gold.

"I do not have a child of my own, but mothers pray to me to protect their daughters. I take girls under my wing to protect them from the eyes and hands of men," the Goddess of the Wild said, her palms upturned in supplication and respect. "You have seen the caprices and cruelty of men, as well as their selfishness."

"Indeed." Demeter looked at her gravely, looking like a grieving widow in her black cloak.

"When I was little, Father had me on his knee and told me that I could have any wish I wanted. I told him that I wished to be the mistress of my own life and body, beholden to no man. He granted the wish and must honor it, for I was wise enough to make him swear by the Styx. It is too bad that he will not honor a woman otherwise," Artemis said with a disgusted shake of her head.

oOo

Demeter remembered the wish that Zeus had offered Kora. She should have suggested that to her daughter! Zeus said that her daughter could claim it any time, which meant...

The Goddess of the Harvest got a sudden glint in

345

her eyes. Surely she could not be denied a message to or from her daughter! That was well within her right! It wasn't at all an unreasonable request. Kora could use that wish to make her sire annul this... indecent union!

"I understand your wrath, aunt. You have every right to be angry. But you are not just hurting Zeus. Everyone suffers from your rage. Humans and animals alike starve because you would not allow the fruits of the earth to be harvested. Men have become so desperate and hungry that they go to the forests and strip it bare of both plants and animals... I beseech you. Lash out at Zeus, not the world!"

"The only way to get through that thick skull of his is to take away what he loves most – his precious humans." Demeter's eyes narrowed, her lips twisting into a grimace. "But... there is something you can do for me, for the sake of your creatures..."

"Name it."

"Go back to Zeus. Tell him to remember that he gave Kora a wish years ago and that she has not yet used it."

Artemis's lips curved in an understanding smile as she nodded, being wise enough to not press her argument any further. "Then there is a way out for her yet."

oOo

"What you ask for cannot be done," Zeus said as he stared at his daughter with solemn regard. He had all but forgotten that wish he had granted his other

346

daughter all these years ago. Of course, if she still desired something – a gift, perhaps, to make her feel better about being down there, then the King of the Gods would give it to her. Defying Hades's will was another matter entirely.

"How can you deny Demeter or Kora?" Artemis demanded.

"Were it any other man who kidnapped her, I would not permit it. But this is Hades we are talking about/"

"So?"

"*So!* This is Hades. The God of Death. Even a god must fear Death."

"He is your brother. And Demeter's brother. Surely he can be appealed to. He refuses Demeter audience, does he not?"

"He says that she will not be admitted to the Underworld until she is ready to accept her daughter's fate."

Artemis groaned as she rolled her eyes and threw her hands up in the air.

"My sentiments exactly," the King of the Skies commented.

"Excuse me, I could not help but overhear," Hebe said as she brought up some ambrosia and nectar. Generally, gods did not like to have their conversations intruded upon, but Hebe was a quiet and efficient girl who often dispensed surprisingly good advice. Zeus smiled at her indulgently, and Artemis regarded her with an encouraging nod.

"You say you gave Hades your blessing to have her, correct?" the Goddess of Youth asked.

"Indeed."

"Did he sound in all intent, to have her as his proper queen, and such? Hermes says she even has a new name."

"Yes. He claimed that he would have no one else as his bride."

"Aha." Hebe stroked her chin, and the other two glanced at her with curiosity. Her dark eyes twinkled. "Perhaps one way to lure him – and her – up here is to have a wedding. They are not properly married yet, are they?"

"I... do not know. Hades did not say anything about a wedding celebration, but I assume we would have one up here once Demeter got her good sense back. After all, he is a proper man. That is, if he has not already married her amidst the dead souls."

Artemis and Hebe exchanged a sideways glance as their father said that.

"You should send Hermes down there and ask him what he intends to do. That knowledge might aid you," Artemis offered. "I need to speak to him myself about something else, and will be glad to relay this message."

"Go ahead." Zeus waved his arm dismissively, glad to be free of the situation for the moment.

Artemis rose from the seat, biting back a wry smile as she inclined her head in a respectful bow, before impulsively kissing his cheek in a display of affection. He beamed up at her, and she skipped away, inwardly gleeful at how predictable her father could be at times.

Hermes absolutely hated these trips to the Underworld. He could zip along the paths of the Underworld with relative ease, still having some of his super-speed here, but he always had to fight the urge to look over his shoulder. The onyx Palace loomed before him, its front gates opening for him like a gaping maw to devour him.

He soared along the grand marble hall and through the arched doorway – topped with a sinister marble replica of Kerberos – and entered the throne room, sliding to a stop in front of the thrones. The one on Hades's left was empty. Thankfully, the Lord of the Dead appeared to be in a patient mood. His shoulders were relaxed, and he leaned against one side of the throne slightly, appearing as if he expected this meeting to be brief and of little import. Hermes frowned for a moment. *Hmph.*

"I have a message from Zeus. He has a question, and he would appreciate an answer."

"Certainly." Hades looked almost bored.

"He would like to know what you have planned in way of a wedding ceremony. Zeus would be honored to host the wedding feast, and–"

"I have my own plans regarding such matters. I have been to Olympus often enough to see what debacles these weddings of our family can be."

"Still, Zeus would like to know if she is married proper, or will be."

"Mind your business. Tell Zeus to not worry about the wedding arrangements. Things will be done in due time."

"Very well." Hermes bowed. "I have one more question."

"Why should I deign to answer another?"

"Of course, you do not have to, but Artemis would like it if you did."

"Oh?" Hades raised an eyebrow at the mention of his niece.

"She... wishes to know if you would do a small favor for her."

"What is it?"

"She would like to remind Persephone of a wish that Zeus gave her a long time ago."

"That is it?"

"Yes."

"Hmm. Very well. You may go now."

"Yes, sir." Hermes quickly bowed out and was on his way out of the Underworld before Hades could change his mind.

o0o

Persephone sat on a stool in front of her mirror, wearing a robe of deep green velvet, her feet bound in slippers of the same material reinforced with thin straps of leather. The teeth of her silver comb pulled through the thick waves and knots of her hair as she used her other hand to try to manage the wild tangle. What would it be like to cut off her hair? Just take a pair of shears and lop it all off at the nape of her neck? Sometimes she hated having to take care of her hair, combing or braiding it, since her hair was frizzier than her mother's and had the tendency to form curls at the ends.

"Do not try to pull it down like that," she heard Hades chide gently. She looked up, seeing him in the reflection as he stood there in a black robe that was loosely tied in the front, revealing his chest. He reached out with his hands, lightly running his fingers through her hair and letting the natural waves bounce free.

"It makes me look so wild," Persephone pouted, shaking her head.

"Ahh, but I have seen you frolic plenty of times like this. It reminds me of these times. Besides, there is something comely about how you look with your hair loose." He stroked the top of her head affectionately. The memory of frolicking in the meadows caused her to give out a quiet sigh.

"I miss frolicking."

"You can do it in Elysium, or the Blessed Isles, or any of the gardens," he replied calmly.

"It is not the same." she shot back just as evenly. He shrugged, still stroking her hair. He had seemed about to say something more, but he remained silent.

oOo

Zeus and Hera stared as they listened to Hermes as he brought them the newest bit of information from the Underworld. So Hades intended to do things properly, although who knew when he would. The Lord of the Dead seemed indifferent to the passage of surface-world time, and had his own way of doing

351

things. He didn't want a wedding on Olympus? Damnit. Zeus didn't think he would be too happy going to an Underworld wedding. There would be nothing to eat there but for the Food of the Dead, unless food was brought in from above. What mischief might ensure that one of the gods accidentally eat a piece of the forbidden food if such a gathering was held in the land of the dead?

Food of the dead. Zeus mused that subject. Hades was apparently not ready to hold such a banquet, and... Zeus blinked.

"I have an idea," Zeus muttered, stroking his beard.

"All of us know better than to eat the Food of the Dead. Demeter might have given her daughter that admonition. If there is a chance that she has not yet eaten the food of the dead, then I could get her back for Demeter..." Zeus said with increasing enthusiasm. It was not guaranteed to work, but it was definitely worth a try. Hellas was in dire enough traits, and if this went on, the extinction of the descendants of Deucalion and Pyrrha was imminent.

Chapter XXXVIII

oOo

Hades smiled to himself as he glanced over at Persephone. She gazed at the souls before them calmly, assessing them as she listened to their stories. In the beginning, she had been completely silent, listening as they petitioned Hades. He appreciated her respectful silence but didn't want a dummy queen sitting next to him. He would ask her what she thought after hearing a story, and encouraged her to ask questions to the soul if she wished to understand the situation better. She had been shy at first, speaking only when he prompted her, but as she spent time sitting on her throne, she gained confidence as Queen of the Underworld.

Without Demeter to constantly shelter or supervise her, Persephone was free to say anything she wanted, and ask any question. Thanks to his own magic, Persephone's nightmares hadn't bothered her for a couple of weeks now. She would be upset if she knew, but as long as her sleep was peaceful, why should she care, and as long as she was happy, so was he.

He felt her hand rest atop his for a moment, squeezing. He welcomed these little touches, and when she drew her hand away, he took the opportunity to grab it gently, pressing his lips to the back of it.

She smiled at him. She looked exquisite in a gown of soft gray velvet, hematite-studded silver pins and jewelry completing her look. She looked almost like a ghost in all the gray, her pale skin white against her garb. Her hair was completely swept off her neck, sitting atop her head and the back of it in a tangle of coiffed curls held back with a crown of silver set with the same polished stones. Against the black and white marble and the wrought metal thrones and the various gray-hued souls, it looked as if color had drained from this world but for the color of her hair and the barely perceptible light that radiated from within her.

When the last soul bowed to them and filed out of the throne room with a shade, Persephone turned to her husband.

"It has been a long day." Her smile was faint and suggestive. "I was thinking about relaxing with a hot bath..."

"Hmm... certainly not by yourself?"

"Most certainly not." Her eyes sparkled.

"Delightful." Hades had an enraptured expression, gazing at her as he regarded her with a smile.

"Look at the lovers." A soft laugh made its way across the grand room. They looked forward to see Hekate standing there, her arms loosely crossed as she stared at the couple. Persephone blushed and quickly sat upright. Hades frowned, not liking the sudden interruption.

"Sorry for appearing so suddenly, but I heard you were holding Court and thought I would get a quick appointment. I need to speak with you, Hades. It is good to see you, Persephone. Perhaps we could go visit Nyx tomorrow? We will talk more later."

Hekate's eyes flicked back to the King of the Dead.

"I will see you in a little bit, then," Persephone whispered. Hades nodded as she slid out of her throne and left.

"What is it?" Hades asked casually, leaning his head against one hand as he glanced down at Hekate. The goddess stepped forward, wearing a deep purple gown, her thick, curly ebony hair pulled back with a matching purple sash. The regal color served her well in this situation, and she squared her shoulders.

"We need to talk about Demeter." Her voice was no-nonsense. The Lord of the Dead let out a slow, short groan.

"Do not waste my time."

"Surely you know of the chaos Demeter is wreaking. People are starving to death! There is fighting over what little food is left. The Spartans are attacking neighboring villages for food. The temples are filled with the wailing of the mortals, begging for food and help."

"That is my sister's doing, not mine."

"You know why she does it!"

"Ahh... but I have told Hermes to assure her of Persephone's safety. I would not lie, you know that. She refuses to be satisfied with my words. I have even given her a simple codicil for seeing her daughter again. She refuses my generous offer. Is that my fault?"

"You kidnapped her daughter! How can you refuse the blame?" Hekate was indignant.

"I do not deny that my decision was rash. But you cannot change things that have already happened.

What have I done? I have but taken one woman, a woman who has known only my affection and respect. You can see for yourself that she is well-cared for. Am I the one causing the famines? Have I lifted a hand to harm any of the humans above? You know that I am the God of Death, but I do not involve myself in the ways the mortals meet their end. The gods above are more responsible for their deaths than I am!" His dark sapphire eyes glinted fiercely as he leaned forward. "My brother quakes before her wrath, but he does not apologize for the crime he has committed against her."

"You can be so damned logical when it suits you."

"Never forget that, Hekate." His tone was dry. "Do not presume to think that I am ignorant of the goings-on of the world above. But I will not be part of Zeus and Demeter's quarrel. Both of them are extremely stubborn, but I am not to be blamed for that."

"You are stubborn as well."

"Is that news? I think not."

"Come now, Hades. Please do not let this continue. Hellas is being ravaged. The gods are desperate, but Demeter will not be moved. She has but one demand, and only you can fulfill it."

"I have demands of my own, and she knows them. And do not think she has just one demand. Zeus has his own part to fulfill."

"What is this, tit for tat?"

"Not on my part, like I said. Zeus and Demeter have their own problems. I am not part of it, nor will

356

I be." His tone was resolute.

"Do not be an ass." Hekate frowned. Hades scowled right back, and the room took on a sudden chill.

"I have made my decision. Do not speak of this subject any further."

"But..."

"*Hekate.*" The Lord of the Dead uttered her name with an edge that plunged them both into silence as the shadows around them rippled violently. His lips were set in a tight line.

She swallowed and bowed her head. If Hades had been privy to her thoughts, he would have known that she was considering whether she should have gone to Zeus first, rather than Demeter, and also feeling the weight of remorse that she considered her burden for her part in Demeter's wrath.

"Leave now," Hades commanded. She retreated without protest.

Hades let out a low sigh, leaning back. Calling him an ass, of all the nerve! Was it his fault that his brother was the stupid ass? He hissed softly as he rose from his seat, hands clenched into fists. The affairs of the surface world could be so needlessly complicated sometimes. Could he be blamed for not wanting any part of it? Fortunately, now he had a companion that served as an excellent distraction from such unpleasant matters. He quickly pushed Hekate and her words out of his mind as he strode off in pursuit of Persephone.

oOo

As the days passed, Persephone experienced another monthly cycle. By now, she was used to it, and even almost welcomed it, using it as an excuse to keep Hades at bay since his physical attentions could be very.... distracting, not to mention thrilling. There were times when she questioned whether she ever wanted to return to the surface world or not, and Hades's loving attention made that all the more difficult, so she was relieved to abstain from it for a while. After a handful of days, Persephone ached for his touch. She had been tempted to give him modest concessions, but abstaining from any form of intimacy was the only way she could manage to stay resolute for so long and keep a clear head. His touch was so thrilling that she *needed* these monthly interludes of solitude.

Hades had done everything to her sexually except for intercourse itself. She ached for him, and he knew it. But she remained virginal, if in only the barest sense of the word. His hands and mouth had explored every inch of her body, literally. And she had come to know his own body as well. But she did ache for his manhood in ways that could not be satisfied by other means, no matter how lovely they felt.

At this moment, she walked along the shore of the sea in Elysium, enjoying the lapping of the waves at her feet. Her mantle was down, revealing her hair done up in a loose bun.

oOo

Hades watched Persephone from under his helmet as she walked on the sand. Her gown and mantle were a deep blue, setting off her creamy skin. He desired her, and he felt his manhood twitch. He licked his lips, wanting what she wanted.

Persephone slowly looked over her shoulder. He often observed her from his unseen state, and though they both knew that she could sense him, he did it anyway for their amusement. There was something thrilling about touching her, too, when she could not see him; teasing her with shadows or invisible caresses in the most surprising of places, to which she playfully pretended to struggle, mock-outraged. The thought made him harder, and he licked his lips again, shivering as he thought about what he could do to take her... fully.

"Hades..." she breathed. "You should know better than to play hide-and-seek around me," she playfully chided. He pulled his helmet off, cradling it under one arm and shaking his hair from his face.

"I hear no objections," came his remark.

oOo

Persephone smiled faintly at that. There was no denying how she felt around his presence, whether it be at a distance or in the heights of intimacy. Other men did and would find her desirable, but she was certain no one could ever make her feel the way Hades did.

Under the light, it was easy to see the blue in Hades's dark eyes, and she gazed up at him, loving the sapphire glints she saw. Unconsciously, she drew closer to him, and he held out an arm. She could not stop herself from stepping forward and leaning against him, her hands touching his chest as his arm draped loosely around her shoulders.

"I love you, Persephone," he whispered as he kissed along her temple.

"I know." She closed her eyes, burying her face against his chest. Heat seemed to radiate from him, and she pressed herself to him. Warmth suffused her nerve endings as she wrapped her arms around him.

"Aidon... I need you." She hugged him more tightly, wanting him to simply fill her with his heat and surround her with it. Passion and desire was a source of solace for her in this dead realm, for it was only the living that felt what could seem an inferno in their flesh.

"Seph." She looked up to see him staring down at her.

"I need you," she whispered again, feeling the rhythm of her heart through her veins, and the beat of his own heart against her chest. His hand reached up to cup her face.

"I've always needed you," he replied as he ran his thumb along her cheek, and she leaned her face into the warmth of his hand. She nodded slowly but firmly, holding his gaze.

o0o

As always, Persephone felt a bit dizzy as they materialized in the bedroom of the residence on the

Blessed Isles, a temporary aftereffect of teleportation. He kept her steady with an arm around her middle, letting her orient herself before he guided her to the side of the bed. She leaned against the bedpost as he unpinned his cloak, tossing that to the floor.

"So what did you have in mind for tonight, love? A nice massage? Some shadow-play? You teasing me, or the other way around?" he asked, his voice purring in that low way that never ceased to cause her to feel the hot stab of sexual quickening. The mental images that came from his words caused pleasant memories to tickle her consciousness, and she stared at him with pure want, ready to cast aside the last shred of her sexual innocence. Her clitoris ached, and she wiggled around her hips slightly, shifting her weight from foot to foot. He tugged off the pins that held up his tunic, causing his entire chest to be bared before her appreciative gaze.

"I need you, Hades. All of you." she hissed, her womanhood throbbing with the delicious burn of arousal. He reached out, removing her pins as well before his hands moved down to her bare breasts. Her neck and throat were peppered with hungry kisses, and her girdle was tugged off before he pulled away her clothing, leaving her bare before him.

She stood there pale and beautiful with moisture glistening just under the dark red curls that sat at the juncture between her legs. She reached with one hand to finger herself.

His hand, strong and firm, gently plucked her slim hand away from her pussy. Only when he was in the mood to watch did he let her pleasure herself in

361

front of him. But not this time. She whined in frustration, trying to free her hand, but his grip was too strong.

"No fair," she moaned, twisting around.

"It is fair, my love... I will pleasure you to heights you can only reach through my touch..." He kissed at her neck and then raised her hand, licking her juices from her slender fingers. His face was a mask of bliss, and he shuddered, teasing her with his hands before motioning her to get onto the bed. She was fully aware of his ravenous gaze as she settled herself amidst the blankets.

"What would tickle your fancy tonight, lady Persephone? Ah, the very sight of you..." He gestured towards his own aching erection, which made for a very visible tent under the fabric of his tunic.

"There is one thing that I have wanted... that we have both wanted for a long time." She lifted her pretty chin, making for a splendid sight against the deep scarlet blankets that lined the comfortable bed.

"And... what might that be?" Hades asked as he loosened his belt, letting his tunic fall to the floor.

"I want you to take me in the way I know you have always wanted to. I am yours, Aidon."

oOo

Hades stared at her for several moments before feeling an almost overwhelming rush of exhilaration. *Yes*.

"You are offering me yourself? As a lady to her lord?" Hades whispered, barely reining in his

362

enthusiasm, his voice tight with self-control.

"Yes." She was smiling faintly.

"Oh, Persephone...." He quickly climbed onto the bed, his movement smooth and sleek much like an overgrown cat.

"My lord." She moaned softly, splayed on the bed, naked and inviting. He blanketed himself over her, pressing a gentle kiss to her forehead. He settled his knees before lowering his hips, rubbing his aching manhood against her slit, causing her to arch and whine softly. Keeping himself propped up with one arm, he kissed the side of her face and neck, teasingly pressing into her a fraction of an inch before pulling out.

"Mmph... Tell me..." He breathed, the tip of his manhood now at her opening, creating a light prodding motion, "Tell me how much you need me." He slid in about an inch, encasing most of the swollen glans within her tight flesh. She groaned softly when he pulled out.

"Hades. I need you. I cannot imagine anyone else for myself. I only want you and your touch. Please. Do not torment me. Take me. Make me yours."

He smiled down at her, his loving gaze showing her how much he enjoyed her words. He pushed back in, further now feeling her stiffen a bit at first before he stroked her arms, glancing at her with concern. She nodded, and he slid further, biting back a groan at the tightness that surrounded him.

o0o

363

There was a bit of soreness as she adjusted to him, and she bit her lip to muffle a small whimper. He remained within her, and she looked up into his eyes. Despite the lingering pain, she wanted more. She wrapped an arm around his middle as she reached with her other hand to cup his face before sliding her fingers down his throat and shoulder.

Her breath hitched and she bucked against him, her fingers digging into his shoulders. The nails, short and neat, left red crescent marks in his back as she clung to him. This was what male and female had done for countless eons, as a natural process. She let out a soft moan as his body pressed into hers, and she arched her back, clenching around him.

o0o

Fuck. She was so tight and wet. It felt as if her body was trying to swallow him up. After several moments of just enjoying it, he started to thrust slowly. She responded more than eagerly, her gasps and wails filling the bedchamber. She was so delicious in every way, her noises making him ache even further.

He thrust deeply and rocked his hips in fierce motions, unable to keep himself in control. Various forms of intimacy were enjoyable, but there was nothing like mating, of raw and wild passion brought together in the pure simplicity of heated union. She cried out his name, arching against him as he slid one hand to her hip to steady her as she wiggled against him.

He thrust more wildly, spurred by her cries for more, and when he wasn't looking at her face, her bouncing and jiggling breasts had his rapt attention. She was enthusiastic about this, thrusting her hips back at him, clawing at his chest even as she begged for more. Her hair had come undone from the sash it was bound in earlier and now flowed along her shoulder in wild, silky tresses.

oOo

When he came, it was glorious, this hot explosion within her, causing her to give out a sudden gasp at the unexpected pleasure of his climax against her inner flesh. It was also plentiful, filling her up, causing warmth to radiate through her insides.

Hades wasn't done, as she was soon to discover after he had allowed her a short rest.

"I hope you found this experience to be meeting your expectations," Hades whispered as he kissed and nuzzled the side of her neck.

"Rest assured, it exceeded them." She gave out a contented sigh when he wrapped his arm around her waist, pulling her into a tighter embrace and showing her that he was still aroused. Even though she had been well-fucked mere minutes ago, the thought of another coupling excited her. Hades sat up, and she found herself positioned so that she was facing him while sitting in his lap. He leaned back, propped up by several large pillows. She steadied herself by placing her hands on his chest, and wiggled around, feeling his groin press against her own. She wiggled her hips upward, letting his manhood stand to full attention before lowering herself again. Keeping one hand on his chest, she reached down with her other one to grasp his engorged passion.

"Seph..." He wiggled as she slowly lowered herself, using her grip on him to help steady the hard flesh as she slid it within herself. He felt her clenching around it, and she let go of him, sliding down with a suitably provocative wiggle to her hips. His hands slid up her thighs to her sides, squeezing gently.

"It feels so good," she purred, flipping her hair over her shoulder. She shifted her hips around, causing frissons of pleasure for both of them.

"All for you," he replied, stroking her sides before he bucked his hips upward. She gave out a low gasp before grinding downward, and he growled at her before he repeated his motion. The young goddess twisted and writhed against him, clenching around him as he held onto her. Reaching down with a hand, he found her sensitive nub and pressed against it, causing her to whimper as she continued writhing against him.

"Who is your lord?" he whispered. She stared up at him with eyes that gleamed with raw need.

"You are," she moaned, grinding against him as he continued to manipulate her, pressing against her aching clit. With a cry of exultation, she came, slumping forward and burying her face against his chest as she caught her breath. He stroked her hair and back, putting off his own orgasm for the moment as he ran his fingers along her body, feeling her faint

366

trembles. After she had calmed a bit, he gently pushed her off him and hoisted her up so that she was on her hands and knees. She gave out a shuddering moan when he slammed into her from behind, his hands on her hips with an iron grip as he thrust into her roughly. She did not protest, and reveled in the pure animal force of Hades's passion. This was not the refined Lord of the Underworld or the dreaded Dark One. He was simply an impassioned male who was enjoying himself with the one he loved, and he certainly wasn't the only one enjoying this scenario.

His roar of climax was much like a beast's own, and that thrilled her. It flattered her to know that she alone could drive the Dark God into such throes of ecstasy. Even after he had spent, he continued thrusting, remaining hard, his flesh plunging into her welcoming body as she kept herself steady – at least, as much as she could – enjoying the small aftershocks of orgasm that his continued attentions brought her. She gave out a low, shaky sigh when he finally pulled out of her. When she felt him gently press on her hip to make her lay down, she did not resist and let her body flop down. As she closed her eyes, she felt him stroke her cheek.

"My love, you were simply stunning," she heard him say. A faint smile tugged at her lips.

"Thank you." She curled up on the bed, exhausted from his fierce attentions and simply wishing for some rest. She knew that lovemaking was supposed to be intense, but she had never imagined it would be like that. It had been nothing short of incredible, and she felt her entire body suffused with the heat she often longed for.

"Seeing you with that delightful flush on your cheeks makes me want you all the more," his voice purred into her ear.

"Please, Aidon...." She felt a hand massage her breast. "You... you are incredible... and overwhelming."

"Overwhelming? Do forgive me, I cannot help but desire you so much."

"Of course I forgive you."

"Just lie back, and let me love you." His lips rained down along her face and breasts, and his hands massaged her as he rolled her over onto her back. Under this treatment, she was only too happy to surrender to him again, feeling his heated flesh plunge into her with that savage and addicting rhythm. From her position, she could study his face and see the exciting mixture of desire, ecstasy, and need illustrated in his features. He bared his teeth in a handsome growl when he finally approached his climax and clenched his jaw as he continued thrusting. When he was done, she lay there, leaking the evidence of his passion from her still-throbbing womanhood. She seemed not aware of anything around her, and was just barely conscious if even that.

oOo

She did not notice when Hades summoned a shade to fetch him something. The shade was back within a moment, bearing the object that its master

368

had commanded. It faded back into nothingness as the Lord of the Dead turned back towards his bride, pomegranate in hand. He peeled back one section, revealing the dark inner flesh. Its many facets glistened wetly as he looked down at his blissful prisoner.

"Persephone, you must be very thirsty... are you not?" he asked. Her lips were parched. She nodded slowly, her eyes remaining closed. He reached out to taper a finger along her lips. She kissed at his fingertips with a soft whimper. He leaned his head down to suck several pomegranate seeds out of the fruit, leaving their juice on his lips. When his lips touched hers, her tongue darted out to lick the juice off his lips. With a smile, he plucked out a seed.

When he pressed his moistened fingers to her lips, she started kissing and licking them, and sucked the seed in between her teeth. She swallowed, and continued to suck his fingers.

He withdrew his fingers and wet his lips with the pomegranate again, giving her another seed he had been holding carefully with his lips as he dropped it into her mouth. He plucked out one seed and then another to feed her by hand, her nimble tongue flicking out to taste the juice as she swallowed seeds. The darkly splendid juices refreshed her and sweetened her lips as she partook of the treat, feeling the satisfying crunch of the seed between her teeth.

o0o

He sat back, setting the fruit aside and looking

down at her as she lay there loosely curled up, her hair a lovely, tangled mess around her peaceful countenance.

"Sleep well, my love," a voice whispered into her ear as the seeds slid down her chest and into her stomach, rooting themselves into her destiny.

She was lulled into sleep, the flavor of pomegranates lingering on her lips along with its juice. Hades smiled down at her tenderly, stroking the side of her face before he sat back, eating more of the seeds. Her loins were still warm from the passion they shared, and her body was slumped in the exhaustion of an orgasmic afterglow. Hades admired the dark tint that the juice left on her lips and fingers.

o0o

Amidst the barren fields, Persephone heard an anguished wail. She spun around, seeing her mother standing tall, reaching truly Titanic proportions as she glared down at all the desolation before her, sickle in one hand, her other hand – the one that was usually holding wheat – empty. The earth trembled with Demeter's grief and wrath. Above her head, the heavens churned, bringing about bitter cold wind that lashed at the thin shift that Persephone wore.

"Mama!" she called out, but Demeter seemed to not hear her.

"For so long as my child remains in the Land of the Dead, the Earth itself will also be dead!" Demeter's voice boomed through the air, sounding much like thunder. Then she saw flashes of other

gods, pleading with her mother, beseeching her to let go of her wrath, only Mother turned them all away. The world became darker and colder and still, Demeter raged on...

oOo

The Queen of the Underworld gave out a gasp as her eyes snapped open for a moment, registering her surroundings before she closed them again. As she stirred and slowly oriented herself, she felt a warm and muscular form against her own, an arm draped across her back. There was a vague soreness between her legs, and she rolled onto her back, opening her eyes as she stared up at the ceiling. Memories of the night before filtered into her mind. Hades had taken her, and oh gods, how incredible it had been! When he had put himself into her, it had felt just... *right*. It had been just the two of them – everything else had faded away, leaving them in their own private universe – and they had come together in an infinite series of glorious moments.

And then as she had been floating along on the haze of the afterglow, he had given her wonderful sweetness. Lips against hers, and cool kernels that she had welcomed with both hunger and thirst, savoring its flavor and juice. Hades had whispered such loving words, and she had welcomed him...

She blinked as she struggled to sit up. When she propped herself up on an arm, she saw the husk of a pomegranate, a few seeds left in the cream-colored husk, standing out against the ruby-hued comforter.

371

As she licked her lips, she tasted the dried-up juice that had left a thin and sweet but slightly sticky film.

The dream flashed before her eyes, and she looked down at the stain on her fingers. *Seeds.* She now remembered the feel of them sliding past her tongue, down her throat...

"Persephone..." she heard him say. Her hands trembled as she looked up at him.

oOo

END OF BOOK TWO

Notes

o0o

The exact details of the Tantalus, Sisyphus, and Danaid myths were modified by me, but not overly so, since I tried to keep the main elements of each tale. You can look them up on various sources if you wish to read the full tales of each, but I made a few interesting connections between several little-known facts.

Princess Danae – the imprisoned maiden in the tower that was featured briefly near the beginning of this story – was the descendant of the final Danaid, Hypermenstra – 'blameless one' –   since she eventually came to love the man she was given to after he respected her wish to remain a virgin on their wedding night. The couple created a new dynasty. Danae's name is no coincidence, and the dynasty that Hypermenstra gave birth to was the Danaian dynasty. The great heroes Perseus and Hercules were descendants of Danae, so one cannot help but wonder what would have happened if Hypermenstra's husband had chosen to take her by force, ensuring that all fifty bridegrooms died as King Danaus wanted. Greek history would have been very different, then!

Tantalus was the forebear of House Atreus, his descendants committing many sinful and depraved acts. Some of Tantalus' descendants performed dishonorable deeds which included incest, cannibalism, and murder, earning them curses which would be carried through their bloodline, and as the generations went on, curse after curse was added. The descendants of this house included Menelaus and Agamemnon, though these curses ended when Orestes redeemed himself after praying to Apollo and Athena and doing as they told him.

oOo

I imagined Nyx to be more exotic-looking than the members of her extended family, almost like an Indian woman. Of course, she would still have Greek facial features, but I imagine the Goddess of the Night to have dark, dusky skin. I just couldn't imagine her with pale skin, though I have seen beautiful artworks that depict her as such and I do think she can look nice either way.

As for Hekate, I imagined her as a more cheery character than she is often depicted in mythology, at least to her friends and loved ones. Mythology makes her such a fearful character, and some versions even make her older than the Olympians. Being associated with witchcraft inevitably brought her negative connotations with the rise of Christianity, so I wanted to make her personal character unique.

In Rome, she was known as Trivia – literally 'three roads' – due to her being the guardian of the crossroads. In medieval times, 'trivia' came to mean the three ways (trivium) in education – grammar, rhetoric, and logic – think of our own current-day three R's. This was more of a primary school education, with the higher-education quadrivium

374

being arithmetic, geometry, music, and astronomy, back then considered more challenging than trivium. Trivia came to mean what we know it as today in the 1960s, at Columbia University as part of a game, where people challenged one another with such 'trivial' questions. It was further popularized by the game shows that were becoming popular in this era. And of course, now we have 'Trivial Pursuit' and Tri-Bond.

I hope you feel smarter for having learned trivia about Trivia!

About the Author

M.M. Kin has been interested in history and mythology since she was young and has been an avid reader for as long as she can remember. Her other interests include hiking, kayaking, and world domination. 'Seeds' is her first series, and she is currently at work on more books.

She can be contacted at ememkin@gmail.com

Made in United States
Orlando, FL
04 June 2023

33811040R00207